Del

Delphi in Space
Book Two

Bob Blanton

Cover by Momir Borocki
momir.borocki@gmail.com

Delphi Publishing

Cover by Momir Borocki

momir.borocki@gmail.com

https://www.facebook.com/StarshipSakira/

Table of Contents

Chapter 1	*Welcome Back*	*5*
Chapter 2	*Remember When*	*11*
Chapter 3	*Back in the Saddle*	*20*
Chapter 4	*Board Meeting – Nov 12th*	*28*
Chapter 5	*First Steps*	*34*
Chapter 6	*Birthday Girl*	*37*
Chapter 7	*Taking A Break*	*41*
Chapter 8	*Flying Lesson*	*45*
Chapter 9	*Board Meeting – Dec 3rd*	*49*
Chapter 10	*Treaty update*	*54*
Chapter 11	*Training Catie*	*59*
Chapter 12	*Paintball*	*65*
Chapter 13	*Board Meeting – Dec 17th*	*70*
Chapter 14	*Disclosure*	*75*
Chapter 15	*The Tour*	*85*
Chapter 16	*Christmas*	*91*
Chapter 17	*Nightmares*	*114*
Chapter 18	*Production Starts Up*	*117*
Chapter 19	*Board Meeting – Jan 7th*	*121*
Chapter 20	*The New Mayor*	*125*
Chapter 21	*Missing them*	*129*
Chapter 22	*Board Meeting – Jan 21st*	*134*
Chapter 23	*Linda Sends Help*	*138*
Chapter 24	*Soccer Friends*	*143*

Chapter 25 *Board Meeting – Feb 4th* *147*

Chapter 26 *Spies on the Beach* *157*

Chapter 27 *Board Meeting – Feb 18th* *166*

Chapter 28 *Jungle Paintball* *175*

Chapter 29 *Emergency Aid* *181*

Chapter 30 *Pilot Training* *188*

Chapter 31 *Board Meeting – March 4th* *196*

Chapter 32 *Parts for All* *201*

Chapter 33 *Design Review* *205*

Chapter 34 *They're awake* *208*

Chapter 35 *Board Meeting – March 18th* *214*

Chapter 36 *Take Down* *222*

Chapter 37 *Board Meeting – April 1st* *243*

Chapter 38 *Lynx Test Flights* *249*

Chapter 39 *Board Meeting – April 15th* *253*

Afterword *259*

Acknowledgments *260*

Chapter 1 Welcome Back

"Welcome back, Captain."

Marc's eyes fluttered open. "Dr. Metra." Marc recognized the doctor from her image on the video messages she had left him. He was on the Sakira, or at least he assumed he was. It was the alien spaceship that he and his brother, Blake, had found five months ago.

"Ah good, you remember my name," Dr. Metra said. "Tell me how you are feeling?"

"Pretty good," Marc said. "What have you done?"

"You mean besides fix that stupid gunshot you gave yourself?"

"It was an accident."

"Please, ADI might accept that from you since a Digital Intelligence doesn't have any guile, but I know better. Now to answer your question, I repaired the damage to your intestines; took care of the entry and exit wounds. You had some cartilage damage to your right knee and your left shoulder; I suspect childhood sports. I took care of them as well as a few other minor injuries."

She moved around to the other side of the bed Marc was lying on, her eyes flicked upward as she operated the HUD in the wraparound glasses she was wearing. "Then I noticed that you had a little plaque buildup in your arteries, that was easy to take care of. You also had a small buildup of plaque in your brain, nothing serious, but I took care of that as well; you should notice a slight improvement in your speed of recall. I also took care of the skin damage that exposure to the sun has done to you. You had some mild hormonal imbalance that comes with age that was causing you to have gray hair and a few other minor inconveniences that I took care of as well. Evolution didn't seem to care anymore about your species once you had ample opportunity to procreate than it did mine. I also repaired some stress wear on other joints, especially in your left hand. And the lenses of your eyes were starting to stiffen. I treated that, as well. You have excellent vision, by the way."

Dr. Metra moved closer, leaned over, and put her face up to Marc's. "What I can't treat, nor can I understand, is whatever it was that made you do something so stupid as to shoot yourself."

"You'll have to blame my daughter," Marc said.

"Please! . . . Children may be trying, but they are never so trying as that!"

"That's not what I meant. I promised her that I would get you out of stasis," Marc said.

"And this was the best plan you could come up with? Why not simply wait for me to come out on schedule."

"Well, that was going to take too long," Marc said.

"It shouldn't have been more than a few weeks, months at the most."

"No, it was going to be thirty years," Marc said.

"Thirty years," Dr. Metra's ears came forward, showing her surprise and shocking Marc.

Dr. Metra noticed the startled look, "Oh, you didn't notice the ears before."

"No, I didn't," Marc said. "I just noticed those ridges on the bridge of your nose, they make you look like a Bajoran."

"A Bajoran?"

"It's from a science fiction show, Star Trek: Deep Space Nine," Marc said. "Except for the ears, you look like Major Kira."

"Oh, I watched Star Trek," Dr. Metra said. "I did like that Mr. Spock, he reminded me of my first husband."

Marc laughed.

"So, you found the Sakira early," Dr. Metra said.

"I guess you could say it was early. This is 2018."

"Well, that explains the discrepancy in the schedule. But why did your daughter need me? Does she have a disease or condition I can treat?"

"No, not her, her great grandparents," Marc said. "They have Alzheimer's. She was querying ADI about the various medical treatments the Paraxeans have when she realized that you had a cure for it."

"Very industrious of her. How old is your daughter?"

"She's twelve; actually, she turns thirteen next month."

"Well, I wish I could help her, but you should know that I must return to stasis now that you are well."

"ADI."

"Yes, Captain."

"I am declaring that Dr. Metra is critical to my mission. She is not to return to stasis."

"Yes, Captain. The doctor is now on active duty. Protocol no longer requires her to return to stasis."

"You can do that?" Dr. Metra asked, very much surprised.

"Yes, as you can tell."

"But you couldn't bring me out of stasis?"

"No," Marc said, "some other protocol prevented it."

"I was aware of that. But I was not aware that the captain could change my status after I was out of stasis," Dr. Metra said. "That puts a whole new spin on things."

"Yes, it does."

"I hope it doesn't create any unintended consequences," Dr. Metra said.

"ADI says we're good."

"Let's hope she's right."

◆ ◆ ◆

"Will she remember you?" Kal asked Blake. They were at the airport in Rarotonga waiting on the arrival of the lawyer Marc had hired.

"Hey, six foot four, handsome devil like me, how could she forget?" Blake said.

"She probably knew you back when your left side was the good side," Kal said. "I don't think your right side will hold up to that memory you're cherishing."

"You do remember that you still work for me," Blake said.

"Sure, but only because I want to," Kal said.

"Oh right, I forgot you're now part of the idle rich. This is just a hobby for you."

"Some hobby," Kal said. "Hey, here they come." Kal motioned to the passengers who were now coming down the stairs from the Boeing 777. It took a few minutes before they started coming through customs.

"What does she look like?" Kal asked.

"Blond, five-foot-six, generally gorgeous," Blake said. "Didn't you look up her profile?"

"Picture wasn't all that great," Kal said. "I think she wanted to look like a kick-ass lawyer, not a hot babe."

"Marc says she is a kick-ass lawyer," Blake said. "I think that's her."

The woman coming through immigration pulling a carryon waved to Blake.

"Must be," Kal said.

Blake and Kal walked over to meet her halfway, "Ms. Newman?" Blake asked.

"Yes," Samantha Newman said. "You're Blake, right?"

"Yes, and this is Kal Kealoha, our head of security," Blake said.

"Nice to meet you," Samantha said. "Please call me Sam."

"Are we waiting for more luggage?" Kal asked.

"No, I shipped the rest," Samantha said. "It'll be here in a couple of weeks; Marc said to travel light. Where is he by the way?"

"Off in Hawaii, last I heard," Blake said. "He did tell you he wouldn't be here, didn't he?"

"He said he probably wouldn't be here," Samantha said.

"Well, I haven't heard from him for a week, so who knows where he is. He left a bunch of stuff for you at the hotel, which means you'll be busy right away," Blake said.

"He is so thoughtful," Samantha said.

Blake gave Samantha the key to her room and the layout of the hotel and who was staying in each room. "I'll see you in the office when you're ready," Blake said.

It was only fifteen minutes before Samantha made her way into the office. "How are the accommodations?" Blake asked.

"A bit rustic," Samantha said.

"Sorry," Blake said. "This was the nicest place we could find where we could get a big block of rooms."

"Well, I'll manage," Samantha said. "So, where is my desk?"

"The one by the window," Blake said. "This one's Marc's, I use it when I need one, but mostly I work out of my room."

"Okay, so I have three files here," Samantha said after she sat down and glanced through the stack of files on the desk. "Your corporate charter, the outline of the agreement he wants me to negotiate with the Cook Islands government, and some preliminary patent filings. Anything else I need to look at?"

"Marc asked me to find a hospital ship we could buy. We're setting up a clinic here, and he wants to be able to start handling patients faster than we could build a clinic," Blake said.

"Buy, would you consider leasing a ship?" Samantha asked.

"We'll probably only need it for a year or so," Blake said. "But it'll likely need to be upgraded. I haven't found any modern ones available in our time frame, but I didn't look at leasing one."

"We'll probably be able to find a modern one for lease. There are several that get used in natural disasters when they are leased by the Red Cross or other relief organizations. I'll check and let you know."

"Here is your comm unit," Blake said as he handed one to her. "If you'll register your fingerprints with it, that will activate it. It will act as your computer; it's a lot more powerful than it looks. The keyboard and display on your desk are linked to it already."

"What about security?" Samantha asked.

"We have our own private network," Blake said. "Your searches on the internet will be untraceable. The comm has an amazing voice-recognition system. It starts out almost perfect for normal commands, and it doesn't take long to learn your accent and speech pattern. Most of us give our comms a name, that makes it easy for it to know we're issuing a command. Just say 'call' and any of our names, and it'll ring us up. Catie will set it up for you so you can replace your phone if you like. She'll also show you how to use the earwig and these fancy glasses."

"Looks like I have my work cut out for me," Samantha said. "I'll get started right away."

"We usually eat at seven," Blake said. "There's a nice restaurant just down the street if you would like to join us. It will give you a chance to meet Liz and Catie."

"Sounds fine," Samantha said. "I probably will work here until then. I had a nap on the plane, so I should be able to stay awake past dinner."

"Okay, I'll stop by to pick you up," Blake said.

Chapter 2 Remember When

As soon as Dr. Metra released Marc from medical, he sent her and the Sakira to the Cook Islands where he had set up base. ADI had made a fake identification for Dr. Metra that showed she was from Costa Rica. ADI had assured him and Dr. Metra that the documents were perfect and would have no trouble passing the scrutiny of the governments of the Cook Islands or New Zealand.

Marc had the LX9, the captain's cutter from the Sakira, take him back to Honolulu. The LX9, or Lynx, as his daughter preferred to call it, made the trip underwater to avoid detection by Honolulu radar. It had to start the trip underwater anyway since the Sakira was under four hundred meters of water where it had been hiding for over thirty years. When they got to the small bay next to his hotel, he had ADI surface the Lynx so he could exit. He went into the cargo hold where his wave rider was. He'd used it to get to the Lynx five days ago; now he'd use it to get back to his hotel. It was dark, so nobody would notice the virtually invisible Lynx as it coasted along on the ocean surface.

Marc had ADI open the cargo hold, partially flooding it. He revved the wave rider up and shot out of the hold. The wave rider bounced hard as it caught a wave, but quickly righted itself. Marc rode it to the beach where he parked it. He'd have one of the cabana boys take care of it in the morning, but now he needed to get some rest. He had two busy weeks planned for himself. But first, he had to start the ball rolling with Catie's great grandparents. As soon as he got back to the hotel, he called his ex-wife.

"Dr. McCormack please," Marc asked the receptionist at Linda's office. "Tell her it's Marc."

"Yes, Mr. McCormack," the receptionist said. "One moment please, I'll see if she's available."

"Marc, is everything okay?" Linda asked. "I haven't heard from Catie or you for a few weeks."

"Everything is fine," Marc said. "We've been in Portugal and very busy."

"Yes, I've noticed. You've been on the news, pretty impressive bringing that ship up."

"It was exciting," Marc said. "But we've left Portugal. Catie is back on Hawaiian Standard time now."

"Back in Honolulu?"

"No, the Cook Islands actually, but same time zone."

"Why are you in the Cook Islands?"

"It's a long story, but back to why I called," Marc said. "We've formed a business relationship with a doctor down there. She has a very promising treatment for Alzheimer's."

"Oh my god," Linda gasped. "What do you mean by promising?"

"Nineteen out of twenty patients showed remarkable improvements. In fact, it was so remarkable that they all passed the cognitive test. Before the treatment, they were all in severe decline."

"That is amazing," Linda said as she shifted to doctor mode. "What kind of treatment and what are the risks?"

"Minimal to no risks," Marc said. "I've actually had it myself, kind of proof that it's safe. The treatment is a series of injections over a few weeks. Catie wants your grandparents to have the treatment. She's the one who found the doctor."

"That would be wonderful, but is it safe?" Linda asked. "I know you just said you took it, but long-term effects?"

"She has data on long-term effects," Marc said. "I can't explain more, there's a lot of confidential information involved; you either have to trust me or not. I need you to decide if it's okay for me to offer it to them."

"My mom's the one who has to decide," Linda said.

"We both know she'll go with whatever you recommend."

"I need to think about this," Linda said.

"Think about it. I'll be in San Diego tomorrow, then I'm flying to Boston. I hope that I'm flying back with your parents. There's another Alzheimer's victim there that I am going to offer the treatment to as well."

"What does it cost?"

"It's part of the trials, so it's free, but you've seen the news, it doesn't matter what it costs."

"I guess you're rich now, so it's pocket change for you."

"It would be pocket change for Catie as well," Marc said.

"Oh, I didn't realize that," Linda said with surprise. "Come by tomorrow, and we'll talk."

The next day it only took a brief discussion before Linda decided that the treatment's risks were worth it. Her grandparents were in their early eighties and in addition to Alzheimer's, had several health issues that Marc said his doctor could treat. Besides, their quality of life was falling rapidly as the disease progressed. It seemed that almost any risk would be worth it. She called her office and told them she was going to be gone for a few weeks due to a family emergency. Then, she packed a bag and accompanied Marc to Boston.

"I'm Marc McCormack," Marc told the woman who answered the door. "I'm looking for Dr. Zelbar."

"He's my husband," the woman answered. "What do you want?"

Mrs. Zelbar was an attractive woman; Marc estimated her age at early forties. He'd known that Dr. Zelbar had married one of his graduate students, but he hadn't realized it had been that recent. If he recalled correctly, Dr. Zelbar would be around eighty years old now.

"I was one of his students about twelve years ago," Marc said. "I was hoping I could talk to him and you."

"He's not really receiving visitors. He's not feeling well."

"Mrs. Zelbar, I know he's been having memory issues, that's why I'm here. I believe I can help."

Mrs. Zelbar looked a little shocked at the offer of help, "Then please come in," she said, "and call me Nikola."

"Thank you, Nikola. How has he been dealing with it?"

"His memory isn't that bad yet," Mrs. Zelbar said. "But without the short-term recall, he can't work anymore. Not working is driving him insane."

"And you as well, I suspect."

"Yes, that's true. He's in the study, please follow me."

"Leo, one of your former students has come to visit you," Mrs. Zelbar said to the old man sitting at the desk.

Dr. Zelbar was a shadow of his former self. He was so much thinner and being hunched over, he looked, *"well, tired,"* Marc thought.

"Hello, Dr. Zelbar," Marc said. "I don't know if you remember me, I took your class in advanced signal processing at MIT."

"I remember you. McCormack. You were always correcting me," Dr. Zelbar said. "I knew I should never have agreed to teach that class. I'm a material scientist, not a damn mathematician. You drove me nuts."

"I'm sorry about that," Marc said.

"No, you aren't. You loved every minute of it."

"Well, I've matured since then."

"I should hope so. What do you want? I'm not much good anymore. I can't remember what I had for breakfast."

"I've heard," Marc said. "That's why I'm here. I've formed a new company, and we need a material scientist."

"I told you I'm not any good," Dr. Zelbar said. "Maybe Nikola can help you."

"I heard you, but I have an offer for you that might change that."

"Well, don't just stand there, spit it out."

"I have access to a clinical trial for Alzheimer's. I'd like to offer you the opportunity to participate in that trial. I'll cover all the expenses. All I ask is that after the treatment, you consider joining my company."

"If you can fix my memory, I'll marry you," Dr. Zelbar said.

"I think you're already married," Marc laughed.

"I know, it's just an expression; I'm not that far gone."

"What is this treatment?" Mrs. Zelbar asked.

"My company is located in the Cook Islands, think of Hawaii, but smaller," Marc said. "The treatment takes three or four weeks, depending on the patient's response. It's just a series of injections that remove the plaque from the brain. I've got my daughter's great grandparents coming back with me for the treatment as well."

"What about me?" Nikola asked.

"You're welcome to come," Marc said.

"There was no question about that, but if it works, would there be a position at your company for me?"

"Possibly. As I recall, you were one of his grad students, so a PhD. in material science?"

"Yes, in molecular science, actually."

"Then we definitely would have a position for you. However, it is a private enterprise, that means no publishing of papers, and you'd have to sign a non-disclosure agreement."

"I would do anything for both of us to be able to work again."

"Then, by all means, we'll have a position for you, whether it works or not," Marc said. "I'm sure we'll be able to figure out how to make him better, even if this treatment doesn't work."

"What do we do?" Nikola asked.

"I would suggest packing," Marc said. "We can take care of all your needs, so I recommend that you just pack personal items you wouldn't want to be without."

"We'll be ready by tomorrow."

"I'm looking for Dr. Tanaka," Marc said to the young woman who opened the door.

"Yes, I was told to expect you," she said. "My father is resting in the den right now. Please, come in."

It was 10:00 a.m., and Marc was in Pasadena, visiting the home of one of the most preeminent nuclear physicists of the modern age. Tanaka was another victim of Alzheimer's, in his case, early-onset.

"Dr. Tanaka," Marc greeted the middle-aged man sitting in a chair in his study.

"Do I know you?" Dr. Tanaka asked.

"No, father," the young woman said. "This is the man I told you about. My friend, Nikola, said he could help."

"Help what?"

"Your memory."

"What's wrong with my memory? Who are you again?"

"I'm sorry, he has gotten so much worse in the last six months."

"I understand," Marc said. "Then, I guess it's you whom I need to talk to."

"Yes, I'm his guardian now. My name is Emiko, by the way."

"I'm pleased to meet you," Marc said. "I'm here to offer both treatment and a job to your father. I have a clinic in the Cook Islands that is doing a clinical study on a new Alzheimer's treatment. It has shown tremendous efficacy, although we only have limited test subjects as of now. Unfortunately, only two with early-onset; however, they both recovered completely."

"Oh my god. That is wonderful!" Emiko said. "What do we need to do?"

"My goal is that if he's cured, he will work for my company," Marc said. "But there is no obligation, I only ask that he consider it. I'll cover all your expenses during the treatment as well as travel back to Pasadena if you decide to come home."

"If you can cure him, he will do anything for you," Emiko said. "He was such a great man before this disease and an honorable one. He would consider it a debt of honor to repay you."

"Okay, I have a plane at the airport. You only need to pack a few bags, whatever you don't want to be without. We can take care of anything else you need. Call me when you're ready, and I'll pick you up," Marc said. "You can come back and get more things later or arrange shipment."

"Oh my god, oh my god! I'll hurry and pack, we'll be ready tomorrow. Oh my god, I have to call my grandfather!" Emiko cried. "Thank you! Thank you so much!"

"Everyone, welcome to Hawaii. We'll be staying at the Aston, it's close to the airfield where we've landed," Marc announced to his passengers. "Please get a good night's rest. Our flight to Rarotonga is at ten o'clock tomorrow morning."

A van was waiting to take everybody to the hotel. It was a slow process getting them all off the plane and into the van. Marc was thankful that Fred had found a new flight steward who was just as polite and helpful as Fatima had been. Jennie Baker had a charming southern accent and was able to guide the Alzheimer's patients through the process without anyone getting upset. Between her and the nurse Marc had hired for the trip, they were handling things very professionally.

Once they reached the hotel, there was plenty of help from the staff, so Marc left the group and checked everyone in. He was looking forward to a quiet dinner and several drinks when his reverie was interrupted.

"Dr. McCormack?" a young man asked.

"She's over there," Marc said. "The blond lady who's leading the elderly couple to the elevator."

"No, it is Dr. Marc McCormack that I am looking for," the young man said.

"Then, you've found him," Marc said.

"I am Tomi Nakahara. My father is Dr. Masa Nakahara; perhaps you've heard of him?"

"I recently came across the name. Nuclear physicist from Japan."

"That is correct," Tomi said. "My aunt is a good friend of Emiko Tanaka's grandmother. We have heard that you may have a treatment for Alzheimer's."

"I may," Marc said cautiously.

"If you do, I would beg of you to include my father. We heard of the most gracious offer you have made to Dr. Akemi Tanaka. My father is a colleague of his and suffers from the same ailment. He has already tried to commit Seppuku; we are desperate for a treatment."

"I would be happy to try and help," Marc said. "It is possible. I can come to Japan next week and discuss it with your father."

"Please, Dr. McCormack. I've brought my father here. He will be most overjoyed to join his colleague, Dr. Tanaka."

"Our plane is full," Marc said, "but I can come back soon."

"I fear for my father's life," Tomi said. "I must watch him every minute. I am only able to be here without him because I have someone from the hotel sitting with him, and I have told him of the offer you have made to Tanaka San. If I go back to our room and tell him that he must wait . . ." Marc looked at the desperation on Tomi's face.

"I can make room for one more person," Marc said, "but that is all."

"That is enough," Tomi said. "I can trust Emiko to watch after my father. I am not important. I can come later on a commercial flight to help."

"Alright," Marc said. "We leave the hotel at ten o'clock tomorrow morning."

"Thank you so much," Tomi said as he bowed over and over. "I am your most humble servant. Anything you ask of me will be done."

Marc went to the restaurant and started dinner with a double shot of the finest Glenfiddich they had. *"At least now I have an excuse to get my wave runner to Rarotonga,"* he thought.

"Okay everybody, next stop Rarotonga," Marc said. He looked down the aisle at the completely full plane.

"But what about you?" Linda asked as she looked around for an empty seat.

"I had to give up my seat for Nakahara San," Marc said. "Don't worry, I'll meet everyone in Rarotonga."

"How?"

"I'll fly there," Marc said.

"It'll take you days," Linda said.

"I'll be there by tonight," Marc said. "Don't worry, Blake and Catie will take care of everything until I get there."

Once the plane was in the air, Marc contacted ADI. "ADI, I need the LX9 here at 18:30."

"Yes, Captain."

It would only take him an hour to get to Rarotonga once he was aboard the Lynx. Marc thought about how nice it was to be able to do Mach five in a comfortable passenger jet. Blake had been taking care of things in Rarotonga for the two weeks Marc had been gone. He had gotten them clinic space that they would use until they acquired a hospital ship. He had even arranged to have their yacht, the Mea Huli, shipped to Rarotonga.

"Admiral."

"Yes, Lieutenant," Admiral Michaels said.

"You asked for an update whenever we got unusual activity on Dr. McCormack."

"Yes, I did. What's going on now?"

"He just flew his ex-wife and her grandparents, along with four elite scientists to the Cook Islands. Three scientists and the grandparents all have Alzheimer's. The intercepted communications imply that he has a cure," the Lieutenant said.

"That's interesting," the admiral said. "The Cook Islands?"

"Yes, sir. His team has been there for sixteen days. They also ordered their yacht to be delivered there as well."

"Let's send someone down there to keep closer tabs on him."

"Yes, sir."

Chapter 3 Back in the Saddle

Following his fast trip from Honolulu, Marc rode his wave runner to the beach behind their hotel on Rarotonga. Catie and Blake were waiting to meet him.

Blake grabbed Marc's suitcase off the back of the wave runner. Marc crawled off and peeled off the fly-fishing suit he was wearing over his clothes. Blake grabbed it as well and headed for the hotel. "I'll dump these in your room."

"Hey, that's pretty clever," Catie said. "I was worried we'd have to sneak you into the hotel because you'd be wearing a wetsuit."

"I thought about that," Marc said. "It was hard to find this in Hawaii, not that much fly-fishing goes on there, but apparently some people like to use them for surf fishing. How's your mother?"

"She's okay. She was with the grans a few minutes ago. She should be at the restaurant waiting for us by now. She wants to talk with Dr. Metra."

"I assumed she would."

"What are you going to do about the ears?"

"So, you've met her?"

"Duh, I made a trip out to the Sakira as soon as she showed up here," Catie said. "Man, that is a cool ship."

"I didn't think you could resist," Marc said. "I thought about restricting access."

"Oh, that would have been so mean," Catie said. "Uncle Blake and I spent a whole day on her just looking around. Those Foxes are really cool."

"Foxes?"

"The FX4s," Catie said.

"Oh, I'm sure they are. I haven't seen them yet."

"What's wrong with you!" Catie squeaked as she punched her father on the shoulder.

"I've been busy."

"Anyway, the ears?"

"She's going to wear a headscarf," Marc said.

"Like a Muslim?"

"Or a Hindu, or several other groups of women. It's not that unusual."

"What about the nose?"

"She said she was going to alter it, so it looks more human," Marc said.

"Oh, why not the ears?"

"Ears must be special, or hard to alter," Marc said. "She was pretty clear she wasn't touching them."

"They are pretty cool," Catie said. She laughed as she remembered Dr. Metra showing her how she could move them. "Are you going to join us for dinner? We're already supposed to be at the restaurant."

"I'm ready," Marc said.

Marc followed Catie to the restaurant. "Hello, everyone."

Linda, Emiko Tanaka, Nikola Zelbar, and Liz were all seated at the table; Blake was hurrying in behind Marc.

"Hi," Linda said.

Emiko jumped up and greeted Marc with a bow, "I am most honored to see you again," she said.

"I'm pleased to see you again, too," Marc said. He looked at Linda, "Are our patients settled in?"

"Yes, Dr. Metra has them all in bed. She's going to administer the first treatment tomorrow."

"Good to hear," Marc said as he sat between Catie and Linda as his daughter had arranged.

"You weren't kidding when you said you'd be here tonight," Linda said. "How could you make such good time?"

"Charter flight," Marc said.

"It must be nice to be rich."

"Oh, it is," Marc said. "Catie seems to like it as well."

"I can tell," Linda said. "She's wearing capri pants from Walmart and some top she probably bought at the local gift shop."

"And she has a thousand-dollar phone and a pair of tech glasses worth twice that," Marc said. "She has different priorities than you."

"Well, I'm just glad she's happy, and she does seem really happy."

After dinner, Marc had a meeting scheduled with Samantha.

"Sam?" He called out as he knocked on the office door.

"Come on in," Samantha said.

"You didn't join us for dinner."

"It seemed like it was going to be a family affair," Samantha said. "I thought I'd stay out of the way."

"How are things going?"

"Good, I've made the necessary contacts with the government, and I've been doing research on the patents you asked about. I don't see any prior art." "Neither do I see the kind of documentation you would need to file."

"I'm planning on keeping them as company secrets," Marc said.

"That doesn't give you much protection from corporate espionage."

"Hence the island location. Are you okay with the accommodations?"

"They're okay," Samantha said. "Blake told me that Kal was looking for a more permanent location."

"Hopefully they'll find one soon," Marc said. "Hotels get tiring. You're all set up with a comm and specs?"

"Yes, Catie set me up. She's pretty amazing for a twelve-year-old."

"Yes she is. I recommend you avoid referencing her age in front of her."

"I noticed she gets a bit peeved if someone does," Samantha said. "She fits right in with everyone, and you wouldn't think she was so young if it wasn't for that small voice of hers and her youthful looks."

"How's the contract?" Marc asked.

Samantha turned her computer display so Marc could see it.

"You're not using your specs." Marc had expected Samantha to have him link with her comm so they could share a view.

"I pace myself with them," Samantha said, "I'm still getting used to them. I prefer the display and keyboard for now. I might be too old to change."

"I seriously doubt that," Marc said.

"Thanks for the vote of confidence. As you see, I have all the documents prepared so you can move your corporation to the Cook Islands, but I suggest we wait until we're a little further along in the negotiation about the control of Manuae before we file."

"You're the lawyer, just tell me what I need to do."

"I'll have papers for you to sign tomorrow, then I'll be meeting with the prime minister. We'll see where things go from there," Samantha said. "Don't expect it to happen very quickly."

"I know better. You're planning on working more tonight?"

"Yes," Samantha said. "Working with governments is very slow, but it takes an enormous amount of effort to keep things moving."

"Then I'll leave you in peace," Marc said. "If you want me, just ping me on your comm."

"I will."

Marc waited a few days after everyone had received their first treatment before he went to check in on them.

"Hello, Nikola, how's Dr. Zelbar doing?"

"He's doing much better," Nikola said. "He's remembering things more readily and asking about the status of some of his old projects."

Nikola led Marc into Dr. Zelbar's room. The Alzheimer's patients were housed in small two-room suites where they could have a family member staying with them if they wished.

"Leo, look who's come to visit," Nikola said.

"More likely, come to see when I can get to work," Dr. Zelbar said.

"Leo," Nikola scolded.

"He's partially correct," Marc said. "But remember, it's your choice. You can go back to Boston if you like."

"We're not in Boston?" Dr. Zelbar said with surprise.

"No, Leo," Nikola said. "We're in Rarotonga in the Cook Islands. Remember I told you that yesterday. This is where the clinic is."

"Oh yes, I remember," Dr. Zelbar said. "Some tropical paradise," he scoffed as he looked around the hospital room.

"We need to stay here until you get better," Nikola said.

"I think another ten days," Marc said. "Then you can move to a nice hotel on the beach."

"What do I care about a beach," Dr. Zelbar said. "What I need is a lab."

"The hotel will be very close to your lab," Marc said.

"Good," Dr. Zelbar said as he went back to reading a book. Nikola led Marc out into the second room where she was staying in order to be close to her husband.

"He is getting better," she said. "He's just frustrated, and honestly, he's always been a bit cantankerous."

"I remember," Marc said. "How are you doing?"

"I'm okay, going a little stir crazy."

"Would you like to start on one of our projects?"

Nikola's eyes lit up. "Oh, I would love to have some work to do."

"This one is pretty straightforward. We have a theoretical design for a new battery, and we need to figure out if it will work. It's a lithium-ion, ceramic mix. We actually figured out how to mix the two, but we don't know the optimal structure."

"Oh, that sounds very interesting," Nikola said. "I could start on it right away."

"I'll send you the details we have. Blake has a small lab set up for you so you can start anytime you want. My assistant, Masina, will be able to handle almost anything you need. If she can't, she'll put you in touch with either Blake or me."

"What about the non-disclosure?"

"The production process is the key here," Marc said. "You'll be analyzing the results and tuning the process to create the best design; I think we'll wait on the non-disclosure until you're both ready to consider it. If you decide to go back to Boston, we'll take over the work. You've signed an employment contract already, so that takes care of everything else."

"Oh good," Nikola said. "So, you think another ten days?"

"Yes, but you can move to the hotel anytime you like," Marc said.

"No, it's best if I stay here," Nikola said. The nurse who was passing through the room to check on Dr. Zelbar nodded her head in emphatic agreement.

Marc walked down the hall to check on Dr. Nakahara and Dr. Tanaka. Their children had decided that they should room together. The two physicists were old friends, and everyone hoped that they would help each other through the process.

"Hello, Emiko, Tomi," Marc said as he knocked on the door to the suite.

"Hello, Dr. McCormack," Emiko said.

Tomi jumped up and gave Marc a deep bow. "I am forever indebted to you."

"I am happy we could help," Marc said. "When did you arrive?"

"I arrived on Tuesday," Tomi said.

"I hear that they're both responding well."

"Yes, father is like he was before," Emiko said. "It is the most amazing thing I have ever seen. Nakahara San is doing better as well."

"Yes, he is improving," Tomi said. He sounded a bit disappointed that the improvement wasn't as dramatic as Dr. Tanaka's.

"Dr. Metra told me that all her cases of early-onset Alzheimer's responded to the first treatment dramatically, as Dr. Tanaka has done. She's assured me that your father is doing well and should make substantial improvements after the second treatment. She says he's shown about the same level of improvement as my daughter's great grandparents have."

Tomi's face relaxed. "She told me he was doing well, but I was worried she was trying to protect my feelings."

"I believe the next treatment is in a few days. That's supposed to be the time when you normally see the biggest change," Marc explained. "Are the two of them still happy to be sharing a room?"

"Oh yes," Emiko said. "Father has taken it upon himself to quiz Dr. Nakahara, to help him improve his memory. Dr. Nakahara seems to find it quite amusing. Sometimes he pretends not to remember just to see my father become frustrated."

"That sounds very promising. How are you two doing?" Marc asked.

"We are doing well," Emiko said. "We are helping the nurses with the other patients. Tomi has been helping do some of the work setting up the new labs and equipment."

"I'm glad to hear that," Marc said. "Have you thought about what you would like to do later? Will you go back home?"

"I would like to stay here," Emiko said. "I am studying to be a doctor, and your Dr. Metra says that she can help me. I can enroll in a medical school in Auckland. Then, I would be close to father, and she says she will try to set things up so I can do my internships here."

"We'd be happy to have another doctor on the staff," Marc said. "We are planning to be a city soon. What about you, Tomi?"

"I have a degree in environmental science," Tomi said. "I have talked to the Minister of Finance and Economic Development's office about potential employment here. I've always been interested in low-environmental-impact manufacturing."

"That's interesting. You may know that we've agreed with the government here to have a minimal environmental footprint," Marc said. "I'm sure we could use you."

"I have just graduated, but I would be most honored to join your company."

"My daughter is working on a new sewage treatment system for underdeveloped countries. We plan to install several here in the Cook Islands. Perhaps you would be willing to work on it with her?"

"I would be most honored."

"I'll have my assistant, Masina, contact you. She can set both of you up with the necessary computers and company phones. If you're going to be staying with MacKenzie Discoveries, we need to get you set up. She'll also give you the contact information for my daughter, Catie."

"Thank you," Tomi said.

"No, I should be thanking you," Marc said. "We are working hard to attract talent, so this is a bonus for us."

Chapter 4 Board Meeting – Nov 12th

"Good afternoon everybody," Marc said as the team settled down in the lounge of the Mea Huli. The Mea Huli had arrived the week before from Portugal, and everybody was happy to have her available again.

"I think it's time we started to apply a bit more structure to our process," Marc said. Samantha quietly applauded, while everyone else looked at Marc like he'd grown a second head.

"I want to hold a meeting as a team at least every two weeks; we'll call them board meetings. We'll each give updates on the status of our work, pick up and give out new assignments, . . . provide suggestions, . . . offer help." Marc kept slowing down as he continued to be greeted with dead silence from the room.

"Come on guys, a little support would be nice," Samantha said. "You're running a multibillion-dollar company here. A meeting every other week shouldn't be too much to ask."

"I'm okay with it," Catie said, "although I don't see why we can't just use our specs."

"Because we want everybody to hear the updates at the same time, and when they're not being distracted by other matters. That way, we'll get the best understanding, and everyone will be able to ask questions and offer suggestions," Marc said. He was a bit ticked off at the lack of response.

"I'm good with it," Blake said. "We've had lots of meetings before. We were all shocked by the thought of a *'board meeting'* and a regular schedule." Blake used air quotes to stress, board meeting. "We've been used to playing it fast and loose."

"We'll still have impromptu meetings when the situation requires," Marc said. "And I realize that right now, this may be more for my sanity than for the rest of you, but a little organization can't hurt."

"That's right," Blake said. He got up and got the bottle of Glenlivet fifteen-year-old scotch he kept on the Mea Huli. Blake poured a round for everyone. "What?" he said in response to Marc's scolding look. "We have to toast the first board meeting." He paused at Catie, looking to Marc for approval. Marc nodded, giving in to the inevitable, but indicated just a splash for her with his fingers.

"If that's what it takes," Marc shook his head and laughed, he was happy that everyone was following Blake's lead in celebrating the new board.

Blake stood up, "To our Chairman!"

"To our Chairman!"

"Okay, now let's get down to business. As everybody should know, we've started our medical clinic in a small, leased office here on Rarotonga. Most of you have met Dr. Metra when you got your physical. She's the doctor Catie found who has developed the Alzheimer's treatment. She is now starting to treat the patients whom I brought in last week. Dr. Metra," Marc said, indicating she should start out.

"Good day," Dr. Metra said. "We have five patients whom Dr. McCormack brought in to continue the clinical trials for our new Alzheimer's treatment. They have all settled in, and each received their first treatment last week and their second treatment yesterday. They are all having an excellent response to the treatment so far. We'll give them a third treatment next week; although, I think only one of them will actually need it. But an extra treatment won't hurt, and with two of them going home the following week, I don't want to take any chances. The temporary clinic should be able to handle twenty patients at a time. We need a few more nurses to care for the patients. That is especially true if we need to offer any other treatments or emergency care. Right now, I only have the two nurses and the caregivers we have hired from the local population. But, to be able to handle more patients, we should really have twelve more nurses."

"I'll get on it," Samantha said. "I think we have an attractive package to offer nurses."

"Thank you," Dr. Metra said.

"Hopefully, Dr. Zelbar will be working on the polysteel process soon, but he will need lab space," Marc said as he looked at Blake.

"On my list," Blake said. "I found a warehouse here in the port that should work until we can put something on Manuae. We can just put up prefabbed walls to build offices and labs inside it. I have a big order of that stuff coming in on a freighter next week."

"Great," Marc said. "I've identified four other scientists who should be of help to us. I'll be going out next week to make the offers," Marc continued. "How are we coming on more permanent accommodations for them, or do we want to continue to house them in the hotel?"

"I'd suggest leaving them in the hotel," Liz said. "We don't want to be penny wise and pound foolish. As I recall, these scientist types aren't the best at doing their own meals and laundry. The cost of a hotel over an apartment will be dwarfed by any loss in productivity or schedule. For those who want a bigger place, we can deal with as they request it."

"Makes sense. Sam, facilities on Manuae?" Marc asked.

"We are still negotiating the contract, which means we can't break ground yet. It looks promising. There hasn't been any issue related to building a few structures on Manuae. Especially with your promise to remove them and restore the island by the end of the lease," Samantha reported.

"We're going to remove all the structures," Liz said. "Where are we going to be living after that?"

"Ah, a moment of truth," Marc said. "Blake, you're on."

"We'll be living in Delphi City," Blake said. He flicked his eyes up, using his HUD to turn on the big display at the front of the lounge.

"That looks more like a town than a city," Kal said.

"Well, it will grow," Blake said. "This is just the first quad, which will be eight hundred fifty meters on a side. Four quads will make a section, and each section will be sixteen hundred meters on a side. The end quads are fifty meters longer because of their overhang. We're shooting for the first quad to be completed within the year. Section One should be finished about six months after that."

"When the first quad is completed, we'll be able to start adding production there and start putting in dorms for the workers and some lab space. For quad three, we'll focus on residential and retail space."

"If a section is going to be sixteen hundred meters, will we be able to put a landing strip for the G650?" Kal asked.

"The G650 needs seventeen hundred eighty-five meters when it's fully loaded," Fred said. "We can probably handle a short one like that if we lighten the fuel load."

"I plan to add a ski jump at the end, so it'll be able to take off in the sixteen hundred meters we have for it," Blake said. "I've run the numbers with Gulfstream, and they agree."

"Sweet," Fred said.

"Those columns look kind of small," Liz said. "Is that to scale?"

"They are, and it is," Blake said. "The columns are five meters in diameter, and they have buttresses up to the crossbeams to help stabilize them. They're made of polysteel, so they're strong enough."

"What's polysteel?" Kal asked.

"It's the new mix of carbon and steel that the Zelbars are working on," Marc said.

"Aren't we counting our chickens before they hatch?" Samantha asked.

"I didn't know you were a farm girl," Marc said. "What, I don't get a laugh?"

"It wasn't that good, Daddy."

"I'm surrounded by critics," Marc said. "Moving forward. Yes, we are assuming a lot, but we have got lots of time; we'll adjust the design if we don't get the results we're expecting."

"Back to the columns," Blake continued. "They actually don't have that much side force on them. The platform will be constructed of polysteel and have two levels. It's basically a ten-meter-deep basement for our entire infrastructure; sewage, electricity, power, etc. We'll cap it with solid polysteel decking that we'll construct all the buildings on top of."

"And parks," Catie said.

"Yes, and parks. Catie has informed me that we have to dedicate thirty percent of the space to greenbelts, parks, and trees. She's asked to manage that design since it appears she doesn't trust me."

Catie stuck her tongue out at Blake. "I just want to make sure it gets enough attention," Catie said. "I know how busy you are."

"Any questions or suggestions?" Marc asked. "We'll be reviewing the design at each meeting. We're still a ways from being able to start production of the polysteel."

Marc looked around the room. Nobody was asking for attention, so he moved on. "Next: Kal, how is recruiting going?"

"Using my contacts, I've found five guys who fit the profile we're looking for. They're tired of doing private security and mall guard crap. They're smart but too antsy to go to college, more the outdoors type," Kal said. "They'll be here in two weeks. Liz and I will run them through some basic training and see who we want to keep."

"Good," Marc said. He liked the fact that Kal was going to do a secondary interview process on them with Liz. They couldn't afford to bring in anyone who wasn't solid. "Anything else security related?"

"Yes, I'd like to get us out of the hotel as soon as possible," Kal said. "I've been looking for a private house or estate. It's much easier to handle security when you don't have to filter out all the other guests who should be there in order to identify the ones who shouldn't."

"Good idea; I assume Blake's been helping you look for a place," Marc said.

"He has," Kal replied.

"Liz, do you have time to start coordinating the work of our scientists?" Marc asked.

"Of course. Do we have any of them working yet?" Liz asked.

"Dr. Nikola Zelbar has started working on the batteries. Tomi Nakahara is going to be working with Catie on the new sewer system we agreed to design for the government here. We'll especially need it up when we start having people on Manuae," Marc said.

"Sewer system?" Blake asked. "I don't remember that."

"Catie, why don't you explain?"

"Well, you know that one of the biggest problems low-investment areas have is how to handle all the sewage. They don't have regular plumbing like we're used to. It's too big and expensive to put into the small villages and other remote places. This design will take any waste that's plumbed to it or dumped in it and process it. I've been working on one for the Mea Huli, and this will be almost the same. Then people either use the public restrooms that are plumbed to it, or they can have a special private toilet similar to the one that guy designed for Bill Gates' prize. But this one lets you throw toilet paper into it."

"Where else would you throw the toilet paper?"

"In a trash can next to the toilet," Catie said. "Kind of gross, isn't it? But it's pretty common in a lot of underdeveloped countries and regions. The toilet I'm designing will separate out the water, dehydrate the waste and package it into a bundle that you can carry and dump into the public system. That system will process it into a sterile organic mix."

"That sounds like a lot for you," Samantha said.

"Well I have ADI subcontracting a lot of the design," Catie said. "I'm just coordinating it. If Tomi likes it, I'd be happy to hand it off to him."

"Thanks, Catie. Fred, do you have anything?"

"Nope, I'm just a pilot, boat driver, and extra security guy," Fred said. "But I'm willing to pick up whatever you need me to do."

"Don't worry, Marc will be handing action items off to you soon enough," Blake said. "Count your blessings while you can."

"With that, let's close this meeting. The next meeting will be the week after Thanksgiving," Marc said. "So, with the extra week, I expect lots of progress."

"Hey, that's a holiday week," Blake said. "Catie and I are taking it off."

"I remember giving Catie the week off, but when did you get it off?" Marc asked.

"I'm a junior partner, I gave myself the week off," Blake said.

"Damn, I knew making you a partner would come back to bite me," Marc said. "Fred, we're ready to go home." Marc loved the banter with Blake. It kept the meetings light and engaging.

Chapter 5 First Steps

"Dr. Zelbar, how are you feeling?" Marc asked.

"Great, I've haven't felt this good in years," Dr. Zelbar replied.

"Have you considered my offer?" Marc asked.

"Yes. Nikola explained it to me again. We're ready to sign up. Where is that document you want us to sign? We need to get to work before we kill each other. And it's not as if you don't already have Nikola working for you."

Marc and Nikola exchanged glances.

"Ha, I knew it, she's been purring like a kitten, and she only does that when she's working on something interesting."

Marc laughed, "I guess I've been found out. But there is no hurry, there is plenty of time."

"No, there isn't," Nikola said. "I'm going to kill him tonight if he doesn't stop complaining about nothing to do."

"Alright," Marc said. "Here are the documents; please review them with your lawyer before you sign them."

"Forget that. Where do I sign?" Dr. Zelbar said. "If you're happy with them, I'm happy. All I want to do is work."

"Me too."

Marc called a couple of nurses in to witness the signing. They looked thrilled to be seeing Dr. Zelbar getting ready to leave.

"We don't have a lab set up for you," Marc said. "But I'm sure you'd prefer to do that yourself. We have a temporary space here in Rarotonga. Hopefully, we'll be able to move to a more permanent location in a few months."

"I don't care about that," Dr. Zelbar said. "Now, what do you want us to work on?"

"We had a small accident a few years ago," Marc said. "A welder working for me had some mixture of something like graphite fall on the sheet metal he was spot welding. The result was a blend of steel and carbon that looks very promising."

"That's just carbon steel," Dr. Zelbar scoffed. "It's been around for centuries."

"Yes, I know," Marc said. "But, analysis of the steel shows an unusual bonding of the carbon and iron atoms. Much more carbon than iron, and it appears to be stronger and much more durable."

"Well, that's at least interesting," Dr. Zelbar said in a huff.

"Leo, be nice," Mrs. Zelbar said. "How were you able to analyze the material?" she asked Marc.

"We got about a square centimeter of material. It was obvious that something was different when the welder tried to grind it off. The grinder had no effect on the area. So, we cut it out, and I had a friend do spectroscopic analysis on it. I have the results. I can send them to you."

"Please," Mrs. Zelbar said.

"Wait. Just because you're the one with the degree in molecular material, doesn't mean you get to take over," Dr. Zelbar said.

"Of course not, we'll work together," Mrs. Zelbar said. "It just so happens I already have my computer and email set up. We'll get you set up today and we'll start analyzing this material right away." She smiled at Marc.

"Alright, now get me out of this place."

"I'm not sure the treatment is complete," Mrs. Zelbar said.

"The doctor says that the last treatment can be done on an outpatient basis," Marc said. "He just needs to come back one day next week for a few hours. Why don't I go ask the doctor to come in and expedite your release?"

"That would be wonderful, wouldn't it, Leo?"

"What? Whatever. Now, if the carbon atoms bonded to the iron to form . . ."

Mrs. Zelbar smiled at Marc again and mouthed 'thank you.' Marc gave her a head nod to indicate he'd like a moment with her in the hallway.

"What can I do for you, Dr. McCormack?" she asked once he had closed the door.

"You say he's much better?" Marc asked.

Mrs. Zelbar laughed. "Pretty much, he's more fun when he's involved with a project."

"How's your battery project going?"

"It's keeping me busy," Nikola said. "It gives me a chance to get away from him for a while. I didn't realize I was so happy until he mentioned in there that I've been purring."

"Well, I have another project if you'd like it."

"Of course. I could use a second project. What is it?"

"You won't be too busy on the steel project with him?"

"Not so much. I'll help, but Leo will insist on doing most of the work. I'll handle the overflow and be a sounding board when he gets stuck. It always works better when I have a project or two of my own going at the same time."

"I have the preliminary designs for a new fuel cell," Marc said. "I need to have feasibility proven and a proposal for manufacturing it. Similar to the battery project, but I think it's more complex."

"That sounds perfect. Just send the data along with the carbon-steel data," Mrs. Zelbar said. "This sounds like I'll be having as much fun as Leo."

"Hey, Blake, you have a minute?" Marc said as he walked into Blake's office.

"Hey, the next board meeting isn't until after Thanksgiving. I still have time to get my stuff done," Blake quipped.

Marc laughed at his brother. "Hey, I'm here to talk, not to check your homework."

"Take a seat," Blake said. "What's up?"

"I wondered how you were doing. How is this working for you?"

"Oh, you mean, how do I like working for hard taskmaster?"

"Is that how you feel?"

"No, you drive yourself harder than anyone else," Blake said. "I'm doing fine. Work is interesting, working conditions are pretty nice," he said. "The people I work with are all smart, hard workers, and I get to see my niece every day."

"Anything you'd like to change?"

"I'd like to get back to flying," Blake said. "But that can wait for a while. I know you don't want anyone to know about the Lynx, much less those Foxes."

"We do want to wait on that," Marc said. "I'm going back to Boston for Thanksgiving. Do you want to come?"

"No, I'll go with you for Christmas, but I'm just getting to know the people around here," Blake said. "The ladies are receptive to my charms, and I have a few more bars to check out."

"Okay," Marc said. "Let me know if things need to change. I can't lose my wingman."

"Hey, I thought you were my wingman!"

"Only when we're at a bar," Marc said.

"Hey, how about Sam?" Blake asked. "Is there something going on there?"

"No," Marc said. "She's just the best lawyer I know. Why do you ask?"

"I don't know, she seems to look a little more upbeat when you're around. Thought you guys might have some history."

"Nope, just my lawyer."

"Well, maybe you should think about that. She's a pretty nice lady besides being a ruthless lawyer."

Marc chuckled. "That ruthless lawyer part scares me a bit."

"Chicken."

"Speaking of chicken, you want to go out for lunch today?"

"Sure."

Chapter 6 Birthday Girl

"Here's the birthday girl!" Marc said as he started clapping.

Catie's ears turned red, and she blushed at all the attention as everybody stood up and clapped along with Marc. They were having the party at the Flambé, one of the best restaurants on Rarotonga. Her great grandparents were there. They'd had their second treatment with Dr. Metra and were doing much better.

"Hi, Mommy," Catie said as Linda walked up and gave her a hug.

"How does it feel to be a teenager?" Linda asked.

"Not really any different," Catie said. "It's not like there's some sudden change that happens overnight."

"We should talk about that," Linda said, giving Catie a knowing smile. "But for now, we should celebrate."

"People," Marc shouted to get everyone's attention. "We're going to run this birthday party starting at the end; presents first, then dinner, then cake. That will give us all something to chat about besides work."

Catie's great grandparents, Agnes and Duncan, came over. "Young lady, we've missed too much of your life with our health problems, but we want to catch up," Duncan said. "Now I hear you're coming with us to stay at your mother's for Thanksgiving. Your father says you should be able to stay a whole week."

"I will Grandpa Pa," Catie said.

"Sweetie, these were my mother's," Agnes said as she handed Catie a black velvet box. "I want you to have them."

Catie opened it to reveal an exquisite pearl necklace with matching earrings. "Oh, Grandma Ma, they're beautiful."

"Just like you. Now you'll need to actually start wearing dresses once in a while so you can show them off." Agnes wrinkled her nose as she looked at Catie in her Capri pants and Polynesian top.

Catie laughed. "Hey, this party is supposed to be casual dress."

"You have casual dresses," Agnes said.

"I promise to start wearing dresses more often," Catie said.

"Good!"

Linda came over and gave Catie a small velvet box.

The diamond earrings sparkled when Catie opened the box. "Mommy, they're beautiful."

"What your gran said," Linda said with a laugh. "We'll buy you some dresses while you're staying in San Diego with us."

"Thanks, Mommy."

"I'm feeling a little shabby trying to follow those presents," Marc said. "What do you give a girl that has everything?"

"Oh, Daddy."

"Well, Fred and I went together on this one," Marc said. "He's going to give you flying lessons, or at least flying hours, until you're qualified on the G650."

Catie clasped her face with both hands, "Wow!"

"It will take about four or five months to go through all the training," Marc continued. "We can't let you solo until you're sixteen, but we're hoping we have a way around that. But he'll get you the hours and everything else certified."

Samantha walked up and gave Catie a hug. "I'm working with the government to get an exception for you. I think I can get a family and or a cargo-only exception for flights between the islands out here."

"Oh, that would be so cool," Catie squealed.

Liz walked over and handed Catie a small package.

Catie opened it to find a stainless-steel cylinder about three inches long, "What is it?"

"It's a pocket Bo Staff," Liz said as she pulled one out of her pocket. She pressed the end of it, and it expanded into a five-foot-long staff. "I'll teach you how to use it."

"That's going to be fun," Catie said as she gave Liz a hug. "Thanks."

Kal walked over with a small padded case. It was only about one-and-one-half feet square and two inches thick. "Here you go, Cat," he said as he handed it to her. "You're going to be needing this in a couple of weeks."

Catie opened it up; she only saw a small gray cylinder and zippers for pouches. She gave Kal a questioning look.

"It's probably easier to just pull out the manual," Kal said as he pointed to a slot in the case.

Catie pulled the manual out, "A paintball rifle. But . . ."

"My present is putting the paintball arena on the top of the construction list," Blake said. "It will be ready when you get back from Thanksgiving."

"Wow, for me?"

"Well, it's early for you," Blake said. "Kal and Liz will be using it to train their security guys as we hire more of them."

"Wow, thanks, everybody," Catie said. "This is the best birthday ever." Catie looked at her great grandparents and beamed.

"Alright," Marc said. "Let's clean up this mess, and then we can sit down and order dinner."

Chapter 7 Taking A Break

That Sunday, Fred flew Marc, Catie, Linda, and the grans to San Diego on the G650. "I'll be back to get you on Saturday," Marc told Catie. "Have fun." He said goodbye to the grans and to Linda as they deplaned.

Then Fred flew him on to Princeton to do some more recruiting. After that, they'd go to Boston, where Marc would spend Thanksgiving with his parents. He chafed a bit that he had to have Kal with him as a bodyguard. There had been a big argument about whether to send Liz with Catie, but in the end, they agreed that she was unlikely to be a target in the states. Marc paid for some discreet security from a private company just to be sure.

Marc waved to Linda as Catie climbed the ramp to the G650. "How was Thanksgiving?"

"Great," Catie said. "We had lots of fun." Catie gave her father a hug and a kiss as she boarded.

"Welcome back," Jennie said. "Now, if you'll be seated, we'll be taking off in a few minutes."

"We're here in the front row," Marc said. Catie gave Kal a quick hug as he walked by her to the second row to take his seat.

"Hi, Kal, you miss me?" Catie asked.

"I always miss you," Kal said. "Liz has been antsy without you and me to work out with. We need to get back there and calm her down."

"I miss her too," Catie said. "Daddy, I see your recruiting trip was successful," Catie said as she looked at the small group at the back of the plane. She waved at them before she sat down.

"Yes, I came up with three new scientists," Marc said. "One of them has a spouse who's also a scientist, and one has a spouse who's a doctor. Should be nice additions." Marc sat in the seat next to Catie.

"Cool. How were Nanna and Poppa?"

"They were fine. They're looking forward to seeing you at Christmas. Dad is still teaching at Boston College, and Mom is still teaching high school. She wanted to know how you were doing with your studies."

"What did you tell her?" Catie asked.

"I said you were doing fine, but if she really wanted to know how you were doing, she should grill you on her next call."

"You didn't say *grill*, did you?"

"Oh, yes, I did. So be ready for at least one quiz," Marc laughed.

Catie punched her father on the shoulder, "You're so mean."

"Have to have a little fun when I can. Tell me what you did in San Diego?"

"Well, the grans took me to the Old Globe Theatre and we saw How The Grinch Stole Christmas. They produce that every year."

"And?"

"I didn't think I would like it, it's for little kids after all, but it was really good. The costumes were amazing, and it is a good story. I think the grans liked it even better than I did."

"What else?"

"We all went to the zoo, that was a long day. We had to get a cart for the grans at the end; they were getting tired. But we all had fun."

"Did you do Sea World?"

"No, not enough time," Catie said. "Mommy and Grandma Ma made a huge turkey for Thanksgiving dinner. They really had a good time in the kitchen. I watched football with Grandpa Pa."

"Did you really?" Marc asked.

"Well, I sat with him. I worked on my math, mostly. But he didn't notice."

"Who won?"

"I don't know. Grandpa Pa was happy, that's all I know."

"Did you visit any old friends?"

"Nobody was around," Catie said. "And I didn't have that many anyway. I just hung out with Mommy and the grans."

"Anything else?"

"Shopping, I've got enough dresses to last the rest of my life."

Marc laughed, "We'll need to go to more fancy places so you can wear them."

"You don't need to," Catie said. "It's okay if they just hang in my closet."

"But the grans will want reports," Marc said, giving Catie a knowing look.

"Darn. Oh," Catie's eyes got big, and she gave her father a big smile, "Mommy has a new boyfriend."

"She does? Did you get to meet him?"

"No, but I heard her talking on the phone. She was all gushy and stuff. I think she's a little happier now."

"That's good."

"By the way, those security guys were good," Catie said.

"You noticed them, did you?"

"Not at first, but the same guy in two different places kind of tipped me to it."

"Did your mother see them?"

"No, just me."

"That's good," Marc said. "Now, I think we should talk."

"We've been talking."

"I know, Smart Alec. I mean, talk about you and how you're doing."

"I'm doing great," Catie said.

"Are you really? It has been a whirlwind six months," Marc said. "You were kidnapped, and we've been continuously moving around. And now you're a bit isolated at the hotel where you're living with your father, who's busy and hardly spends any time with you. How can that be doing great for a thirteen-year-old girl?"

Catie thought for a few minutes, then took a deep breath, "Well, I spend as much time with you as I want to. I only have to walk into your office, which is next door to my room at the hotel where I do most of my work and my homework. You never tell me to get lost, well, almost never."

"You deserve it when I do," Marc said.

"Probably. Anyway, I don't feel isolated. I have Liz to talk to any time I want. Uncle Blake is always good for a laugh or some help if I need it. Kal and Liz work out with me all the time. I get to work on the most interesting projects in the world. The kidnapping was not cool, but you got me back, and I always knew you would. I have ADI to help me and to talk to. Her personality is growing, so that's fun and interesting. What kid wouldn't want to be me?"

"Sure, and what kids do you know?"

"I've never had that many friends," Catie said. "We've only been there five weeks, so I haven't had time to meet many anyway. When I go to the beach, I hang out with the kids there. This one guy has been teaching me to surf. So, I could have as many kids for friends as I want, I just haven't met anyone that I want to have as a close friend. And I've been practicing what you told me about establishing a relationship with someone, so we will have something to build on later. The Finance Minister's son and I are okay friends, he's the one teaching me to surf."

"I worry that you're growing up too fast."

"You know that Mommy says I was born a twenty-year-old."

"Yeah, we've always talked about that. You've always been so smart, and you've been around so many of her colleagues and mine that you've always acted more like an adult than a kid," Marc said. He sighed, then continued, "But you're more important to me than any of this other stuff. So, if you're not happy or you want something you're not getting, you come and talk to me. Okay?"

"Deal."

Chapter 8 Flying Lesson

"Are you ready for this?" Fred asked Catie as they headed to the G650.

"I was born ready," Catie said.

Fred just laughed at her, "It's going to be different than flying the simulator. Even with those three-D glasses, it'll be different."

"I know," Catie said.

"Blake has bought a full-blown simulator," Fred said. "He assumes that he'll be able to modify it for the Lynxes."

"We should, we're using the same controls," Catie said. "The rest is just software, and ADI is the best programmer in the world."

"I'm sure," Fred said. "Once the simulator is here, we'll put you through more difficult scenarios."

"Good morning, Captain, Hello, Catie," Jennie greeted them as they climbed the ramp into the jet.

"Hi, Jennie, you're coming up with us?"

"Somebody has to make your coffee," Jennie said. "Besides, I understand we'll be picking some people up from Auckland."

"Oh," Catie's eyes shined. "I didn't know we were going that far."

"These jets are expensive to fly," Fred said. "We don't want to take this baby up without getting something else out of it besides flying time."

"Who are we picking up?" Catie asked.

"Some construction workers Blake hired," Fred explained. "Now go up, sit in the copilot's chair, and handle the preflight. I'll check with the crew chief."

"We're good to go," Catie said when Fred made his way into the cockpit.

"Good, let me double-check your work," Fred said. "I know you have probably done this a few dozen times on the simulator, but humor an old man."

Catie frowned as Fred went through all the preflight checks, but didn't say anything.

"I'll let you handle the radio," Fred said. "I'll do the takeoffs and landings for now. Today, we just want you to get the feel of handling her."

"Okay," Catie said with disappointment.

"Get on the radio," Fred chided, "I'm ready to fly."

"Clearance, MacKenzie One to Auckland."

"MacKenzie One cleared to Auckland airport, AZ423, depart runway one, squawk 0-2-3-3."

"MacKenzie One cleared to Auckland airport, AZ423, depart runway one, squawk 0-2-3-3." Catie echoed.

"MacKenzie One readback correct, MacKenzie One taxi into position one left."

"MacKenzie One taxi into position one left."

"MacKenzie One cleared for takeoff."

"MacKenzie One, cleared for takeoff," Catie responded.

"Let's go," Fred said as he pushed the throttle forward.

"MacKenzie One good afternoon, radar identified maintain seven thousand."

"Roger, maintain 7 thousand."

"MacKenzie One, after noise abatement turn heading 0-9-0."

"Right, heading 0-9-0 after noise, MacKenzie One."

"MacKenzie One climb to flight level 2-3-0."

"Climb to flight level 2-3-0, MacKenzie One."

"Wow, that's a lot of talking just to take off," Catie said.

"I guess it is, but you get used to it, and they don't want you running into any other planes," Fred explained. "You have to repeat everything, so they know you've heard them. Check and double-check, and you'll be safe."

"MacKenzie One contact Auckland Center on 1-2-7-0."

"Auckland Center on 1-2-7-0 MacKenzie One, good day."

"Auckland Center, MacKenzie One, climbing to 2-3-0."

"MacKenzie One identified, maintain 2-3-0."

"Thank you, MacKenzie One."

"Okay, are you ready to take the controls?"

"Sure,"

"Then take them," Fred said.

"I have the controls."

"You have the controls."

"Now let's fly some slaloms for a bit, that way, you can get a feel for her," Fred said.

Catie immediately starting banking the G650 to the right. After a bit, she eased it back to the left, carefully keeping an eye on the heading and altitude.

"Auckland Center, MacKenzie One, requesting transition to 3-0-0."

"MacKenzie One, cleared for ascent to 3-0-0."

"MacKenzie One, cleared for ascent to 3-0-0."

"Take her up," Fred said.

Catie pulled the yoke back and adjusted the flaps. The nose of the G650 pitched up, and they started to climb. "Textbook," Fred said.

The flight to Auckland lasted two-and-a-half hours. Catie was greatly relieved when they started to chat with the control tower again.

"I can see why you talk so much," Catie said. "It's so boring just flying."

"You have to enjoy the scenery and the freedom," Fred said.

"I'd rather be doing loops," Catie said.

"So, would we all."

"Auckland, MacKenzie One, flight level 3-0-0 with clearance to 3-3-0 our discretion, we are requesting runway thirty-two."

"Cleared to land, MacKenzie One."

"Wow, that was cool," Catie said after they landed.

“I’m glad you enjoyed it. Tomorrow we’ll take her up and just fly around the island. Once we’re out of the air control lanes, we can have some fun.”

“Oh, that sounds better,” Catie said.

"MacKenzie One, contact ground 1-2-1 decimal 9."

"MacKenzie One."

"Ground, MacKenzie One is with you for gate 1-8."

"MacKenzie One is cleared into gate 1-8."

"MacKenzie One."

Chapter 9 Board Meeting – Dec 3rd

"I hope everybody had a nice Thanksgiving break," Marc said, "but back to work."

"Scrooge," Blake said.

"I try," Marc said. "How's the hunt for a house going?"

"I think we've found just the place," Blake said. "Kal likes it from a security perspective, we just need to take Sam out there to give us a woman's perspective."

"Hey!" Liz said.

"I guess I meant an *I refuse to camp*, woman's perspective," Blake said. "You're too easy to please." Liz gave Blake a smile that might have meant she was okay with his excuse or that she planned to get even. "Anyway, it's a mansion that's being rented online as a vacation rental. It's close to the harbor and the Mea Huli, so we should like that. There are enough rooms upstairs for everyone if Catie and Liz are willing to bunk together. It has a study, a maid's quarters and a bedroom downstairs. If we convert all three, then we'll have plenty of office space. It also has a small cottage on the grounds for the security team. We could kick Kal out there or give up one of the offices if Liz and Catie want their own rooms, but they've been sharing the hotel room all this time."

"I notice you didn't suggest that Fred bunk with Kal or you," Liz said. "You guys have been sharing a suite."

"I'd make Kal go to the cottage first," Blake said.

"I'd move to the cottage first," Kal retorted.

"I'm okay bunking up; how about you, Catie?"

"Sure, Roomie," Catie said. "You hardly snore at all."

Liz threw a coaster at Catie, "I do not snore!"

"I said hardly at all," Catie said.

"Back to the mansion," Marc said loudly.

"We could use the dining room to hold board meetings if you're okay with security," Kal continued.

"We'll see," Marc said.

"I'm available after the meeting to go look," Samantha said.

"Great," Blake said. "Kal, do you want to take her?"

"Sure, I'll take along a couple of my new guys and have them case the area some more. We'll want to do some gardening too," Kal said. "The owner seemed amenable to us spending the bucks to tame some of the jungle around the place."

"Sam, how about our contract with the government?"

"I've got a big meeting with them on Wednesday. We'll see how that goes. It looks promising."

"I'll keep my fingers crossed," Marc said. "Kal, how about security?"

"Liz and I ran the five candidates I brought out through their paces. We decided to keep four of them," Kal said.

"Why did the one wash out?"

"We got a bad vibe off him," Kal said.

"Although I'd be okay with him watching my back in the field, I wouldn't want my friends hanging around with him when he's off duty." Liz nodded, seconding Kal's assessment. Marc was happy to see that they were in agreement.

"Anything else?"

"Paintball arena is ready. I thought we'd go up against the new guys."

"Have fun," Marc said. "Liz, anything?"

"I really like Dr. Nikola," Liz said. "Blake has everybody set up in that warehouse, and the scientists seem to like the arrangement. They have lunch or coffee brought in and hang out arguing about stuff while their experiments run. That plasma torch is something else. Those two physicists you have are just doing everything on the computer or the whiteboard. I don't know when they'll want any equipment."

"Just be ready," Marc said. "Now some new business. Dr. Metra says she can handle more patients. I think it's time we started to offer the Alzheimer's treatment to private patients."

"Hear, hear!" Fred called out.

"How do you want to advertise?" Samantha asked.

"I'd like to start with discreet inquiries," Marc said.

"What?" Samantha asked, wrinkling her nose.

"I'm assuming that word will start getting around from the families of the fifteen patients we've treated so far," Marc said. "Catie's great grandparents have gone home, people will notice that they've been doing better. Dr. Tuba has declined our offer of employment. He is planning to return to the University of Washington and start teaching again. I expect that we will start getting inquiries from others about the potential for treatment. Sam, I was hoping you might find a way to let some other people know about our treatment."

"I can," Samantha said. "What would we be charging for the treatment?"

"Five hundred thousand dollars," Marc said.

"Are you insane?" Samantha gasped.

"It costs over fifty thousand dollars a year to care for someone with Alzheimer's, more for the clientele we're talking about," Marc said. "Over a trillion dollars a year is spent treating Alzheimer's patients worldwide. To be able to save all that expense, plus get a loved one back, has to be worth a lot. We can't handle that many cases right now, we might as well demand as much money as we can."

"You're cutthroat," Samantha said. "I can't believe you." She slumped back in her seat and crossed her arms.

"Sam, we need more money. We're only going to be able to help maybe twenty-five patients a month. I'd be happy to do it for free, but then we'd be inundated with people. How would we decide? Plus, the publicity it would generate would be problematic. If we focus on wealthy and powerful people, there wouldn't be an issue about publicity; in fact, it's likely that nobody knows they have Alzheimer's. If any of you hears of a case we should take for free, we will. But until we're in a place where we can offer it more widely, I think this is the best path."

Marc looked around the table for support. Only Samantha was furious, but nobody else seemed interested in jumping in to defend his position.

"How long before we can offer it to more people?" Catie asked, throwing her father a bone.

"Six months to a year," Marc said. "We have to be more secure when we do. We have to develop a process for managing it at remote locations if we want to handle more than twenty-five a month. We can't make everybody come to the Cook Islands. There is some very proprietary technology associated with the treatment that we cannot afford to get out."

"But you could handle a lot more than twenty-five patients a month," Catie said.

"When we get the clinic built on Delphi City, we will be able to handle more, but even then, it will only be about two hundred a month."

"But you could make some of them for regular people," Catie said.

"I'd be happy to," Marc said. "Why don't you and Sam work out how to handle those kinds of inquiries and referrals. We'll set aside fifty percent for those cases."

"Okay," Catie said. Samantha relaxed a bit and quit glaring at Marc. Marc decided to wait a few days before asking her about handling the paying cases again.

"Fred, how is the training program for the new Lynxes coming along? And, any luck finding a couple of pilots?"

"We have a flight simulator for the G650 on order. Catie assures me that it can be modified to allow us to train the pilots for the Lynx. I've got a few feelers out to some guys who look promising. I should hear back soon."

"Okay," Marc said. "Let's go home."

That afternoon, Samantha grudgingly approved the house. It was a beautiful place, but the appliances and fixtures were dated, and probably had not been the best when they were installed. The next day they moved in. Everyone immediately started calling it the compound. Kal had the jungle trimmed back and a fence installed to help keep out unwanted visitors. There were always at least two of his security detail wandering around outside. They never came into the house, but their presence was still felt.

After the first night, everyone agreed it was better than the hotel, even after they had to eat Blake's cooking for breakfast.

Chapter 10 Treaty update

"Samantha, are you busy?" Marc asked as he poked his head into the lawyer's office.

"I'm always busy," Samantha replied. "I assume you're looking for an update?"

"I am."

"Come in and sit down."

"Where's your assistant?"

"This is Saturday," Samantha said. "I assume she's at home or at the beach."

Marc looked a bit startled as he did a quick check in his head. "I guess I lost track of time."

"It happens." Samantha gave Marc an enigmatic smile. "So, what do you want to know?"

Marc rolled his eyes at her. "Like there would be anything else on my mind."

"You might want to take me to dinner."

"Am I forgiven?"

"Mostly," Sam said. "Dinner would help with that too."

"I'm up for that," Marc said with a nod. "I will take you to dinner, even if you don't have good news."

"Great, you should call for reservations now. Someplace extra special since I have good news."

Marc laughed and used his HUD to ask ADI to make reservations at Antipodes. "Antipodes okay with you?"

"I hear it's excellent," Samantha said. "By the way, what does Antipodes mean?"

"It's a word for Australia and New Zealand," Marc said. "Means the exact opposite side of the earth from where you are."

"Interesting. Now that we have the pleasantries out of the way . . ."

"And you've got yourself a dinner invitation."

"Yes, that too. I've gotten the government to agree to the main terms you've asked for in the contract. They've accepted the fifty-million-per-year lease rate. And they have agreed to our paying it out over the fifty-year term of the lease, as long as you purchase bonds to guarantee the payment. It will cost you one-billion to buy the bonds. Then you will be required to make another billion in investments within the first ten years, a minimum of one hundred million in the first year.

"It also requires you to establish a medical clinic focused on treating and developing treatments for chronic, genetic, and debilitative diseases where any Cook Islander will be treated for free. We're still working on the tax rate, but they seem flexible. I've structured it like a treaty, as you asked. That was easier than expected; I guess they feel more comfortable with the language. One unexpected thing is that you'll be appointed mayor of Manuae."

"What!"

"Well, there has to be some government structure, police force, etc. Since everyone on the island will be working for you, it simplifies things if you're the mayor. Of course, you're only going to be paid one New Zealand dollar per year."

Marc laughed. "Being mayor on top of everything else I have going on. That's all I need."

"It won't be any different than what you're already planning to do. You can delegate to your staff."

"What's the holdup, then?"

"We're waiting on approval from New Zealand."

"Why are they involved?"

"You do know that New Zealand is responsible for the defense and foreign policy for the Cook Islands?"

"Yes, I do."

"So, since we're structuring it like a treaty, they've stuck their nose in."

"Is that going to be a problem?"

"I don't think so," Samantha said. "The investment and subsequent growth should spill over to New Zealand. They're probably just doing some due diligence and giving some key members of the government a chance to update their portfolios."

Marc shook his head, "Should have expected that."

"Of course, it also leaves a little more time for some of the officials here in the Cook Islands to update theirs as well."

"How long?"

"Two weeks?"

"Probability of success?"

"I'd say ninety-five percent," Samantha said.

"Captain, I concur," ADI told Marc.

"Great. I'll pick you up at seven, Sam."

"Looking forward to it," Samantha said.

Marc knocked on Dr. Metra's door jamb. "Do you have some time?" he asked.

"Captain, I always have time for you," Dr. Metra said. "What can I do for you?"

"I wanted to discuss the Alzheimer's treatment."

"Are Catie's great grandparents okay?" Dr. Metra asked.

"They're doing fine," Marc said. "I want to discuss expanding the treatment capacity. We're planning to bring a lot more patients in."

"That shouldn't be a problem."

"I would like to understand our options if we want to have remote treatment sites."

"I think we could manage that," Dr. Metra said. "We would have to make more parts and such."

"I'd like to discuss how we can do it without the secret getting out," Marc said.

"I see," Dr. Metra said. "First, let me explain some of the limitations of the treatment."

"Okay," Marc said as he settled into the chair in front of Dr. Metra's desk.

"In order for the nanites we use to penetrate the blood-brain barrier, they have to be extremely small," Dr. Metra said. "Here on your planet, we are limited by how small we can make the nanites."

"What do you mean by here on our planet?"

"I mean in gravity," Dr. Metra said. "The printers we use to make them work best in micro-gravity. It is not possible to make things as small under normal gravity as you can in micro-gravity."

"I see, but we are making the nanites here," Marc said.

"Yes, but in order to make them small enough, I have to make them less capable. I have to give them less of a brain," Dr. Metra said. "If we were making them in micro-gravity, I would be able to give them a lot more smarts and still keep them small. Then they would do the treatment after only one shot without any further help. But because I have to make them, shall we say 'dumb', I have to guide them to where they need to be, and I have to wait between treatments for the patient's body to flush the nanites out."

"How do the smart nanites eliminate the need to wait?"

"They don't," Dr. Metra said. "But I can program them to wait. I would program one third to go active each week. They would then just enter the brain on their schedule, remove the plaque, and then they would be flushed. The next week the next third would do the same. Because the ones we're using are dumb, I have to space the treatment out, and I have to guide them to the brain."

"That's what you use that scanner for," Marc said.

"Yes, it creates a field that attracts the nanites."

"So, we would need to make more nanite printers and more of the scanners," Marc said. "How hard would it be to train someone to use the scanner?"

"We can make a simpler scanner that would be automatic. They would just need to put the patient under the scanner for one hour after the shot."

"Anything of interest in the scanner?" Marc asked.

“Not really, it just emits a field. If you want to disguise what it does, we could have it emit several different fields.”

“What about the nanites,” Marc asked, “how can we prevent someone from analyzing them?”

“They’re just lumps of minerals after the treatment.”

“What about before?”

“They’re quite small, but I suppose that someone would be able to examine them,” Dr. Metra said.

“Why are they like lumps of minerals after the treatment?” Marc asked.

“They destroy the plaque by emitting an electrical charge that slowly uses them up.”

“Okay, but is there any way we can have them do that without having to come into contact with plaque?”

“We could add a small timer,” Dr. Metra said. “Actually, a self-dissolving fuse that would only last for two hours or so.”

“That sounds like it would work,” Marc said. “Can we make the printers and the scanners here in gravity?”

“For this level of functionality, yes,” Dr. Metra said.

“How could we protect the nanite printer?” Marc asked.

“I wouldn’t know, but I’m sure you or someone could work with ADI to make sure it was tamper-proof.”

“I’ll work on it,” Marc said. “For now, I’d like to keep this discussion between the two of us.”

“You’re thinking ahead, I see. Keeping it private between us won’t be a problem,” Dr. Metra said. “You’ll let me know when you want me to do any work on it.”

“I will,” Marc said. “Thanks for your time.”

“I always enjoy the company.”

Chapter 11 Training Catie

Catie was running for her life. She was just three hundred meters from the compound, but she was gasping for breath. She dug down deep and pushed for all she was worth, but it wasn't enough. Liz whacked her on the butt as she sped by, leaving Catie in the dust.

Catie stumbled to a stop and stood there gasping until the security jeep that was following them drove up. She grabbed a ride in the jeep for the last two hundred fifty meters. Liz's backup was laughing under her breath. Catie scowled at her, and she stifled the laugh, driving to the compound in silence.

"Hey, you should have walked the rest of the way as a cool down," Liz said.

"I figured you would rather I cool down inside the compound than out," Catie snapped. She got out of the jeep and started doing some light stretches. "How could you have so much left that you could blow by me that way?"

"You started out too fast," Liz said. "You have to pace yourself."

"You told me to run for my life!"

"Yes, you have to sprint to establish distance, but then you have to dial it back so that you're just maintaining that distance. Nobody can sprint for fifteen hundred meters, especially after running four miles."

"Now, you tell me."

"Lessons learned the hard way are always remembered best."

"So, I've got a lot of lessons that I'm going to remember really well," Catie said as she symbolically rubbed her butt.

"You do pretty well," Liz said. "It seems to me you figure most things out before they bite you."

Catie just grunted. "Hey, if we can run down the street like that with only one security guy in the jeep, why can't I go running without you?"

"Because this way, there are two of us to protect you."

"But you're not armed. I know your Krav Maga skills would do a lot, but it seems like I would be okay with just the jeep."

"Who says I'm not armed," Liz said.

"Well, I don't see any weapons."

Liz reached her hand to the left strap of her sports bra and flicked her wrist. Her Bo-staff extended to five feet. She tapped Catie on the butt with it.

"Ow! Another hard lesson."

Liz dropped the Bo-staff, reached around behind her back and whipped out a knife, in a single motion she threw it. It stuck in the tree Catie was standing next to.

"Ooh, do you have any more?"

"Let's just say I like three," Liz said. "Where's your Bo-staff?"

"It's in the jeep," Catie said.

"Not going to do you much good there, is it?"

"I guess not. Show me how you keep yours?"

Liz showed Catie the small pocket in her sports bra that she had used to hold the Bo-staff. "I have all my sports bras modified like this."

"What about the knife?"

"I use the space between my shoulder blades. I've got enough muscle that there's a gap there that holds the sheath perfectly," Liz said. "Look." Liz turned around so Catie could see the knife sheath attached to her sports bra. "It's padded, so it doesn't chafe."

"I see, so should I have mine modified like this?"

"Well, you shouldn't carry a weapon that you don't know how to use," Liz said.

"So, teach me how to use a knife," Catie said. "Especially how to throw one. That's really cool."

"Okay, I'll teach you, but I don't want you carrying one until I say you're ready."

"That's okay," Catie said as she rubbed her butt where Liz had tapped her with the Bo-staff. "Can we start today?"

"Do you have time? I want to do our Bo-staff lesson first."

"I have time. Do you?"

"Sure, I'm not all that busy yet," Liz said. "Don't tell your father, or he'll dump some onerous chore on me."

"I won't, but he'll know how busy you are at the next board meeting."

"Yeah, I know. I want to help more, but there are a few things he's got going on that I'd rather he gave to Fred or Kal," Liz laughed.

Catie ran and got her Bo-staff from the jeep, while Liz went to the house to get their headgear.

"Enough," Catie yelled. After twenty-five minutes with the Bo-staff, Catie was tired of getting whacked on the butt or the back of her thigh. "I'm too sore to take any more hits."

"Then you need to do a better job of defending," Liz said.

"I'm trying," Catie whined. "You're just a sadist!"

"Okay, I'll give you a break," Liz said. "Let's do a couple of drills."

"Okay," Catie said as she took off her headgear and shook out her hair. She was sweating profusely. Liz took off her headgear, her hair was completely dry. *"It's not fair,"* Catie thought.

"You're getting better," Liz said. "You got me a couple of times."

"Yeah, like two versus thirty," Catie said.

"You're still favoring your left leg," Liz said. "You have to stay balanced and look at my center of mass, not my Bo-staff."

"Then how do I block it?" Catie asked.

"When you see I've committed to a move, you block it. You should be able to tell where I'm aiming by my hands," Liz said. "And they don't move as fast as the end of the staff, so your eyes will be able to track things better."

"I know, you keep telling me that," Catie said.

"Okay, I'm standing there, I'm going to attack, and you're going to just tell me where I'm aiming," Liz said. "I won't actually hit you."

"That will be nice for a change," Catie said.

"Ready?"

Liz shifted her weight and snapped her Bo-staff forward.

"Left leg—no waist," Catie yelled.

"Look at my center, not my hands. The hands are there; you can see them but don't focus on them. If I don't put any weight into it, it won't hurt, and it'll be slow enough for you to block anyway," Liz instructed.

"Okay," Catie said as she took a deep breath. She shook herself and relaxed, focusing on Liz's center of mass.

Liz shifted her weight.

"Head!"

"Right Leg!"

"Left knee!"

"Head!"

"Left ankle!"

"That's better," Liz said. "Does it make more sense now?"

"I think so," Catie said.

"Now get prepared, I'm going to do feints this time," Liz said.

"I'm ready."

Liz twitched her Bo-staff to the left, then came in from the right. Catie easily blocked it. "Hey, that was easy," she said.

"Did you see the feint?" Liz asked.

"I did, but not that much, it was just like a shadow," Catie said.

"See, looking at the center gets rid of all that noise," Liz said. "Your brain doesn't have to worry about as much. Some people are twitching the end of their staff all the time, but if you can ignore it, then they're just wasting energy and slowing themselves down."

They spent another ten minutes on the drills before Liz called a stop. "You still up to practicing with the knife?" Liz asked.

"Yes!" Catie said. "A few minutes at least."

They collapsed their Bo-staffs, then Liz went to the tree and pulled her knife out. "I like this double-edged knife," Liz said. "It's a good throwing knife, and it's good in hand-to-hand as well." Liz handed Catie the knife. "Hold it with the blade sticking out the back of your hand."

"Like this?"

"Yes, that's the grip you use when you're fighting with it," Liz instructed. "Then you can punch and block, and you're unlikely to stick yourself with it. If you hold it the other way, you're going to be pulling it out of yourself."

Liz threw a punch at Catie, which Catie automatically blocked. "Hold that block," Liz said. "See, how if you just twist your hand and tilt it a little, you trap my arm. That's why you hold it that way. Now when you throw it, you hold it the other way."

"That's kind of awkward to switch when you're fighting, isn't it?" Catie asked.

"You're either throwing it or fighting with it," Liz said. "You should never switch. If they're far enough away that you would throw it at them during a fight, then they must be running away."

"Okay," Catie said.

"Now we'll work on a two-turn throw," Liz said. "For you, that should be about fifteen feet from the target. Hold the knife by the handle, set yourself, then shift your weight and throw it, don't bend your wrist. Let go of the knife when it's vertical."

Catie held the knife and did a couple of simulated throws.

"That's good, release it this time," Liz said.

Catie did the throw, the knife hit the tree, but it didn't stick. Liz ran and grabbed the knife. "Step back about eight inches," Liz instructed. "Then try again."

This time Catie's throw almost stuck in the tree.

After Liz retrieved the knife, she had Catie back up another four inches. "Try it again."

This time the knife stuck.

"Hey, it doesn't seem that practical to adjust your distance so you can stick the knife," Catie said.

Liz laughed, "No, but we need to practice with your natural throw first. Then we'll work on adjusting your technique so you can modify the distance." She ran and got the knife. "Try again."

Catie threw the knife, and it stuck again. "Throw this one now," Liz said as she handed Catie another knife.

"You did have two," Catie said.

"Yep. Now throw."

After another ten throws, Liz called a stop. "You'll need to work on it for a while, get your muscles built up, and smooth out the technique. Then we'll start working on varying the distance. I'll put up a board tomorrow and bring more knives."

"You mean you don't like running to get the knife every time."

"No, I don't," Liz said. "This is about training you, not wearing me out."

"But then I might have a chance when we fight," Catie said.

"I think you'll need a bit more than that," Liz said. "You're getting better, but you're still just a neophyte."

Chapter 12 Paintball

"Okay, this is going to be four on four," Kal explained as they gathered at the new paintball arena. "The opposition is the four guys we just hired. They're a bit cocky, and we need to help them focus on their training."

Catie, Blake, and Liz nodded their heads. Marc had begged off, especially since there was only room for four players. "The layout is similar to the one we used in Hawaii: four hallways, two or three rooms off each hallway, and a central area that has walls for barriers. Each team enters from the opposite ends of the arena; we'll be coming in from the north."

"What are the rules?" Catie asked.

"Don't get shot," Kal said. "And if you do, you're out."

"Anything else?"

"Bad guys don't follow rules."

"Great!" Catie pumped her fist.

"We'll play it the same as last time. Catie, you're left-handed, so you're on the right side; Liz, you play left. Blake, you're center fielder; once clear you take control of the hallway or room; I'll cover our six."

"Surveillance pucks? Comms?" Catie asked. Surveillance pucks had been their secret weapon in Hawaii. They were from the Sakira and provided a three-hundred-sixty-degree video of the area directly to their comms. They would stick to anything, and the comms were smart enough to correct the view, so they weren't seeing things upside down.

"Both teams have them," Kal said. "Are we ready?"

Everybody gave him a thumbs up. "We go in expecting them to be already in place, don't get sloppy. We'll go left."

Blake opened the door. Catie slid a surveillance puck along the floor into the hallway. The hallway was clear, so Blake entered while Catie and Liz covered. Once in the hall, Catie picked up the puck and stuck it to the wall above the door. It would give them a continuous feed of the hallway in both directions. She segmented the view into a couple of small windows in her HUD and set an alarm to alert her if there was any movement.

Kal followed behind, walking backward as Blake started toward the first corner. Catie walked along the right wall, and Liz the left. There weren't any rooms off of the hallway in their direction.

Blake held up three feet from the corner. He was inspecting the sides of the walls for signs of a surveillance puck sticking out. He nodded to Catie to tell her that it was time for her to put a puck into the next hallway.

Catie pulled a pair of pucks out of her bag. They were each stuck to opposite sides of a toy block that acted like an axle that kept the fifteen-millimeter-thick pucks from tipping over. She set them on the floor and pushed them. They rolled along the floor into the hallway.

"Clear," Catie whispered into her comm. The volume in the other comms was much higher than her whisper. It was a feature that they had found useful. They didn't want the other team to hear them, and whispers were problematic. Since the earwig was designed to pick up even the faintest whisper, they set the transmission to a constant voice level.

They moved quickly to set up control of the next hallway. Catie placed a puck on the back wall so they would get the best view of the hallway. She also put one on the wall of the opposing hallway to give them a better view of the hallway they were exiting.

"Two rooms on the left, one room on the right," Kal said. "Let's clear the left-hand rooms first."

Blake nodded and moved to the door on the left. Staying to the side he waited for Catie and Liz to take up positions, Catie knelt down beside him against the wall since the door handle was on the right side. Once Liz was in position, Blake tested the handle to see if the door was locked. The handle turned, but the door wouldn't budge.

"Jammed."

"Hall is still clear."

Blake lay down on his back close to the door with his knees bent. He waited until Catie gave him a high-sign on his HUD, then he reared back and kicked the door in. He quickly rolled to the side while everyone took cover. Catie tossed a puck into the room.

"Room looks clear."

"Make sure," Kal instructed. "Two of you go in, Blake and I'll cover the hall."

Catie and Liz entered the room. While Liz covered her, Catie balanced a puck on the end of her rifle and used that to stick it to the ceiling. With a bird's eye view, it was easy to verify that no one was hiding behind any of the furniture. Catie used her specs to get the surveillance puck to release itself from the ceiling, it dropped into her hand. She and Liz made their way to the closet. It was unlocked; Liz covered high, while Catie opened the door and tossed the puck in.

"Room's clear."

They followed the same procedure for the room next door and cleared it. As Catie was coming out of the room, her HUD pinged, showing movement at the end of the hallway.

"Incoming."

Blake and Kal ducked into the other room, while Catie and Liz ducked back into their room. "What's up?"

"Someone just eased a puck along the edge of the wall at the corner; about 1.5 meters up. It's just peeking out into the hallway."

"So, they know where we are."

"I'd say so," Catie replied.

"I can take the puck out," Kal said. "Everybody be ready in case they try to rush us."

"Got you covered," Catie said as she lay down and took aim down the hallway.

Kal could see the puck location on his HUD. One of the paintball guns Kal carried was more like a sniper rifle than the machinegun-like rifles favored by most paintballers. He used the angle he got from being across the hall from where the puck was to take aim without exposing himself too much. He squeezed off a shot.

"Nailed it," Catie said.

"Okay, do you think you can roll one all that way?"

"Sure," Catie said as she pulled out her double puck. She lined it up with the hallway and gave it a solid push. It rolled until it hit the wall at the end of the hall. They immediately got a quick view of the opposing team in the other hallway. They appeared to be discussing what to do about their disabled puck. They also didn't seem to notice the puck that had rolled down the hall.

"I don't see another puck," Catie said. "And they're holding the one you shot off the wall."

"Sloppy," Kal said. "They're back about three feet; I say we ease down there and take them high-low." Kal took out one of his door jammers and jammed the door to the room they hadn't cleared. "Okay, let's go."

Catie jumped up on Blake's back, and they eased down the hall. Kal exchanged his sniper rifle for an automatic one. They carefully made their way down the hall along the right side. When they got to the corner, Blake stopped just shy of it. Liz crouched down and waited. Catie took her paint gun and set it to automatic. She used the surveillance puck to aim it, poked it around the corner, and let go. As soon as the opposition spotter was distracted by Catie's fire, Liz launched herself into the hall on the floor, firing even before she landed.

"Out!"

"Out!"

"Out!"

"Out!"

They had taken all four opponents out in the quick exchange. Catie's rifle had paint on it, but she was clean. She hopped off of Blake's shoulders and collected her rolling puck. She wanted to grab it before the other team saw it.

"Okay you Yahoos," Kal said. "What were you doing?"

"We were strategizing," the lead guy said. "We had a lookout."

"That's what your comms are for. You can strategize and discuss things while you're all keeping watch."

"Then, you might have heard us."

"You can level the volume," Catie said. "Just use your HUD to set the comm unit to transmit everything at the same level. Then you can whisper."

"Ohh."

"Yes, oh!" Kal said. "You've had the gear for over a week, didn't you familiarize yourself with it?"

"Yes, but we missed that."

"How did you see our puck?"

Kal nodded to Catie. "You can set your HUD so that the comm unit alerts you anytime there's movement detected by the puck. I saw it peek around the corner."

"We want a rematch."

"But you're all dead," Kal said.

"A zombie rematch then," another one said, making them all laugh.

"First, why don't you do some scrimmaging among yourselves, that way you can figure out how to best use the gear. The arena's been open a week, now I suggest you use it."

"Yes, sir!"

Chapter 13 Board Meeting – Dec 17th

"Meeting will come to order," Marc said as everyone got seated around the Mea Huli's sundeck. "Samantha, you're the key to our actually getting started with anything."

Samantha smiled. "I like to be the linchpin. I've got the contract about ready. There are some minor wording issues to work out. Then we'll need the final signoff by the parliament before everyone is ready to sign. We should be ready to break ground on Manuae the first of the year."

"Great! Blake, are we going to be ready to break ground?" Marc asked.

"We have tentative approval to put in a two hundred forty square meter building. Two-thirds of it will be dedicated to polysteel production. The rest divided between batteries and fuel cells," Blake said. "We've got the building sitting offshore on a ship. We just need the concrete foundation, plumbing, and a concrete slab poured. There's another ship offshore with the concrete. They'll pump it directly into the forms when we're ready."

"Crew for the excavation and plumbing?"

"They arrived in Rarotonga on Monday. They're checked into the hotel, and from what I can tell, they're hoping we're delayed a few weeks," Blake laughed. "They're having a good time."

"They can have a good time on their time off," Marc said.

"They're going to be working twelve-hour days, six days a week," Blake said. "They'll be too tired to have much fun once we start."

"I don't remember being tired ever stopping us from partying on our day off. I'm sure they'll work it out," Marc said. "Kal, how's security shaping up?"

"We've started training, as everyone should know," Kal said. "The new guys have been properly humbled, and are dedicated to working twice as hard, so they're not embarrassed again. I'm still keeping my eye out for new talent, but we need to get these guys in shape before we get any bigger."

"Okay, any issues on the labor front?"

"Nothing as of now; we're still early in the hiring cycle."

"Thanks. Liz, how's the battery process coming along?" Marc asked, moving the updates along.

"We just started production here on Rarotonga. We're doing a lot of training now, so things are slow," Liz said. "I've asked Blake to set up a permanent facility for packaging the cells into actual batteries. Since there's nothing proprietary there, I assume we'll leave it on Rarotonga."

"I agree," Marc said. "I'm sure that makes the local guys happy."

"Yes, they were a bit frustrated when they realized that much of what we're doing is going to move to Manuae," Samantha said. "This will show them how everything we do will still have a positive local impact on Rarotonga."

"And our polysteel?" Marc asked, shifting the focus back to Liz.

"Bit more complex there," Liz said. "The Zelbars have been running experiments, and they say they're making progress, but I can't tell. They're really going through the power right now, and those CO_2 scrubbers are working overtime."

"I assume we're saving the scrubber cartridges," Marc said.

"Yes, Dr. Nikola assures me we can run them back through the system once they have it actually depositing the carbon," Liz said.

"Well, it is a big step, and will take time," Marc said. "Catie, how's the treatment plant going?"

"Tomi has really taken over doing all the work. I help when he needs ADI to get some design done for him," Catie replied. "He's installing the prototype here on Rarotonga. It will handle the sludge delivered from the various septic tanks around the island, as well as anything they plumb to it. That will demonstrate the feasibility under pretty harsh conditions."

"That's good, how's the toilet design going?" Marc asked.

"He's ready to build a prototype," Catie said. "He sure spent a lot of time on the material selection. He said it's because he wants as many of the parts to be made in the local communities as possible instead of having to import them. I'll let you know when he needs someone to test it out."

"Oh, you can skip me on that," Samantha said. "The Mea Huli is about as primitive as I want to get."

"That bathroom and toilet are better than the ones at the compound," Liz said.

"Exactly," Samantha said.

"How is the progress on our polysteel coming?" Marc asked ADI. He was working in his new office at the compound.

"Doctors Zelbar are achieving a small amount of bonding. They are close to the right mixture, but the arc strength they are using is too low," ADI said.

"Won't they just keep raising it?"

"It appears they are fixated on this setting," ADI said. "They have gotten some positive results and are experimenting with various process changes. They want to see if they can achieve the bonding you showed them."

"Sounds like it might be some time before they get where we want them to be."

"I calculate a sixty percent probability that it will take six months and a ten percent probability that it will only take three months. There is a twenty-five percent probability it will take longer than one year."

"That's too long. Can we just turn the power up for them?"

"They recalibrate the equipment and check the settings before each experiment."

"That's nice," Marc said with a frown.

"Change the calibration tool," Catie said.

Marc was a bit startled; he hadn't heard Catie come in. "What are you doing here?" he asked.

"Just listening," Catie said. "If they recalibrate each time, change what they're calibrating to. Like adjusting the scale, so it looks like you weigh less."

"ADI?"

"I could modify the meter they're using so that it reads incorrectly."

"Can you do it in such a way that it will look like a malfunction instead of deliberate manipulation?" Marc asked.

"Of course. I can burn out one resistor enough that it changes the scale," ADI said.

"Then, do it."

"Now, young lady, what are you doing here?" Marc asked.

"I want to talk about Kal," Catie said.

"Okay."

"When are you going to fix his legs?" Catie pleaded.

Marc grimaced, "Soon."

"How soon? Why are you waiting?"

Marc sighed, "I want to have the deal on the island completed at least. Fixing Kal's legs means we have to let the cat out of the bag."

"Tell them about the Sakira," Catie clarified.

"Yes. I really want to be in a more secure position when we do that. Also, once his legs are fixed, it's kind of like broadcasting that we have some really out-there technology. People will notice."

"Not if he wears pants," Catie said.

"True," Marc said. "But why do you think he wants his legs back?"

"So he can surf and swim," Catie said.

"Right."

"But if he promises to wait until we've got the island deal done, and he only surfs and swims off of Manuae or Delphi City, won't that keep the secret?" Catie pleaded some more.

Marc sighed again and rubbed his hands over his face.

"Come on, Daddy!"

"Okay, team meeting tomorrow," Marc said.

"Yes!" Catie squealed and jumped up and gave her father a hug and a kiss.

"Thanks, Daddy!"

"Everything we do keeps pushing up the schedule," Marc muttered to himself.

Chapter 14 Disclosure

"Alright, let's get this meeting started," Marc said. They were aboard the Mea Huli on the main deck with Fred upstairs at the helm. "All of you know Dr. Metra."

Liz and Kal nodded, both looking curious at the inclusion of the doctor in the meeting of the inner circle and on the Mea Huli. Meeting on the yacht without Samantha usually signified highly sensitive discussions.

Marc noticed their consternation. "I've included Dr. Metra because . . . I guess you could say she started all this."

Kal and Liz both sucked in their breaths with surprise. "How's that?" Kal asked.

"First, this is the last chance to bail out," Marc said. "If you're uncomfortable with where we've been headed, now is the time to go join Fred up on the bridge. You're both rich, so you don't need to do this."

"Why would we pull out now?" Liz asked.

"Because it's going to start becoming more dangerous and definitely more controversial," Marc said.

"More dangerous, how?" Kal asked.

"Up until now, we've had to worry about pirates and a little industrial espionage."

"The pirates were pretty dangerous," Kal said.

"Yes, but soon we're going to be getting the attention of some national governments."

"Which ones?"

"Well, we already know that the US government is keeping tabs on us. I expect us to attract the attention of the Chinese and the Russians," Marc said. "We're dealing with New Zealand already, so that means the British will be alerted. The French and Germans won't be far behind," Marc added.

"Oh, this actually sounds like fun," Kal said. "I always wanted to be James Bond as a kid."

Liz looked at Kal askance; then she turned back to Marc, "And the upside?"

"More money, a chance to influence the way the world develops," Marc said.

"Better toys," Catie jumped in.

"Better toys?" Liz asked.

"Like the Lynx," Catie gushed.

"I'm still committed," Kal said, giving Liz a look.

"Me too," Liz said.

Marc took a deep breath and exhaled. "Okay. ADI, are we secure?"

"Yes, Captain," ADI said.

Liz and Kal gave Marc a puzzled look.

"ADI is not our tech genius, well not exactly," Marc said. "She is an Autonomous Digital Intelligence. She is the ship computer for the spaceship that Blake and I found."

"I knew it!" Kal said.

Everyone looked at Kal expectantly.

"I knew it, but I couldn't believe it," he said. "The tech is just too good. And polysteel, come on. No way that was a lab accident; I bet that's the same stuff as the Lynx's shell."

"Not exactly, but close," Marc said.

"Why not exactly?" Liz asked.

"Because you can only make the material that the Lynx is made of in zero gravity," Catie said.

"Oh," Liz said as her eyes bugged out a bit. After a moment, she added, "Makes sense; spaceship, factory in space, they kind of go together."

"Alright, when do we get to do a spaceflight?" Kal asked.

"Yeah!" Catie and Blake added together.

"Later children," Marc said. "Let's get back to the main purpose of this meeting."

"Oh, right," Catie said.

"Catie, do you want to take over?" Marc asked. "You're the one who insisted we take this step now."

Catie's eyes got wide as her lips formed an OH.

"Big ideas, big britches, time to step up and pay the piper," Blake said.

"Alright," Catie said slowly. "You already know about ADI." Everyone nodded. "Well, Dr. Metra is a Paraxean. They're the ones who made the spaceship."

Everyone turned to look at Dr. Metra. She removed her headscarf and wiggled her ears.

"What!" Liz gasped. "An alien."

"That depends on whose perspective you're talking about," Dr. Metra said.

"But not human," Liz added.

"Correct," Dr. Metra said. "But we are very similar in biology."

"How similar?"

"Later!" Catie said, retaking control of the meeting.

Liz sat back a bit stunned that Catie grabbed control, "Sure."

"Everyone has seen the work with the Alzheimer's patients," Catie continued. "That was Dr. Metra's work. While we were raising the Chagas, I did some research with ADI on their medical capabilities. I was hoping that they might have better technology for prosthetics than we do."

"Thanks," Kal said.

"Anyway, we can give you new legs," Catie said as she looked at Kal.

"I don't know," Kal said. "It was a lot of work getting used to these. I'm not sure I'm ready to go through that again."

Catie giggled, "I don't mean new prosthetic legs, I mean new legs."

Kal shook his head, totally stunned. "You mean like a leg transplant?"

Catie looked at Dr. Metra and gave her a nod.

"That's partially correct," Dr. Metra said. "What we do is scan your DNA, and in your case, gather as much medical data about your legs from before they were amputated. Then we print new ones."

"Print them?" Kal asked, looking a bit unsettled.

"We use organic material that we create using your DNA and tissue samples we take from you, such as nerves, muscle cells, skin cells, bone, bone marrow. Then we print your new legs on a three-D printer that handles that material."

"You can do that?"

"Yes. Then once your legs are printed, we'll infuse them with blood and stem cells we generate from samples taken from you," Dr. Metra continued. "We do that to reduce the time you're incapacitated. It takes about one week before the printed legs essentially become detached legs. Fully alive and waiting to be reconnected."

"Wow!" Kal said.

"Then we do the surgery. We attach all the main arteries and nerves and bones to your existing legs," Dr. Metra said. Then she gave a very human grimace, "We do have to cut your legs off a bit more to get back to viable tissue that is unaffected by the amputation. We take that into account when we print your legs. After the surgery, it takes one week before your body reintegrates the legs."

"Then, what?"

"Then you do physical therapy for a few days and go home," Dr. Metra said. "You'll need to come in for a few weeks to get a stem cell booster shot, but you should be walking as well as you do now after the initial therapy."

"But what about the bones knitting?"

"We fix broken bones in a few hours. Yours will be completely knitted long before you're walking."

"So, a week and a half, and I'm walking?" Kal asked incredulously.

"Yes!" Catie said. "Really cool, isn't it?"

"Will my brain be able to adapt to the legs again?"

"Usually that happens during the integration phase," Dr. Metra said. "In rare cases, we have to do some brain stimulation to encourage your brain to re-associate the old muscle memory with your new legs. But we're using all the same nerve trunks, so it's seldom an issue."

"When can we start?" Kal asked.

"As soon as Captain McCormack gives the word."

"Whenever you're ready," Marc said. "I do have a few conditions, though."

Kal had to bite back an angry retort, "What conditions?"

"We are trying to keep this alien spaceship thing under wraps. I would simply ask that you try to avoid flaunting your new legs around. Swim and surf off of Manuae, wear long pants when you're in Rarotonga, things like that."

"I can do that," Kal said. "For how long?"

"Let's say eighteen months," Marc said.

"Good by me," Kal answered. "But wait. We're trying to build up our security force here, right?"

"Of course," Marc said, wondering why Kal was stating the obvious.

"Especially with this worry about all those governments interfering," Kal added.

"Right."

"Well, I know some guys with wicked skills who would give their left nut to get back into the game. They just need new parts."

Marc frowned at Kal.

"Sorry about the language," Kal said as he looked at Catie, who was giggling. "It's just a saying."

"Okay, you say you know some guys," Marc said. "How many?"

"What about women?" Catie asked.

"We'll attract both. How many do you need?" Kal asked. "It's a tight-knit community; word gets out that there's a job for them, they're going to come calling."

"We can't advertise that we can replace limbs," Marc said.

"We won't have to," Kal said. "I'll just tell them there's some new tech that will let them get back in the game. That they will hardly remember they don't have their leg or whatever."

"Okay, how many?" Marc asked while looking at Blake and Liz.

"I'd say another twenty to start," Blake said. "We can always add more later. What about pilots?"

"That's tougher," Marc said. "Supposedly, we don't have fighters. Let's hold off until we're ready to bring a few in to fly the Lynx."

"Oh!" Catie said quickly. "Uncle Blake, we can fix you up too."

"You can?"

"Yes," Catie said. She turned to Dr. Metra and motioned her to continue.

"Cer Blake," Dr. Metra said. "Catie has already had me print a new eye for you. We can take care of that in about three hours. You should reintegrate it right away; if not, a few days of brain stimulation will do the trick. Your burns are another story."

"They always are," Blake said with a frown.

"It would be easiest to simply replace the arm," Dr. Metra continued. "That's up to you."

"Replace my arm?"

"Hey bro, I'm replacing my legs, what's an arm?" Kal said, needling him.

"Go on," Blake said to Dr. Metra.

"Burns are especially difficult because we have to repair them from the base up," Dr. Metra continued. "I would prefer to surgically remove your cheek and your left pectoral muscle and replace them with printed ones. It would be less discomforting to you. For the rest of your burns, we would need to inject you with, I'll use the term from your science fiction, nanites similar to the ones we use in the Alzheimer's treatment. They would remove the damaged tissue and replace it with new material. We would have to do it in several steps."

"How do these nanites work?" Blake asked.

"They're not as sophisticated as depicted in many of your science-fiction stories. They simply are tiny machines. We inject them into your body, then we can direct them to a particular location. The first ones will extract the problem tissue, dissolving it with acid so your body will flush it. Then those nanites are directed to your GI tract. Your body will process them and . . ."

"I get it," Blake said. "Then?"

"Then we inject more nanites that have the new material in them. It's similar to the three-D printing, but we have to do it under your existing tissue. The first nanites create a void, the second set fills it."

"How long?"

"Each procedure takes a few hours, but they need to be separated by at least a week. It can be longer, so you'll be able to set the pace. The first treatment should dramatically reduce the nerve pain you experience now. I expect it will take ten treatments."

"How can you be so sure this will work?" Liz asked.

"As I said earlier," Dr. Metra said, "our biological makeup is very similar. I have done some experiments to prove that I can print your genetic material. I also have done the procedure on several human cadavers and a few live human patients."

"Alien abductions," Kal joked.

"I don't think so," Dr. Metra said. "I dealt with people who were isolated and had tragic accidents. We were able to almost completely erase the memories. None of the patients I worked on even remembered that they had had an accident."

"So, how similar are our biologies?" Liz asked.

"Except for the ears, you would have to do a genetic analysis to determine we were not the same species," Dr. Metra said.

"So, you get pregnant and have babies just like us?" Liz asked.

"Yes, we're not compatible enough to procreate, but other than that."

"You even have menstrual cycles?" Liz asked.

"Biologically speaking, we do," Dr. Metra said.

"Hey, can we move on to another subject?" Blake asked, looking a little embarrassed.

"Everyone who doesn't have to worry about a menstrual cycle shut up," Liz said sternly. "What do you mean by biologically speaking?"

"We would have what you call menstrual cycles," Dr. Metra said. "But we stop them. It is a form of birth control as well as providing other benefits."

"What do you mean, you stop them?" Liz asked.

"We make a more sophisticated nanite and put one on each ovary," Dr. Metra said. "They regulate the secretion of estrogen and other hormones based on the body's chemistry. That keeps everything balanced, eliminating the need for menstruation."

"What if you want to get pregnant?" Liz asked.

"You can instruct your comm unit to send instructions to the nanites. They then cause you to ovulate. Once you're pregnant, the nanites regulate your hormones to manage your pregnancy."

"When do you start this process?" Marc asked.

"Oh, so now you're interested," Liz snapped.

"We typically start it before puberty," Dr. Metra said. "The nanites are programmed to extend the transition through puberty. That is healthier for the child and delays sexual interest, which is healthier for all."

"What about the guys?" Kal asked.

"There are nanites for them as well. Most parents have them injected before puberty, but most males turn them off once they reach majority."

"No surprise, there," Liz laughed. "Do you have the process perfected for humans, and can you do it after puberty?"

"Yes," Dr. Metra said. "It's a simple injection. I could do it in the clinic anytime."

"I think we have a couple of patients for you," Marc said.

"Oh, Catie already has hers," Dr. Metra said.

"What?" Marc asked.

"I asked her if she wanted them when I did her physical," Dr. Metra said. "She told me she did."

"You did this without consulting me," Marc demanded.

"On Paraxea as well as in the US, a girl is allowed to make her own decisions about such things," Dr. Metra said.

"I'm worried about the risk," Marc said.

"I can assure you there was no risk," Dr. Metra said. "I did tests on this when we first arrived here."

"And you didn't think you should tell me?" Liz asked Catie.

"I wasn't allowed to tell you," Catie said. "I wanted to, but Daddy had to make the call about bringing you guys in on the Sakira thing first."

"Okay, I forgive you," Liz said as she gave Marc a smile and a nod.

"Now can we get back to Uncle Blake and Kal," Catie said. "When do you guys want to start?"

"I think we should do a little recruiting first," Blake said. "But I'd like my eye fixed today if possible."

"The Lynx is following us now," Catie said. "You just have to go aboard with Dr. Metra."

"Hey, can we all go see this spaceship?" Liz asked.

Marc gave a big sigh, "I don't see why not. I'll stay with Fred, Catie can be your tour guide."

"Speaking of Fred," Blake said, "won't he notice?"

"Yes, but we can keep feeding him the new tech line," Marc said.

"Why?" Blake asked. "If we need pilots, he was a hell of a pilot in the Air Force before he got out."

"He'll be training on the Lynx," Marc said. "Let's keep the weapons capability quiet. I need to think about how we handle that. Things are starting to roll over the top of me right now."

"You need more people to delegate to," Blake said.

Marc gave Blake a hard look.

"Don't look at me," Blake said as he gave Marc an innocent look. "I'm all about flying, shooting, and that kind of stuff. I hate paperwork."

"And I don't?" Marc asked sarcastically.

"No, but you love to plan, so you're stuck with it," Blake said. "I just go with the flow."

"Get out of here before I kick you over the side so you can go with the flow," Marc said. He knew he was his own worst enemy when it came to delegating.

Blake rushed out with mock fear, laughing the whole way.

Chapter 15 The Tour

"The Sakira is two hundred fifty meters long by one hundred meters wide," Catie said while they approached the Sakira. "She's elliptical in both axes, much more so in the longitudinal axis. She's eighty-two meters tall."

"Why, ellipsoid? It's not all that aerodynamic," Kal asked.

"Aerodynamics doesn't matter in space," Catie said. "Uncle Blake can explain it better, but it's about structural strength."

"Oh, for structural strength, that makes sense," Liz said.

"It's also about manufacturing; her hull is monolithic."

"Wow, that is something," Liz said.

"What's different about this hull compared to the polysteel?" Kal asked.

"You'll have to ask ADI or Uncle Blake," Catie said. "But the Sakira hull absorbs energy, same as the Lynx's. That's why they're hard to see, they absorb the light."

"What do they do with all that energy? Where does it go?" Kal added.

"The inside of the hull is coated with superconductor strips," Catie said. "ADI controls how much of the energy they absorb from the hull gets redirected to the system capacitors."

"What happens when the capacitors are full?"

"ADI either lets the hull heat up, or she bleeds the energy off," Catie said. "Right now, she has to bleed the excess energy from the fusion reactor. She's bleeding it off into the water stream that moves down the canyon the Sakira is sitting in. In space, she can bleed it off by radiating it away with the lasers or a plasma cannon."

"Why radiate it like that?"

Catie shrugged.

"Stealth," Blake said. "The laser or plasma cannon controls which direction you're detectable in. A laser is a pretty narrow beam. You'd have to be directly in its path to detect it."

"Back to the tour, right now we're in Flight Bay Two," Catie said. "It will take a few minutes to pump all the water out."

"Big waste of air in space," Kal said.

"If they're running ops, the flight bay is depressurized. Everyone has a suit on. This bay can be segmented with a film so that only the area the Lynx comes into has to be depressurized," Catie said. "If they're in a hurry, they just lose the air. When you dock, they just equalize the pressure in the whole bay so you can get out and bring it all back up from seventy-five percent."

"Why don't they do that with the water?"

"Too much pressure down here," Catie said. "The film can only handle two atmospheres."

"Boy, you really studied this stuff," Liz said.

Catie beamed a little at the praise, "I had lots of time while we were dealing with the Chagas."

"When did you find out about the Sakira?" Liz asked.

"Two weeks," Blake said. "We found it in June. Catie showed up the next week, and two weeks later, she's onto us."

"Women have always been smarter than men," Liz said. Catie gave a big head nod agreeing with her.

"Okay, water's gone," Catie said. "Let's go out. The bay is one hundred twenty by thirty meters, seventy-five meters wide if you measure up at the top. It's designed to handle fifteen Foxes."

"Foxes?"

"The Foxes are the fighters; I told you better toys," Catie said. "They're thirteen meters shorter than the Lynx, but they can go faster."

"How much faster?"

"Wait until we get to them, you're making me forget what I want to tell you."

"Okay."

"Anyway, this flight bay is designed to handle fifteen Foxes, or thirteen Foxes and a Lynx."

"Why only thirteen when you add the Lynx?"

"The Lynx is longer, not enough room to turn it around if you have a Fox next to it. As you can see, the bay is a little narrower at the bottom because we're on the bottom half of the ellipse. Flight Bay One can handle twenty-one Foxes," Catie added. "More if you don't leave room for them to turn around."

"Not good if you're fighting," Blake said.

"Right!" Catie said. "Anyway, the Foxes are in the flight bay above us. We only have four, so they're all up there. The Sakira can handle thirty-four Foxes and one Lynx, with maneuverability, or it can transport lots more. It just has the two flight bays."

"Not much for an aircraft carrier," Liz said.

"The Sakira isn't an aircraft carrier, it's a research vessel," Catie said. "It's really not designed for atmospheric operations, or underwater, but it can do it. To land a Fox in atmosphere, you have to sync up speeds and be going fast enough that the Fox has lift, then ease it in. In the water or space, you don't have to worry about lift."

"Nice."

"Airlock is over here. We'll go up to the bridge next." Catie led them through the airlock and to an elevator. "There are two elevators, this one and one just aft of the bridge. There are six decks above us, and a cargo hold below us; it's as big as the flight bay. Then there are three engineering levels below that."

"Big ship," Kal said.

"It sure is," Catie replied. "There's a big environmental plant above the flight bays. It takes care of air and recycles all the waste."

"Ugh," Liz said.

"It's not that bad," Catie said. "They basically turn everything into carbon, oxygen, water, and base minerals. The carbon comes out like ceramic disks. Apparently, they use them and the base minerals to manufacture stuff. If they don't have something, they would go out and mine it from an asteroid or scoop it out of a gas giant."

"Sounds pretty self-sufficient."

"It is. Environmental is also set up to grow food. Hydroponics for plants, vats for meat."

"They grow meat?" Kal asked.

"Yeah," Catie said. "Kind of cool, animals don't need to be penned up or killed."

"Is it any good?" Kal asked.

"Dr. Metra says it is. They add different minerals and stuff, so it tastes like the real thing. She says they can make anything from free-range beef to Kobe beef, from catfish to ahi."

The elevator door swished open into a long aisle with two stories of rooms on each side. "Crew quarters," Catie said. "There's a stairwell on each side so they can go up and down without using the elevator. I guess it makes it easy to avoid the officers."

"Smart thinking," Kal said. Liz gave him a hard stare.

"The galley, mess deck, and rec area are on the next level up. The stairs give them access to that as well," Catie continued. "Above that, there's one level of officer quarters, they're bigger, but basically the same arrangement."

"It figures," Kal said when Catie said the officers had bigger quarters.

Catie laughed. "Above the officer quarters, there's one deck for sickbay and medical labs. The deck above that is lab space; above that more environmental and a few labs. They use the space that's weird because of the elliptical shape for environmental and cargo so that the working area is more rectangular."

Catie led them forward to another airlock. "The bridge is through here, arms locker on the left, captain's quarters on the right. The captain has a second level, a balcony looking over the bridge where he has his office."

"Must be nice quarters," Kal said as he measured the quarters in his head, "Must be something like twenty meters by twenty meters."

"That's as big as a house," Liz said.

"It includes quarters for a couple of guests," Catie said, "as well as a vast dining area and galley so he can host meals."

"It is a house," Blake said. "The second floor allows him to host a party. The wall panel can be made transparent, so they see the bridge, or opaque, so it's private."

Catie poked Blake in the ribs, "Who's giving this tour?"

"Sorry," Blake said.

"What's above the arms locker?" Liz asked.

"ADI," Catie answered.

"The whole space?"

"She's a big girl."

"I guess so," Liz said.

"This is a second airlock that can be sealed if necessary," Catie said as she led them out of the passage. "The captain's chair is on the other side of that wall. You have to go right or left around it to enter the bridge."

"The captain doesn't want someone sneaking up behind," Kal said.

"Smart."

"My god, this is huge," Liz said.

"No kidding," Kal added. "Why so big?"

"I don't know," Catie replied. "To impress people. They could fit twice as many stations in here and still have lots of room."

"Maybe they would have more stations if it was a battleship," Liz said.

"Probably," Catie said. "Two pilot stations up front; navigation to the left; communication to the right. Then a science station to the left, weapons officer to the right."

"Wow!"

"The forward hull can be made transparent," Catie said.

"How can they do that?" Liz asked.

"Hey, diamonds are transparent, and the hull is mostly carbon."

"Makes sense," Kal said. "I've always wondered why diamonds are clear, and coal is black."

"Ask Dr. Zelbar," Catie said. "The deck officers have quarters above the bridge, then there are VIP suites above those."

"Must be nice," Kal said.

Everyone spent time wandering around the bridge. After a while, they went through the captain's quarters and then checked out the quarters for the deck officers.

"What's next?" Kal asked.

"Do you want to see engineering?" Catie asked. "It's just a bunch of stuff I don't understand. Uncle Blake can try to explain it."

"Hey, I don't understand it either," Blake said. "We should be heading back."

"Dr. Metra is waiting for you in sickbay," Catie said. "I'll show them the Foxes while you get your eye fixed."

Chapter 16 Christmas

Linda waved goodbye to Catie as she grabbed a cab. Marc had given her a ride to Boston since they were going that way. They had landed at Laurence G. Hanscom Field in Bedford. It was about the same distance from her parents' home as Logan International Airport, but not nearly the zoo to get into and out of. Catie would spend the first two-and-a-half days with Marc and Blake at their parents' home. Then she would stay with her mother and her grandparents for the rest of Christmas week. Liz would be staying with Catie, and Fred would provide security for Marc while Catie was with her mother.

"Jennie, are you and Susan set?"

"Yes, Susan is going to fly us down to Florida," Jennie said. "We've both had enough cold weather to last a lifetime."

"I know the feeling," Blake said. "If we could only convince our parents to move to Florida or Hawaii."

"Dad likes teaching at Boston College," Marc said. "So good luck with that."

"I know it's hopeless," Blake said. "Here comes Liz with our ride."

Liz drove up in a black Expedition. She pulled up next to the jet, got out, and met Fred, who had already unloaded their luggage and was waiting by the back of the plane. After they loaded it in the SUV, Liz walked over and escorted Marc and Catie to the SUV.

"Hey, what am I, chopped liver?" Blake asked.

"Not my fault that ADI says you're an unlikely target," Liz said.

"Besides, it traditional in Scottish families to sacrifice the younger brother to protect the heir," Marc said.

"I'm the spare in case you get whacked, not the sacrificial lamb," Blake said. He tried to look offended.

"Nobody would ever mistake you for a lamb," Marc said.

Blake huffed a little to show his annoyance as he followed them to the SUV. "Should I drive?"

"I think that'll work best," Liz said. "You're familiar with the area, and it'll leave my hands free."

"I still think you're taking this security thing too far," Marc said.

"Says the man who had his daughter kidnapped in Portugal," Liz said. "Kal and I vote for better safe than sorry. Fred, if you don't mind, sit in the back."

"I'm good with that."

Blake drove them to his and Marc's childhood home in West Cambridge. The thirty-minute drive was quite pleasant, and the roads were mostly empty on the early Sunday morning just before Christmas.

"Fred, while Catie and Liz are with us, you'll have to stay at the Sheraton."

"I'm okay with that," Fred said. "Since I'm free for the first two days, I thought I'd check out Harvard today, and Boston tomorrow. I haven't had a chance to really see some of the Revolutionary War sites."

"Don't be looking here for company," Blake said. "I've seen them all way too many times."

"I'm sure."

Marc's and Blake's parents came out of the house as soon as the Expedition pulled into their driveway. "Wow, nice Victorian house," Fred said.

"Try spending your childhood restoring it," Blake said.

Catie jumped out of the car and ran to her grandparents. "Hi, Nanna, hi, Poppa," she gushed as she reached them.

"Hello, dear," Mrs. McCormack said as she gave Catie a hug. "I've baked cookies."

"This is my friend, Liz," Catie said. "She's staying with me, kind of friend slash bodyguard."

"Hello, Mr. and Mrs. McCormack," Liz said.

"Call me Beth," Mrs. McCormack said as she gave Liz a welcoming hug.

"And call me Walter," Mr. McCormack said as he reached out and shook Liz's hand.

Marc and Blake walked up, pulling their luggage under Fred's watchful eye.

Mrs. McCormack gave each of her sons a hug and a kiss. "Welcome home."

"Hey, Mom," Blake said. "This is our pilot, Fred. He'll be staying at the Sheraton while Catie's here. Then he'll come and stay with us when Catie goes over to the McGinnises."

"We could make room for him here," Mrs. McCormack said.

"Don't worry," Fred said. "I'm looking forward to a few days without having to worry about these three. I've got some friends meeting me at the hotel tonight, and we have plans until Tuesday afternoon."

"If you're sure."

"I am. And here's my taxi. I'll see you on Tuesday," Fred said as he went back to the Expedition and grabbed his bag.

"Have fun, Fred," Catie called out.

"Now come on in, and we'll get everybody settled," Mrs. McCormack said. She kept hold of Catie's hand while she walked back into the house. "We'll have some tea and cookies first, then we have some things to do."

Blake gave Marc a look, hoping that things to do didn't include some project fixing up the house. Marc just rolled his eyes and followed his mother into the house.

"Why don't we go to my study and go over that design you sent me," Mr. McCormack said as he finished his last sip of tea.

"Sure Pop," Blake said. "I'm still playing around with several ideas. It'd be good to get your take on them."

"Go ahead," Mrs. McCormack said. "Catie and I will stay here. I have a couple of her papers I would like to review." When Mrs. McCormack learned that Catie was going to be homeschooled, she had demanded that she at least get to review all of her papers. Catie and Marc had agreed to that, after convincing her that she didn't actually need to run Catie's education. "I see a tendency she has that I think we should address."

"I thought this was a vacation," Catie whined.

"It is, that's why we're only going to review two papers. We'll go over the others via video chat after the break."

"Hey, don't look at me," Marc said. "I had to live with that for eighteen years. She was reviewing all my schoolwork since I was five. She even reviewed my master and doctoral theses before I submitted them."

"A good thing too," Mrs. McCormack said.

"Mom, they really don't grade those papers on the English," Marc said.

"Well, they get published, and other people read them. I would be embarrassed to have people think my son couldn't write better than that."

"That's why I wrote my master's on some classified tech," Blake said.

"And just you wait, it should be declassified in another year . . ."

"Oh brother," Blake said as he and Marc retreated to their father's study.

"Sorry about that, but you know your mother," Mr. McCormack said.

"Hey, it'll be good for Catie," Marc said. "She doesn't focus on her English and writing as much as she does the hard sciences."

"Well, her grandmother won't be putting up with that."

Marc chuckled as he remembered how many times he'd been called to the kitchen table to review some paper. A paper that he thought was ready to submit, only to find out how much work he still had to do on it. "How are you doing, Dad?"

"I'm fine. We both have our health and our jobs. Life is pretty good right now. It was quite an amazing thing, you guys bringing up that ship."

"That was amazing," Marc said as he picked up a manuscript that was sitting on his father's desk.

"What's this, you taking up writing?"

"No, that's Seamus O'Callaghan's book. I'm proofreading the technical details for him. Poor guy is almost blind, so he can't really do it himself."

"He is, what's the problem?" Marc asked as he watched Blake sit down and start to lay out the design his father wanted to discuss.

"Macular Degeneration, and a real shame, he's just fifty-eight years old. Beth hears from his wife that it's killing him. Imagine, you dedicate your entire life to architecture and engineering, building all these beautiful structures, and now you can't see them."

"Do you think I might talk to him?"

"Sure, but if it was his memory that was giving him trouble, I'd have called you. I know what you did for Garth McGinnis's parents."

"We still might be able to help," Marc said. "I'd like to talk to him."

"Well, if you can help him, his wife will be eternally grateful. They've been married for thirty-five years."

"We'll see what we can do," Marc said. He texted a message to Dr. Metra on his HUD.

After watching Blake and his father chat about his project for a while, Marc wandered back to the kitchen. Liz was sitting there, reading the local paper. "Where's Catie?"

"She's in your mother's office, and she is one unhappy girl."

"Why is she unhappy?"

"You'll have to ask her yourself," Liz chuckled. "Something about computers and keyboards."

Marc went to his mother's office. Catie was alone typing on his mother's laptop.

"What's up?"

"How could you give me up like that?" Catie whined.

"Fixing the structure in your paper isn't that bad a curse."

"No, but having to do it on this thing is," Catie continued to whine.

"What's wrong with it?"

"The keyboard sucks, I can barely type two words without a typo; the screen is tiny, and I have to sit at this desk to do it."

Marc laughed, "How would you do it if you were at home?"

"I'd be using my comm and my HUD, ADI would be autocompleting my typing for me; I could be lying on the sofa with just a flat board to project the keyboard on."

"Why can't you do that here? You could at least use your comm."

"Because Nanna comes wandering in here every few minutes to see how I'm doing."

"Oh, you do know that she hums while she walks around."

Catie blinked at her father, and her eyes turned up to the left, "I never noticed it before, I guess you're right."

"Sure, and you could close the door if you wanted to."

"I tried that, she came in and left it open when she went out. It's not like I could get up and close it again."

"No, I guess not. I always used the humming."

"But if she wants to check on my work, it has to be on her laptop."

"Set up a Bluetooth keyboard for ADI, and she'll make sure it's all copied over for you; you just need to move to the desk when you hear the humming."

"Thanks, Daddy, you're a lifesaver. I'll even forgive you for laughing when she brought out my papers."

"Glad I could help," Marc said. He gave Catie a peck on the cheek before he wandered back into the kitchen.

"How's she doing?" Liz asked.

"Better," Marc said. "I pointed out that my mother hums when she walks around the house. Where is she, by the way?"

"She just went out. She said something about taking a casserole to a neighbor."

"Okay, give me the sports section."

"You're going to read the paper?"

"No, but I need it for cover when she comes back." Marc turned the sports section to an inside page and laid it down. Then he turned to his HUD and started reviewing all the paperwork he had piled up.

"How is Catie doing?" Mrs. McCormack asked when she came in from the back yard.

"She seems to be okay," Marc said. "She was working on her paper when I poked my head in."

"Good, I'll just go see how she's doing."

Marc followed his mother to her office. He coughed in case Catie couldn't hear his mother humming.

"Hello, dear, how is it going?"

"Fine Nanna, I'm almost done with this one," Catie said. She was studiously reading the paper on the laptop display.

"Well, let me see what you've done."

Catie moved her chair over as Mrs. McCormack pulled another chair up to the computer and started to read her paper. Catie looked at her father, tilted her head to the right, stuck her tongue out, and held her left hand up like she was hanging herself.

"Catie, don't make faces, it's undignified," Mrs. McCormack said without ever looking up from the laptop.

Marc shrugged at Catie and shook his head.

"I've been teaching teenagers for over thirty years," Mrs. McCormack said. "I can tell what they're doing by the sound of their chair squeaking. And Marc, don't be encouraging her."

Marc waved to Catie and quietly exited the room. "Coward!" Catie messaged him on her HUD.

"You two need to go hang out somewhere else while Catie and I prepare dinner," Mrs. McCormack said. "And Marc, that's the same page you were reading when I came in here ten minutes ago. So, whatever you're doing that you don't want me to know about, go do it in the family room."

"Now I know where Catie gets it from," Marc said as he and Liz settled in the family room.

"You mean, you never noticed before?" Liz asked.

"No, I think she was being subtle before, she didn't want us to know how much she noticed," Marc said. "Now I think she's showing off."

"Or not holding back," Liz said.

"No wonder Dad spent so much time in his study."

"She must be a little intimidating."

"Oh yeah, she can definitely intimidate you."

"I'll be down in a minute," Catie told Liz on Monday morning. "I've got a few homework things to do first," she lied.

"Okay, but I'm not promising any French toast will be left."

"I know how to make it."

"See ya," Liz said, realizing that Catie wanted privacy for some reason.

Catie sat back in the bed; she set her comm so that it would lower her voice to make her sound older, then she dialed.

"Family Aid Boston, how may we help you?"

"I'm planning to make a donation and would like to ask some questions."

"I'd be happy to answer any question that I can."

"Could you tell me how many families you have in your shelter right now?"

"We don't usually give out that kind of information; may I ask why you want to know?"

"I want to do something special for them for Christmas, and I need to know how many families I need to account for."

"Ma'am, we're happy to take almost any kind of donation, but we find that we're more efficient if we just receive the money so we can direct it where it's most needed."

"I understand that, and I plan to make a cash donation also, but I wanted to do something special for Christmas."

"I understand. We currently have thirty-two families in our shelter. We are also currently taking care of over eight hundred families across Boston with various forms of assistance."

"I know, I saw the story on the news last night, that's why I'm calling."

"Okay, how else may I assist you?"

"Can you tell me how many children each of them has and whether both parents are together?"

"I'm not sure, if you would hold please, I'll get our director to talk with you."

A few moments later, another woman came on the line. "This is Rebecca Farnsworth, who am I talking with?"

"I would prefer to remain anonymous," Catie said. "I'm trying to make a donation to the families you have in your shelter."

"Of course, how can I help?"

"I guess I should explain what I want to do."

"That would probably be best."

"Since it's Christmas, I want to give all the parents a chance to buy Christmas presents for their families and themselves. To do that, I need to know how many families there are and the makeup of each family."

"We can provide that information, but I'm curious as to how that will help you."

"I've made arrangements with a local bank to provide debit cards for each family. The cards will only be useful at The Prudential Center and can be used to buy two outfits for each member of the family and one toy for each child."

"I trust our families, but giving them cash cards and expecting them to follow rules like that might be a bit too much."

"You don't need to worry about that," Catie said. Her voice showed that she was frustrated even though she was trying to contain it. "The cards will only work for stores in the Prudential Center and only for merchandise. I'm confident we can track their activities sufficiently. I need to know if you will give me the information I need and whether you can get the parents to the Prudential Center at ten o'clock tomorrow so they can pick up their cards from the bank's representative and do their shopping."

"We certainly can do that," Rebecca said. "It's an unusual gift, but it is generous."

"Okay, so what is the makeup of each family?"

Rebecca listed off the pertinent information for Catie.

"Okay," Catie said. "I've arranged for the bank to have someone meet you at the Prudential Center. Will you be accompanying the families? They want to be able to check the ID of the person in charge."

"I will certainly be there."

"I've also arranged with the bank to pay the rent, utilities, and necessary deposits for each family for one year. This is assuming you can find them appropriate accommodations, something they could afford to continue paying for once they've had time to recover."

"Miss," Rebecca stuttered, "that is probably far more expensive than you might imagine."

"I'm imagining one to 1.2 million dollars," Catie said. "I've deposited one million with the bank, and they will notify me if they need more money once they've determined the burn rate."

"Oh my, that is generous," Rebecca said. "Could I ask you to do an interview with a reporter friend of mine? She would keep your identity a secret."

"I don't think so."

"Would you mind if we had her cover the event?"

"Won't that be awkward for the families?"

"I can assure you the reporter will be discreet and respectful," Rebecca said. "She's an old school friend of mine; she's the same one who did the story you mentioned."

"I guess that would be okay," Catie said.

"Is there anything we can tell them to explain your generosity?"

"Just say that someone who has had more than her fair share of good luck wanted to help some families who have had more than their fair share of bad luck."

"What a lovely sentiment," Rebecca said. "Is there anything else I can help you with?"

"Just one thing, I'm going to make a cash donation also. Does it work better for you if I do it now, or should I wait until after the new year?"

"We're a non-profit," Rebecca said, "so taxes are not an issue. We always prefer to have the money sooner than later, but you should do what works best for your tax situation."

"Okay, then I'll make the transfer now," Catie said. "Done! Thanks for your help, and have a nice day."

"Oh no, thank you," Rebecca said.

Catie immediately phoned her mother, "Mommy."

"Hello, Sweetie," Linda said.

"Can we go shopping tomorrow? I want to go to the Prudential Center."

"We can, it's going to be crazy, though."

"I like crazy," Catie said. "Liz and I can meet you at the Magic Bean. We'll bring all our luggage in our car, so we can just go to Grandma's with you afterward."

"What time do you want to meet?"

"How about eleven o'clock? We can do some shopping and then have lunch."

"We'll see you then."

Catie went downstairs to see everybody.

"Well, hello," her grandmother said. "You decided to join us," she said as she gave the clock a good look to emphasize the 9:30 time.

"I was just finishing up a few things," Catie said. "I'll be all yours for the rest of the day."

"Good, we have to give you up tomorrow, so we want to spend some time with you. Now, do you want French toast?"

"Yes, I would love some French toast," Catie said as she gave Liz a 'see there' look.

"Coming right up."

"Liz, we're going to meet my mother tomorrow for shopping. Could you help me do something so people won't recognize me?" Catie asked.

"It's going to be a zoo so you'll be lost in the crowd, but sure. It'll be good practice. Maybe we can come up with an incognito look for you," Liz said.

"I don't want something flashy; I don't want to stand out."

"That's the definition of an incognito look," Liz said.

"Okay, thanks."

Catie was browsing in the Magic Bean while she watched various families come in to buy toys for their children. She could quickly tell the ones who were with Family Aid Boston because they looked around the store in a kind of awe. Some of them had brought their children with them to pick out their own toy. Generally, the mother would tell them to pick something that they would play with all year since it was their one special toy. The children did not rush to the most expensive toys; instead, they really shopped for that one thing they wanted. Several of the little ones got a stuffed animal. Catie especially liked the stuffed tiger. The mothers steered the older kids toward educational toys or the dress-up and role-playing toys. Lots of Avengers' outfits left the store.

She was standing at the back of the store when she saw her mother and grandmother come in. They looked around the store for a few minutes trying to find Catie. Catie just waited to see how long it would take them to notice her. Finally, they saw her and came back where she was.

"We looked all over for you," Linda said. "Finally, I saw Liz and decided that the young lady standing next to her must be my daughter."

Catie laughed. Liz had taken a curling iron to her normally straight brown hair and given it some light curling. Then she had applied a little makeup to Catie's face. But Catie thought the most significant difference was that she was dressed in high heels, dressy jeans, a light green cashmere turtleneck with a navy jacket over it. Catie would never have thought to combine the clothes like that. Everything except the coat was from her own wardrobe.

"You do look older," Linda said. "I'm not sure I totally approve," she added, looking at Liz.

"She does clean up nice," Liz said.

"I do like that outfit," Mrs. McGinnis, her grandmother, said. "It might even pass muster with your gran, although Mother does prefer young ladies to wear dresses."

"I know, she told me," Catie said. "And told me," she added with a laugh.

"Boys, come in here," Mrs. McCormack called out. "You should see this story."

Blake and Marc came out of their father's study, followed by their father.

"Beth, what is it?" Mr. McCormack asked.

"I want you to watch this news story." Mrs. McCormack rewound the DVR and pressed play.

"This is Marsha Williams reporting from the Prudential Center with a Christmas story to warm your hearts. With me is Rebecca Farnsworth from Family Aid Boston. Rebecca, what can you tell me about what is happening here?"

"We had an anonymous donor call us yesterday and ask us to set this up," Rebecca said. "We have thirty-two families who have recently lost their homes and become homeless. They're having to live in our shelter during this holiday season. This benefactor invited all the families here to the Prudential Center for a little holiday shopping spree. Each family has a gift card that allows them to purchase two outfits for each family member and one toy for each child."

"That sounds wonderful. There are some really nice shops here, what are the families going for?"

"For clothing, the adults are focusing on things they can wear to work. For some, it will be what they will wear to their next job interview. As you know, they say the clothes make the person; so having a nice professional outfit is always a help during a job interview. The children are getting nice, sensible clothes for school. When a family is having a tough time like these families are, the children can feel isolated because their clothes no longer fit them or fit in with their schoolmates."

"How long will these families have to stay at your shelter?"

"Usually, it takes two to three months to find the right accommodations for a family. Some of these families have already been with us for a while. But our benefactor has taken that into account. She has ensured that all these families will be moving to new homes as soon as we can find them. Arrangements have been made to pay all the deposits necessary and even cover utility and rent for the next year. As I'm sure you know, the cost of deposits to move into a house or an apartment is prohibitive. That alone prevents many families with the means to pay the rent from finding a new place."

"That is amazing and extremely generous," Marsha said. "Did your mysterious benefactor say why she was doing this?"

"She told me she saw your story about homeless families last night on the news. She said that she's someone who has had more than her fair share of good luck, and she wanted to help these families who have had more than their fair share of bad luck."

"What an elegant way to put it, but what about all the other families who need help? Surely you could have used the money more efficiently."

"Yes, we could have, but our benefactor wanted to do something special for the holidays, something a bit more personal than simply a check. But she didn't forget about the other needy families here in Boston; she also donated fifty million dollars to our charity."

"Ooh, that is the kind of mysterious benefactor we all need. Well, this is Marsha Williams bringing you this heartwarming story. What I'd like to call Miracle on Boylston Street."

"Catie and I just watched that reporter's story last night," Mrs. McCormack said. "Isn't that wonderful that someone else saw it and was moved enough to do all that?"

"That's where all that money went," Marc said.

"What?"

"Mom, I'm pretty sure your granddaughter is the mysterious benefactor."

"How can that be? She wouldn't have that kind of money."

"Well, she used to," Marc said.

"What do . . . , oh, the ship," Mrs. McCormack said.

"Yes, the ship," Marc said. "She's just donated her share."

"It was that much money?"

"It was a lot more, that's just what we paid out. The rest is in the company," Marc said. "Of course, she still owns her share of that."

"Oh, good. I wouldn't want her to be broke."

"She's anything but broke, a lot more cash-poor than before, but definitely not poor."

"She does have enough cash money?"

Marc laughed, "She held back five million dollars. But Christmas isn't over yet."

"Don't worry, Mom," Blake said. "If Catie runs out of money, she can always pick some more up playing poker."

"Or gin," Fred added. He'd been sitting with Mrs. McCormack, keeping her company when the story came on.

"Oh yes, there's always gin," Blake laughed. "Hey, you never told us how much she took you for that night."

"That's because I was embarrassed," Fred said. "She took me for over three thousand dollars."

"You're not teaching my granddaughter how to gamble," Mrs. McCormack scolded Marc.

"I didn't teach her," he said. "And the way she plays cards, it's not really gambling."

"Ohhhh, she memorizes the cards, doesn't she?"

"Yes, she does. I don't know where she learned that little trick, I certainly didn't teach her."

"Well, I might have shown her how remembering the odd card with a nick, or a fold would help, back when I was teaching her to play gin," Mrs. McCormack said sheepishly. "But that was before we realized she has that amazing memory."

"Oh, so you're the one I have to blame for all the money she took off of me playing Texas Hold 'em," Blake said.

"You shouldn't gamble," Mrs. McCormack scolded. "But Texas Hold 'em. That wouldn't be gambling for her at all."

"Not after about ten hands," Marc laughed.

"Now you know where your daughter inherited all her sly and sneaky ways," Mr. McCormack said. "When I first met Beth, she was supplementing her income playing gin."

"Well, they don't pay teachers enough, especially back then," Mrs. McCormack said. "Anyway, I don't do that anymore."

"I think that's because nobody will play with her," Mr. McCormack laughed.

Marc texted Catie, "Your grandparents and I are proud of you."

Blake texted, "I'm proud of you too."

"Time to open presents," Mrs. McGinnis said. "We have eggnog and cookies on the coffee table."

"I think we should start with the guest of honor," Mr. McGinnis said.

"We're starting with Mommy?" Catie quipped.

"No, the youngest is always the guest of honor," Catie's great grandmother said.

"Seems like it should be the other way around."

"Well, the other way around defines who's in charge," Catie's great grandfather said. "Now, be quiet."

"Starting with your fun gift," Mrs. McGinnis said. "Here's your gift," she handed Catie a large, wrapped box.

Linda's family had a rule that came from many generations back. Each person received only one fun or special gift; all the other gifts were clothes or work-related. Catie had resented the rule when she was seven and realized that everybody didn't have the same rule. That was until her mother took her to visit a homeless shelter and had her work in a soup kitchen for a whole weekend. She got over her resentment right away.

"It's so big."

"Well, open it!"

Catie tore the wrapping paper off, revealing a beautiful jewelry box.

"It so beautiful, what is it made of?"

"It's a mahogany frame with rosewood insets and drawers," Mrs. McGinnis said. "Now open it. The lid has a mirror in it."

Catie opened the lid showing the mirror inset into it. It also showed a padded shelf with hooks to hold earrings.

"It tilts up so you can see them dangle."

Catie tilted the shelf up, underneath it was a set of boxes. The right-hand side was for holding rings, the left-hand side was for studs.

"This is really nice," Catie said. "It will hold all my jewelry."

"Open the second drawer," Mrs. McGinnis said.

Catie opened the drawer to reveal a tennis bracelet with diamonds and emeralds.

"Oh, this is too much," Catie said.

"You can't give an empty jewelry box, it just isn't done," Mrs. McGinnis said. "Besides, it was an excuse for your grandfather to shop for you."

"But where will I wear something like this?"

"I'm sure with all that work your father is doing with the government down there in the Cook Islands, you'll have opportunities."

"This is from us," Catie's great grandmother said as she handed Catie a velvet box wrapped in a ribbon.

"But I already got my fun gift," Catie said.

"You're a woman now, and jewelry is part of a woman's clothing," her great grandmother sniffed, obviously put out that she hadn't been selected to give Catie the fun gift. "Besides, we gave you an heirloom for your birthday, this way, we got to shop for you."

Catie untied the ribbon and opened the box. Inside was a necklace with matching earrings. It was a gold chain with a fan-shaped gold pendant with turquoise inlay.

"Oh, my, these are beautiful."

"Well, put them on, we want to see whether we got our money's worth."

The day after Christmas, Catie, her mother, and her grandmother were walking down the street when a moving van pulled up in front of the house across from her grandmother's. "Oh, I guess our new neighbors are finally moving in. I'm still not sure about their kind moving in here."

"What kind?" Linda asked. Just then, a blue Ferrari pulled into the driveway, and a large, black man got out of it.

"Oh, mother, you don't mean because they're black?"

"No dear, because they're rich. He drives a Ferrari, and his wife drives a Bentley. They've spent a couple of million fixing that house up. If people like that keep buying around here, they're going to drive up the property taxes."

"That will take a while, and you really don't have anything to worry about."

"I know that, but some of our neighbors aren't as fortunate as we are."

"Well, you'll have to lobby the city council to protect them."

"It is on my list. We need to head back home now, Catie and I have some cooking to do."

The next day, Catie was knocking on the neighbor's door while balancing a dish of lasagna in her other hand.

"I think it's another casserole," a man's voice said with a groan.

"Shhh," a woman's voice scolded, "they'll hear you. Come on, answer the door."

The door opened, and the man she'd seen get out of the Ferrari looked out at Catie. "Can I help you?"

"My grandmother and I made this for you. We know how hard it is to move, and wanted to give you guys a night off from cooking."

"Invite the young lady in."

"Please come on in. By the way, my name is Malik," he said as he opened the door wide so Catie could enter the house.

"I'm Catie. My grandmother, Betty, lives in the house across the street from you."

"I'm pleased to meet you," Malik said as he relieved Catie of the dish.

"I'm Jasmine," the woman said as she walked over and extended her hand to Catie. "Alyssa, come down and meet the neighbor," she called out.

Catie shook hands with Jasmine as a young girl about her age came bouncing down the stairs.

"Hi, I'm Alyssa, but you already heard that," she said.

"Hi, I'm Catie. My grandmother lives across the street."

"Oh, so you don't live around here?" Alyssa's face fell a little.

"No, just visiting, but my grandmother says the family at the end of the block has children and the family around the corner from them does too. Then you're just five blocks from the school, and lots of families around there have kids."

"Malik, put that casserole in the kitchen," Jasmine said.

"It's lasagna," Malik said as he replaced the cover after sneaking a peek.

"Well, that will be a nice dinner," Jasmine said. "Alyssa, why don't you put on a coat and walk outside with Catie. It's nice outside, and some fresh air will do you good."

Alyssa grabbed a jacket and led Catie outside. "Did you have a good Christmas?" she asked. "I guess I should have asked if you celebrate Christmas, first."

"Yes, we celebrate Christmas," Catie said. "It was fun. I haven't seen my grandparents for about a year. And my great grandparents came over too. They're always fun. How about you?"

"We spent Christmas at my grandparents' house in Pittsburgh. I got a new bike and some jewelry. And of course, lots of clothes."

"I got lots of clothes too. My gran, that's what we call my great grandmother, thinks I need to wear more dresses, so I've got enough of them for the rest of my life. My grandmother gave me a nice jewelry box, and I got jewelry from my gran, my grandfather, and my father and his parents."

"Where's your dad?"

Catie laughed. "Actually, he's across town staying with his parents. We arrived on Sunday, and I stayed with them until Tuesday; then, I came here."

"That's nice, both sets of grandparents being in the same city. So, your mom grew up here?"

"Yes, right in that house," Catie said. "She even went to Harvard Medical School and lived at home the whole time."

"That must have helped. I hear medical school is tough."

"That's what my mother tells me," Catie said. "Where did you move from?"

"Oh, we lived in Newton, but Mom and Dad both work in downtown Boston and wanted to skip the commute. Besides, they really wanted to live in a Victorian house," Alyssa said.

"That's cool. It is a nice house," Catie said. "Sounds like you'll be changing schools."

"Yeah, I'm going to be attending Buckingham Browne & Nichols School."

"That's supposed to be a really good school."

"That's what they say."

"But no fun leaving your friends back in Newton."

"No, it's not, and my parents work all the time."

"Mine do too. Since I moved in with my dad, I get to spend time with him at work."

"How do you do that?"

"I homeschool. So, I can do that anywhere. Right now, we're living in a house, and we mostly work from there. There are six of us, and we all work for the company."

"You work for your dad's company?"

"Yes, I do small projects and coordinate things. We're just getting started, so it's small. My Uncle Blake works there as well."

"What kind of company is it?"

"We're trying to commercialize some new technology we have," Catie explained. "So, we develop the technology and figure out how to manufacture products that use it. We're working on a new battery right now, so it's really all about manufacturing. But we'll have other things soon."

"My dad has an IT company," Alyssa said. "It's one of the bigger ones here in Boston. My mom is an advertising exec. She's really terrific at it, but she works all the time."

"Maybe you should go to their office to do your homework. Then you'd be hanging out with them. I like doing that with my dad; sometimes we work at the same desk."

"That might be fun. I could definitely do that at my dad's office, and maybe my mom's on Saturdays. It's not that busy then, so it might be okay."

"Sure, then you're just like a coworker, you take breaks with them, make a few comments or jokes here and there. I like it."

"How long are you staying?"

"We leave tomorrow. We're flying to San Diego to drop off my mom, then we're off for the Cook Islands."

"Drop off your mom, can't she fly by herself?"

"Oh sure, but we've got a private jet, so it's nicer and lots faster."

"You have a private jet?"

"Yes, my dad leases it so he can visit clients and people real easy. And we live in the Cook Islands. That means you have to fly to get anywhere."

"Why do you live in the Cook Islands, you don't look like you're from there?"

"No, I don't; people from there all have natural tans," Catie said. "And gorgeous, long, black hair. We live there because my dad wanted a place where we could set up our company that was a little isolated. That way we won't have to worry about industrial espionage."

"My dad worries about that too."

"We're putting the company on Manuae, and it will be the only business on the island. In fact, everybody on the island will be working for the company."

"That sounds crazy; your dad must really be worried about espionage."

"That and the tax rate is really good," Catie said. "Hey, why don't you give me your contact info, and we'll keep in touch."

"Sure, my number is," Alyssa rattled off her phone number, "what's yours?"

"Just texted it to you," Catie said just as Alyssa's phone buzzed.

"How did you do that?"

Catie pointed to her specs, "They're like Google Glasses, only better," Catie said.

"Oh, I wish I could have some."

"If we're selling them next Christmas, I'll send you a pair," Catie said. "But it might be longer, so I'll keep you on the list."

"That would be so cool. It'll drive my father nuts. He's always the first to get any new technology. I usually get his old stuff, if you can call something a year old, old."

"Cool, we can video chat, and you can tell me how my grandparents are doing."

"Oh, you want me to spy for you."

"Uh, I guess I do. They don't always tell us what's really going on."

"Anything else I should spy on for you?"

"Not that I know of, but I'll let you know if I think of something."

Both girls laughed as they continued down the street.

Chapter 17 Nightmares

"Hi, Kal, did you miss me?" Catie asked as she ran into the mansion at the compound. They had just gotten back from their Christmas vacation. Catie was looking forward to a normal routine, without one of her grandparents trying to help her grow into *'a properly dignified young lady.'*

"Miss you? Have you been gone?" Kal asked.

Catie picked up a throw pillow off the couch and threw it at Kal. "You're mean."

"No, I'm not, but I have been enjoying having all this space to myself."

"Where's Sam been?"

"She's been in Wellington for the last four days," Kal said. "Something about networking with the muckety mucks there. I have been throwing wild parties every night."

"Are we having one tonight?" Blake asked as he came through the door.

"Nope, apparently you can't scare up a wild party on a Sunday to save your life. These Cook Islanders really believe in that day of rest thing."

"Maybe you can have one next week, Uncle Blake," Catie said.

"Like we could get away with that!" Blake said. He grabbed Catie's suitcase and carried it and his up the stairs.

Catie followed him with her backpack and the small duffle she had bought to hold all the clothes she had acquired. Her new jewelry box was safely wrapped inside it as well. "Home sweet home," she said as she dropped the bag and flopped onto her bed.

"Were you missing it?" Liz asked as she came in, dragging her own suitcase.

"Yes, weren't you? I like visiting, but I have a hard time when I don't have my own space."

"Just remember your own space ends right here," Liz said, pointing to the space between their two beds.

"Don't worry, I won't invade your space," Catie said. "But you have to admit, it's going to be nice to sleep in our own beds tonight."

"Yes, it is," Liz said. "I'm glad your dad let everyone buy a new bed. The ones they had in this place were okay, but nothing like these."

"Daddy always says, take care of how you sleep, and then you'll have the energy to take care of everything else."

"Smart man."

Catie set her new jewelry box on the dresser on her side of the room. She stood back and admired it.

"Looks nice," Liz said. "Are you going to finish unpacking?"

"I'm going to do that tomorrow," Catie said. "Can we go for a run now?"

"What a perfect idea," Liz said.

"No! Get off of me!"

Catie woke up with a start. She looked at the clock, it read 3:00 a.m.

"No!"

The sound was coming from Liz. Catie got up and went to her. Liz was wrapped up in her sheet, crying.

"No! Leave me alone!"

Catie rubbed Liz's shoulder, "It's okay, Liz, it's okay." She sat on the bed and pulled Liz's head onto her lap. She continued to rub her shoulder. "It's okay."

Liz settled down and quit moving around. Catie just sat there and stroked her back. Then she started singing a lullaby. She remembered her mother used to sing it to her whenever she had a bad dream. Catie sat with Liz until 5:00 a.m. when Liz woke up.

"What are you doing over here?" Liz asked as she blinked herself awake.

"You were having a bad dream," Catie said.

"Oh, I'm so sorry, Catie. I almost never have them anymore."

"It's okay, I don't mind."

"You shouldn't have to deal with my problems," Liz said.

"We're friends, you help me with my problems, why shouldn't I help you with yours?"

"Because I'm the adult."

"That doesn't mean anything; we're two friends being here for each other."

"Thanks, Catie," Liz said. She was terribly embarrassed that Catie had to comfort her. She liked being the tough one, and showing vulnerability was something she just didn't do.

Chapter 18 Production Starts Up

"Hello, Dr. Zelbar, Dr. Nikola," Marc greeted the Doctors Zelbar. "I understand we're ready to start talking about production issues."

"We think that's the next step," Nikola said.

"Great, it's a nice way to start off the new year," Marc said. "Please come in. Let me introduce some new members of our team: Dr. Jonas Scheele and Dr. Patrick McGenty, and his assistant Tomi Nakahara. Gentlemen, Dr. Nikola Zelbar and Dr. Leo Zelbar."

"I know your work," Nikola said as she shook hands with Dr. Scheele. "I think you'll be just what we need."

"I hope so," Dr. Scheele said. Dr. Scheele was one of the leading scientists in the field of plasma engineering and manufacturing processes.

"Let's get down to business, coffee, tea, and pastries will be here shortly," Marc said. "I just wanted to have a short pre-meeting to set expectations, then I'll leave you alone."

"A good idea," Dr. Zelbar said with a slight huff.

Nikola patted his hand and whispered, "Now, Leo."

"We have a team of support engineers and technicians joining us in two weeks," Marc said. "You four are the team leads for the development; the lead for the actual installation of the manufacturing process will be coming with the others."

Everyone nodded their heads waiting for Marc to get to the point of the meeting.

"We have three main manufacturing processes to set up," Marc said. "One for the battery production for which we already have prototype production going, one for the fuel cell elements and then, of course, the most complex one for the polysteel."

"Yes, Yes," Dr. Zelbar said.

"Our agreement with the Cook Islands is that we will be environmentally neutral," Marc continued. "That's why we have Dr. McGenty. He's a leading scientist in the field of environmentally neutral manufacturing. His job will be to make sure we have a full appraisal of the impact we have and how to mitigate it. Now we also have access to an extensive design team that will be offsite. They should be able to provide recommendations and designs as you define the specs. Our goal is to utilize everything that comes into the various plants in such a way that it leaves as a saleable product, or as environmentally safe emissions."

"Does that mean we need a zero-carbon footprint?" Dr. Scheele asked.

"That is the goal," Marc said. "Although it is acceptable to have a negative carbon footprint."

"How are you going to measure this carbon footprint?" Dr. Zelbar asked. "We are going to be using a lot of crude oil."

"That's a good question. One that I hope you all will help me answer," Marc said. "But for now, let's assume that it is a measure of CO_2 emissions. I'm assuming the carbon in the polysteel is bound, therefore, it shouldn't count."

"That is correct," Dr. McGenty said. "We will also need to make sure that there is no residual carbon dust or particulate matter leaving the factory."

"What else?" Dr. Scheele asked.

"Any water discharged needs to be pure, any minerals extracted and sequestered," Dr. McGenty continued. "How will you handle the waste associated with so many people working in one place?"

"We have a septic system design, that Tomi just finished. It takes everything and converts it to fertile soil, water, carbon disks, which we can feed back into the process and a little nitrogen gas and some oxygen," Marc said. "They're being installed in the remote villages around the Cook Islands, and we'll be installing one on Manuae as soon as possible."

"What about refining the materials?" Dr. McGenty asked. "Are you bringing in pure material, leaving the pollutants in someone else's back yard, or will you be refining them here?"

"It depends," Marc said, giving Dr. McGenty a hard look after the insult. "We will be bringing in ores to process where it makes sense. We'll bring in pig iron to make the polysteel, also recycled steel when it's available. We're going to bring in crude oil to feed the carbon into the system."

"What are you going to do with all the sulfur and nitrogen?" Dr. McGenty asked.

"You know, I hired you not only to identify the issues but to help find solutions," Marc said.

"I understand, but you've been thinking about this longer than I have."

"We think we can extract sulfuric acid from the process," Nikola said. "It should come out of the plasma field as a gas along with the nitrogen, water, and some CO_2. We can sell the sulfuric acid."

"The CO_2 can be pushed back into the plasma field; at those temperatures, the carbon will separate and then bond, releasing the oxygen," Dr. Zelbar said. "Some of the oxygen will combine with the hydrogen released from the hydrocarbons, and give you water."

"What about the heavy hydrocarbons, the greases, and tars?" Dr. McGenty asked.

"The plasma field will be hot, they'll all burn up or separate and release the carbon," Dr. Zelbar said. "We just have to capture it all in the polysteel matrix."

"A very virtuous cycle," Dr. McGenty said. "What about power?"

"We plan to contain the plasma field in such a way that we can extract all the heat and turn it into energy to feed back into the process," Nikola said. "The plasma field is mostly self-sustaining, the heat being extracted and fed back into the system."

"That's nice. What about the rest of the power for the production?" Dr. McGenty said.

"We're planning on solar," Marc said. "All the roofs will have solar panels on them."

"The exotic material for the batteries and fuel cell elements?" Dr. McGenty asked.

"We'll use recycled lithium batteries when they're available," Nikola said. "I think the process we have in mind will lend itself to recycled batteries. I'm hoping Dr. Scheele will be able to prove that out now that he's here."

"I'm intrigued," Dr. Scheele said. "I read that you're forming a lithium ceramic."

"That's correct. The batteries will have a much higher power density per gram of lithium, and the additional elements of the ceramic are quite benign."

"And the fuel cells?"

"That is probably our most complex environmental problem," Nikola said. "We will need to find a way to economically and environmentally recharge the fuel cells once they're spent. We don't want them to wind up in some dump or salvage yard."

"It looks like my work here is done," Marc said. "I'll leave you all to it. Ah, and here are the refreshments. The room is yours for the next few days. Tomi has been around for a while, so he'll know how to get anything you need, or contact my admin, Masina, and she'll help out."

Chapter 19 Board Meeting – Jan 7th

"Let's get this meeting going," Blake said. "Some of us have places to be."

"You do?" Marc asked. "And just where have you three been going every evening for the last month?" They were sitting in the sundeck lounge of the Mea Huli while she was running on autopilot thirty miles southeast of Manuae.

"As if you don't know," Blake said.

"I don't. I've instructed ADI only to inform me of Catie's whereabouts when I ask, or if she's in danger. Now that she's thirteen, I have to give her some space." Marc laughed at his joke, but Catie beamed at the implied freedom.

"We've been going to the Sakira to practice on the Foxes," Catie said.

"So, how's the training going?" Marc asked.

"Pretty good," Blake said. "Liz, with her experience as a chopper pilot, has picked it up fast. Catie's been doing the sims for months and makes us all look bad. It's not that different from an F18 in general handling, so I'm doing just fine."

"When can we take them up?" Catie asked.

"I think we want to wait on that," Marc said.

Catie showed her disappointment with a pout.

"We should probably get some air time," Blake said. "As of now, Catie is the only one who's actually flown one."

"Don't remind me," Marc said. He was thinking back to the mad dash they'd made from the Chagas to the Mea Huli when Catie had had to take the Lynx airborne and supersonic to make it in time.

"Come on," Catie whined, "I did good."

"Yes, you did."

"Now the meeting?" Blake said.

"Okay," Marc said. "Catie, why don't you go get Fred and Sam."

"Okay," Catie said as she ran down the ladder to the main deck. Shortly after, she returned, followed by Fred and Samantha.

"Sam, do you have something to share with the board?" Marc asked.

"Yes, I do. We have a signed contract with the Cook Island government covering the right to use the island of Manuae for the next fifty years. It appoints Marc as mayor until the local population exceeds fifteen thousand, and there is a referendum asking for an election. It gives us a very favorable tax position; we'll pay twelve percent tax on the gross sales, no property tax since we're doing all the development, and allows the construction of Delphi City, which will be considered part of Manuae. We're allowed to put in a two hundred fifty square meter manufacturing facility, and dorms for workers to live onsite. We can improve the landing strip to handle larger craft like the G650. It requires that we maintain a neutral impact on the environment and restore the land to pristine condition at the end of the term."

"Perfect," Marc said. "Sam, thanks for all your efforts on this. I know it's been a difficult period dealing with bureaucrats all this time."

As expected, Blake got up and poured everyone a glass of Glenlivet and a splash for Catie so they could toast the deal and the new mayor.

"To our mayor!" Blake toasted.

"To our mayor!"

"Thanks, everybody, I'll try not to mess up too bad. Kal, how are we doing on security?" Marc asked, trying to get the meeting back on track.

"I've got eight guys here now, and six more coming next week. Liz rustled up four from her old crew," Kal said. "That should get us started. We'll begin training the new guys once everyone clears medical." Kal gave Marc a knowing look, sending the message that he was ready to get his new legs.

"Liz, anything to add?"

"We need to work through what we want to do about weapons, but Kal and I are on top of it."

"How is our flight simulator coming along?"

"It's up and running," Fred said. "Catie's really putting it through its paces on both the Lynx setting and the G650 setting. I've done a few hours on the Lynx setting. Those are some amazing jets."

"Catie, how are you doing with our aircraft design team?" Marc asked.

"They decided on using the turbofan design," Catie said as she straightened up in her chair. "I've reviewed it with Uncle Blake, and he agrees that starting with the Rolls-Royce F136 as a base of the design is the best starting place. We can have them modify the engine to our spec; we'll send them the critical parts that only we can manufacture. It will save us over the custom job we did for our prototype. And it saves having to develop all the manufacturing tooling on our own. If everyone is okay with it, I'll have Sam open negotiations."

"That sounds good," Marc said. "What about the cockpit?"

"Same thing," Catie said. "We buy the basic package from a subcontractor, with a few black boxes specified where we'll plug our unique components in. We'll add our components here when we put it all in the Lynx. The team feels we can be ready to put the parts into a real shell within three months."

"So, we'll be flying when?" Marc asked with a smile.

"When are you going to give me a shell?" Catie asked.

Marc looked at Blake. "We're two weeks from starting up the polysteel, but I have no clue how long it will take to dial the process in," he looked at Liz.

"I'm getting two weeks from Dr. Zelbar," Liz said. "But you're right, we won't know until they start."

"When we have the process dialed in, we need to start beam construction for the offshore plant since that's critical path. Give it two months to seed the work, then we can start on a shell."

"Why can't we do it in parallel?" Catie asked.

"We don't want to debug the same process twice," Blake said. "Once we have beam works working, we can set up the second process for sheet and forms."

"But why can't we start that when you're ramping up the beams?" Catie asked.

"Good question," Marc said.

Blake gave a big sigh, "I'll look into it. We'll put in some more manufacturing space to shift the battery and fuel cell production too."

"That's going to be a problem," Samantha said. "The government really doesn't want that big a footprint on Manuae."

"Can we go vertical?" Marc asked, winning him a big smile from Catie and a frown from Blake.

"We could if it's not too tall," Samantha said.

"We could probably do that and only add four meters in that section of the building," Blake said reluctantly. "I'll check it out with our construction team."

"You sound pretty busy. Why don't we ask Fred to start managing the production schedule?"

"I'd be happy to," Fred said.

"Good by me," Blake said. "You can try to keep Ms. Catie happy."

Catie rubbed her nose with a particular finger, and Blake burst out laughing.

"Blake, work with Samantha on the second story; make sure she has what she needs when she goes to the government for approval," Marc said. "We don't want to invest too much before we know if they'll let us go forward."

"How are we doing on battery customers?" Marc asked.

"Tesla will use up all of our capacity for a while," Catie said. "We don't want to stir up new customers until we have more capacity. Tesla is asking for more than we can produce as of now. Is Fred picking up the battery production schedule as well?"

"Send me the details," Fred said after getting a nod from Marc.

Chapter 20 The New Mayor

The Prime Minister of the Cook Islands insisted on having a public gala to celebrate the signing of the agreement. Since Marc was the appointed Mayor of Manuae and the CEO of MacKenzie Discoveries, he was the guest of honor. In typical Cook Island tradition, the event was formal Polynesian. That meant slacks and tropical shirts for men, and long tropical dresses for women.

"I want to wear my jewelry from my grans," Catie said. She and Liz were comparing notes about what to wear for the event.

"The turquoise ones?"

"Yes. What color goes with turquoise, and what do you wear to a Polynesian gala?"

"White or Black is the best color with turquoise," Liz said. "But you can get away with just about anything."

"What about what to wear?"

"Below the knee is the only guidance I could get out of Masina. Other than that, she seemed to indicate that anything went. The men are just supposed to wear slacks and a nice tropical shirt."

"Well, I don't have anything that goes below the knee," Catie said. "I think we have to go shopping."

Liz laughed, "How many dresses did you bring back from Boston?"

"Lots, but none of them are Polynesian style. My grandparents and grans think you should wear something out of *Vogue*."

"Well, let's go shopping."

They went to Nani's Island Wear, which was highly recommended by Masina. The shop was a tropical garden of colors. Bright kaftans hung over all the walls, and there were racks of them on both sides of the store where they entered.

"Wow, look at all these colors," Catie said.

"They do have a wide selection," Liz said as she was flipping through the rack of kaftans. "I'm going to pick up a couple of these while we're here. You should get a couple too."

"Why?"

"Well, when someone comes over, you can throw it over the shorts and T-shirt you prefer to wear around the house. Then you'll be dressed for company and not embarrass your father."

"Oh, whatever," Catie sighed, but she started looking at the kaftans along with Liz.

"May I help you?" the young clerk asked.

"Yes," Liz said. "We're looking for a couple of outfits to go to the gala on Saturday."

"You are so lucky. I wish I could go. It is supposed to be a big party."

"That's what we hear," Liz said. "Catie here wants to wear some turquoise jewelry, so she needs a dress that will go with the color. I'm just looking for something nice."

"Ah, turquoise, that is such a pretty color for you," the clerk said. "I would recommend white; it will go well with the turquoise and will be properly fashionable for a party with our prime minister."

"I don't want to look like a bride," Catie whined.

"Oh no, it won't be all white. It will have a nice swath of tropical flowers in the design. Here let me show you."

After looking at over a dozen dresses, Catie finally settled on a white sleeveless maxi dress with spaghetti straps. It had a wine-red palm border print that came up to just below the hips. Liz chose a one-shoulder cobalt blue dress with a flowered skirt and solid blue bodice.

"Aren't we going to be the belles of the ball," Liz said as she and Catie posed in front of the mirror.

"Are you bringing a date?" Catie asked.

"No," Liz said. "I've sworn off men for a while."

"Oh," Catie said, remembering the nightmare. "Sorry."

"Don't be. I'm warming up to the idea again. Hanging out with your uncle and your dad is helping. They're always such gentlemen."

"Even Uncle Blake?" Catie said with surprise.

Liz laughed, "Sure, he's always making some joke or something, but he never invades my space, and he's always respectful. If you listened to his end of the conversation, you wouldn't know if he was talking to Kal or me."

Catie thought for a moment. "I guess that's right, I've always thought it was just normal."

"Unfortunately, not," Liz said. "Men seem to have this compulsion to treat women differently, and it's not always about being nicer."

"I've never seen my dad treat a woman different than he would a man, except when he's on a date," Catie said. "You know Dr. Metra can help you if you want?"

"How, is she a psychiatrist?"

"No, but she told me how her people treat PTSD," Catie said. "They kind of erase or dull the memory of the triggers."

"Erase the memory?"

"Only if you want her to. Otherwise, she just dulls it. That way, it's still there, but it doesn't sneak up on you. It makes it like something you have to want to recall, instead of having it triggered all the time by things that happen every day. Like loud noises triggering a memory of being shot."

"I'll think about it," Liz said. "I'm not sure I want Dr. Metra messing with my head."

The prime minister went to the stage and stood at the microphone. "I would like to say meitaki maata to all the people of MacKenzie Discoveries. You are a wonderful addition to our islands. For those of you who don't know yet, Dr. McCormack and his company have agreed to invest one billion dollars here in the Cook Islands, setting up manufacturing facilities that will provide employment for many of our friends and relatives. And best of all, they've agreed to do this in such a way that it does not damage the ecosystem of our beautiful home. They will be making this investment over the next ten years, so all of our children will have a choice to stay here in the islands instead of having to go somewhere else to find high-paying jobs."

The prime minister paused while the crowd applauded. "Along with the additional tax revenues, the jobs and the business it will generate, MacKenzie Discoveries will be injecting an additional fifty million directly into the coffers of the government. This will help the government provide better healthcare in our outer islands. No longer will our families have to come to Rarotonga or fly to New Zealand to get basic health care. We will be able to improve our infrastructure with a more predictable source of income. Tourism has been good to us, but it is too variable for long-term planning, and it doesn't create the higher-paying jobs we would want our children to have." Again, there was a round of applause.

"Now I know that all of you would like to get back to the party. The Akirata dance group is coming out shortly, but we wanted to have everyone meet Dr. McCormack and see him appointed Mayor of Manuae."

She signaled for Marc to come forward. After Marc accepted the appointment as Mayor of Manuae, much to his chagrin, he had to give a speech.

"Kia orana," Marc said. "My friends and I have been enjoying the hospitality of your islands. We've been treated well by everyone we have met, and we hope that we are treating the people we meet as well as they have treated us. We are excited to start our venture down here. We want to assure you that we want to be good neighbors and friends. We will be conducting our business in ways that enhance the islands' culture and community. Please feel free to come by and offer help and suggestions on how we can be better members of your community. Our door will always be open. Now in keeping with the island traditions, I think we should all return to the party."

Marc left the stage and came over to Catie and Samantha. "I can see you like giving speeches down here," Samantha said.

"Yes, low expectations," Marc said. "And lots of distractions. Now, as I was saying, we should get back to the party. We don't want to miss the dancers."

Chapter 21 Missing them

"Uncle Blake and Kal are going to be gone for a week," Catie whined. "Should I go with them to keep them company?"

"I'm sure you'll be down there with Liz on the flight simulator often enough," Marc said.

"Liz can't do it. Only one of them can be off station at a time," Catie said. "But I'll go anyway."

Marc grimaced, "That's right. I forgot, but I think that will be good. Talk to Blake. I don't want to have too big a gap in our presence. The two of them being gone will be enough, especially with Kal just coming back from a ten-day recruiting trip."

"Does it really have to be a whole week?" Catie whined some more. "Can't they bring them up to the hospital ship sooner?"

"No," Marc sighed. "Dr. Metra says it will be another month before the Virginia Henderson will be ready. And she was?"

"I know, Virginia Avenel Henderson was the first person to formalize the role of nurses. She defined a nurse's role as fourteen key tasks that they might perform for the patient. That's why they named the hospital ship after her."

"Nice to see you looked it up."

"I wrote a paper on her for my social studies class this term," Catie said. "I might as well get the credit if I'm going to get hassled about knowing the material. But really, a whole week?"

"Dr. Metra has already printed Kal's leg and Blake's arm and cheek, so it's just the surgery and the week of recovery in a sterile environment. She says she'll have them in partial stasis most of the time, so they won't be missing you that much."

"Why is she putting them in stasis?"

"She says it will speed up their recovery, and I'm sure she doesn't want to listen to them complain about how bored they are."

"But I'll miss them," Catie said. "Oh, so Uncle Blake decided to go with a new arm?"

"Talk to him," Marc said. "He said it would get him back to top form quicker. He wants to start training with Liz on Krav Maga."

"How's Dr. Metra going to handle all of the new guys?" Catie asked.

"She'll print the limbs and such on the Sakira, then do the surgery and recovery on the Virginia Henderson. That lets their families and friends visit during the recovery and eliminates questions like, *'where is my brother'*."

"That's good."

"Now, unless you have something else, I have work to do."

"So do I," Catie said. "ADI and I started working on a new design project."

"What are you designing?"

"It's a secret," Catie said. "Probably won't be anything, but it lets me practice some of the stuff I'm learning."

"I'm sure you'll tell me when you're ready," Marc said. "Go to it, then."

Blake and Kal had their surgeries on Sunday; Catie waited until Wednesday to go down to visit them–actually, to see them since they would be in stasis. She was really feeling lonely. Liz was very busy this week since Kal was out, and she had been busy for the previous two weeks while he'd been gone on a recruiting trip. The flight training with Uncle Blake and Liz had been the only fun thing she'd been able to do during that time. With Kal gone, she and her dad were virtual prisoners, since Liz wouldn't trust anyone else to guard them.

Catie walked up to the stasis chamber with Blake in it. He was just lying there; it was as if he was asleep. His face did look better now that the heavy scarring on his cheek was gone, but it was a bit strange to see such a smooth chunk of skin surrounded by the scarred skin Dr. Metra was going to have to repair from the inside out. But she had determined that after two treatments, she would be able to use skin grafts to heal the rest of his face, so he'd only look a little weird for a week after he got out of stasis.

Catie laid her head on the stasis chamber next to Blake's head. She wished that Samantha knew their secret. She was so easy to talk to, but it was hard to talk to her and keep all the secrets they had to hide. It had been easier once Kal and Liz knew, but they were still such a small circle.

"Uncle Blake, I get to do my instrument certification tomorrow," Catie whispered. "Fred says that Sam can get the exemption for me; I'll be able to solo next week. I saw that girl you've been seeing lately, Elei; she was asking where you were. She's really cute."

Catie stroked the glass of the stasis chamber. "Hey, they poured the concrete for the manufacturing plant. They might have the building up by the time you're back. Daddy's mad at Liz because she won't let him just go out to dinner with Sam. She and I have to go with them. We sit at a separate table, but I guess it's hard to call it a date when your daughter is looking at you." Catie giggled at the thought. "He's going to be really happy when Kal comes back. You too, of course."

"Liz is a little grumpy," Catie continued. "I wish you were around to lighten up the atmosphere. You're always so good at that. Fred is grumpy too; I think he's lonely being stuck in the house with Daddy and me, and Liz, who's in a bad mood because she's working all the time."

Catie kissed the glass, "We're waiting for you, Uncle Blake; I'm missing you." She dragged her hand along the glass as she moved to Kal's stasis chamber. "Kal, we're missing you too; I hope you like your new legs," Catie said as she stroked the glass by his face. "Bye, guys."

"Hi, Sam," Catie said as she entered the kitchen. She and Samantha were the only ones in the house. It seemed a little empty with Blake and Kal gone, and with Liz working overtime, handling all the security.

"Oh hi, Catie," Samantha said. "Do you want to join me for lunch?" Samantha waved one of the takeout menus they kept in the kitchen.

"Sure," Catie said, "what are you ordering?"

"A salad," Samantha said. "What do you want?"

"I'll have a salad too, as long as it comes with plenty of bread."

"You're a bad influence on me," Samantha said. "I don't burn the calories the way you do."

"You should come running with Liz and me."

"Hmm, I'll think about it."

Catie called the restaurant and ordered the two salads and extra bread. She sat down at the table and looked at Samantha.

"Do you have a question?" Samantha asked.

"Are you dating my dad?"

"We're starting to see each other a bit," Samantha said. "Is that okay with you?"

"I guess," Catie said. "Didn't I meet you in Boston?"

"Yes, we did once," Samantha said. "I was the attorney who helped your dad buy the Mea Huli."

"Oh, that's right," Catie said. "Were you dating then?"

"No, he never asked me out," Samantha said. "He was still married to your mom when we first met. After the divorce, he was kind of messed up. So even though I liked him, I didn't ask him out."

"So, you liked him," Catie said.

"Sure, he's a really nice guy, good looking, and he can be a lot of fun to be around," Samantha said. "But it was the wrong time, I just figured it wasn't meant to be."

"Then he invited you down here to be our lawyer."

"Yes, I'm sure it was just because he remembered that I did a lot of law dealing with governments," Samantha said. "He didn't seem interested in me in any other way when I first got here."

"What changed?"

"We started spending time together at work; we had a few working dinners, and realized we had other things in common besides work. Then one evening, we talked about whether we should try dating and decided to give it a shot."

Catie nodded, "He seems happier."

"I'm not sure that's because of me," Samantha said. "Things have settled down here, and he's getting to spend more time with you. And he's loving what he's doing with MacKenzie."

"Uh-huh," Catie said.

"Are you still okay with us dating? We're mostly just good friends, so now's the time to change things if it bothers you."

"I'm okay with it. I like you, and I can tell Daddy likes you too. I think you make him happy."

"I'm glad you think so," Samantha said. "I know you have Liz, but you can talk to me about anything if you want."

"I'd like that."

Chapter 22 Board Meeting – Jan 21st

"Hey, Kal, how's it going?" Liz said as Kal boarded the Mea Huli.

"I'm great, how have you been," Kal said, giving Liz a hug.

Liz gave Kal a sharp knee in the thigh, "I've been great."

"That wasn't nice," Kal whispered in Liz's ear as he looked at Samantha.

"Well, I owe you a few," Liz whispered back. "Seems the new legs are working."

"And hurting," Kal whispered as he gave Liz an extra hard squeeze.

"Good morning, Kal," Samantha said. "You're looking energetic as usual. How was your week off?"

"Great," Kal said. "Blake and I got in some fishing and a lot of sack time. But back to the salt mines."

"Out of the way," Blake said as he pushed Kal from behind.

"Jet jockeys are such prima donnas," Kal said as he made his way to one of the lounge chairs.

"Blake, your face," Samantha cried as she ran over to him.

"Nice, huh," Blake said.

"I thought they couldn't fix it," Samantha said.

"New doctor, new techniques," Blake said.

"But you still have a lot of scarring on the neck and forehead."

"Dr. Metra says she can't cut all my skin off at once," Blake said. "She'll be fixing it over the next couple of months. She says I'll soon be as gorgeous as I ever was."

"I'm so glad," Samantha said, tears welling up in her eyes. "And the other scars?"

"She's fixing everything," Blake said.

"She just doesn't know how to fix his mouth," Marc said as he came down the ladder from the bridge.

"His mouth looks okay to me," Samantha said with a puzzled look.

"He's still as big a smart mouth as he ever was," Marc said. He quickly dodged the punch Blake directed at his shoulder.

"Well, there is that," Samantha said. "I hear it runs in the family."

"Okay, let's settle in and get down to business," Marc said. "Samantha, you're up."

"We have a signed contract with the Cook Island government that covers our export of goods and our employment of the locals. We have to add housing on Arutanga to accommodate the increased population. They expect a lot of islanders to migrate there since it is the closest land base where our workers can live."

"On my list," Blake said. "I plan to just use money."

"Works for me," Marc said. "How's our production facility coming?"

"They completed the main part of the building while Kal and I were out fishing," Blake said. "And just in time; we've started putting in the production for the polysteel today. Dr. Zelbar is anxious to get it going, he wants to see it work on a big scale. Dr. Scheele and our manufacturing guy have laid out the process. I'm guessing three to four months before we're ready to start building the city."

"Maybe you'll find ways to speed it up once everything is running," Marc said.

"We'll try," Blake sighed. "Sam got us the approval to go vertical, so I've given that to the contractor. He says two weeks."

"Catie?"

"I'm still waiting on a shell for the Lynx. It sounds like it's going to be a month at least," Catie said. "I'm filling out the design submittal for New Zealand so we can get it certified for their airspace. They have a cross agreement with Australia. We're doing it a little backward, building the plane first, but it might actually go faster. I have no idea what to do with the US and Europe."

"How are you going to hide that little fusion reactor?" Marc asked.

"It's tied into the electrical generator from the engines," Catie said. "The electricity just runs backward when we're using it. It's very discreet, we're using superconductors to hide how much current we can handle. We generate enough power to match the specs when we use fuel, so we won't show them that we can do the same without using fuel."

"I'm helping her with government issues," Samantha said. "I'm working on the contact I'm using to get her licensed to fly. He's anxious to please; I think he's hoping to get a position in the jet-building business. We'll address the US and Europe once we have the New Zealand approval."

"Fred?"

"Tesla is still hounding us for more batteries. The new space will really help us ramp up production," Fred said. "I've already added space in Rarotonga for assembly."

"Kal, how's our labor pool?" Marc asked.

"We're doing pretty good on hiring; we've actually had some people move back from New Zealand to work for us," Kal said. "They miss home, and now that there are jobs, mama's cooking looks really good."

"Glad to hear that," Marc said. "Are we done?" Marc looked around the table. "I guess we are. Blake, can you wait up?"

"Sure," Blake said. Blake got up and poured a couple of glasses of scotch while he and Marc waited for the rest of the board to leave. "What's up?" he asked as he sat back down and pushed a glass over to Marc.

"I wanted to check in with you," Marc said. "How are you doing?"

"I'm great," Blake said. "It's really nice to wake up without any pain."

"I'm sorry, I should have thought of that before," Marc said.

"What do you have to be sorry about?"

"Dr. Metra could have treated you for the pain a couple of months ago."

"Hey, it's been two years, what's a couple of months," Blake said. "I'm just glad to be done with the pills."

"And the scotch?" Marc asked.

"Now, let's not get carried away here," Blake said. "I can cut down, but scotch is good for the soul."

"I hear you," Marc said as he took a sip.

"I'm sorry too," Blake said.

"Why?" Marc asked. He was taken aback a bit; it wasn't like Blake to apologize for anything, much less for something he wasn't aware of.

"For leaving this all on your shoulders," Blake said. "I'm not good at the long-term planning thing, and besides, you don't work that way."

"I know, bad habit," Marc said. "I always have to do it by myself before I bring it out for review. I'm trying to break Catie of that before it becomes indelible."

"How are you going to do that? Mom could never get you to break the habit."

"I think she started too late," Marc said. "Catie needs more friends, people she can talk with about what she's thinking."

"She has friends."

"Who, you, Liz and Kal," Marc said. "She needs to expand that group. Include a few people her own age."

"That's tough. She's what, three or four years ahead in school?" Blake asked.

"Yes, in the nine months since she started homeschooling, she's already doing college level in math and science. She's skipped ahead to senior-level work in all the other course work," Marc explained.

"That kind of cuts out that avenue for friends," Blake said. "We'll have to look out for opportunities as we grow. Something will come up. Until then, the group of us will just have to work on her."

"Thanks," Marc said. "She really looks up to you."

"She has to, I'm tall," Blake said with a laugh. He downed the rest of his scotch and got up. "Don't worry too much, and apply some of that to yourself. We're all here for you as well."

"I know," Marc said as he buried himself back in his HUD.

Chapter 23 Linda Sends Help

Marc's HUD pinged, showing a call coming in from Dr. Metra. "Dr. Metra, how may I help you?" Marc said.

"I have a situation here that really needs your attention," Dr. Metra said.

"Can you tell me more?"

"A Dr. Sharmila Khanna is here asking for a job."

"Okay. So, what's the problem?"

"She is insisting that we treat her daughter."

"I'm not aware of Alzheimer's affecting children," Marc replied.

"Her daughter doesn't have Alzheimer's," Dr. Metra said. "She says she is a colleague of your wife, and that your wife suggested that she bring her daughter here."

Marc sighed and rubbed his face, "I knew I got off too easy."

"What?"

"Nothing," Marc said. "What does the child have?"

"Muscular Dystrophy," Dr. Metra said.

"Can you treat it?"

"Probably," Dr. Metra said. "The girl has an identical twin sister."

"Who doesn't have the disease?"

"Correct."

"Muscular Dystrophy is a genetic disorder, so how is that possible?"

"I assume it was caused by a de novo mutation," Dr. Metra said.

"A what?"

"A de novo mutation is a spontaneous mutation that occurs early in gestation," Dr. Metra said. "It's what drives evolution, but unfortunately, they're not all positive. It is the root cause of many, if not all, genetic diseases."

"Okay, so when will you know if you can treat it?"

"A few days," Dr. Metra said. "I've already asked MADI to start pulling all the relevant data she can find."

"MADI?"

"Catie named my medical digital intelligence MADI."

"Huh," Marc laughed. "I assume you need me to come over and deal with Dr. Khanna."

"If you would, please."

"I'll be right there."

"Thank you."

Marc alerted Kal, telling him that he had to go to the Virginia Henderson. He shook his head with frustration; he wasn't allowed to go anywhere without Kal. "Security my ass, it's more like prison."

Kal met Marc at the front door to their office building in Rarotonga, "I'll drive," he said.

They climbed into one of the jeeps that were ubiquitous to Rarotonga. The sheer number of them running around the islands provided anonymity that Kal and Liz preferred. The Virginia Henderson was only a few minutes from the compound.

"Just you?" Marc asked.

"I think we'll be safe; I've got a guy meeting us about halfway."

Marc shook his head. Ever since Catie had been kidnapped in Portugal, Liz and Kal were especially paranoid. Marc supported the increased security on Catie, but he still thought he could take care of himself, or at least manage with just one bodyguard.

Ten minutes later, Marc and Kal were climbing the ladder onto the Virginia Henderson. It was docked at the end of the commercial docking area. Once in a while, they had to move it. If more than three freighters came in at one time, the third freighter would need the space where Virginia Henderson was usually docked. The Port Authority had been very understanding since they had brought the hospital ship in.

"Dr. Metra," Marc said as he entered her office. "Do you know how your friend got aboard?"

"I lied," a woman behind him said.

Marc turned around to see an attractive Indian woman standing there. She was wearing a typical tropical ankle-length silk skirt with a light-yellow blouse for a top. Two girls were hiding behind her; they were about ten years old, and they were wearing jean shorts and cami tops. All three of them were wearing sandals. It took Marc a moment to notice that one of the girls was using crutches to stand.

"Dr. Khanna, I presume."

"Yes," Dr. Khanna said as she stepped forward and offered her hand to Marc. "Please call me Dr. Sharmila."

"Marc McCormack," Marc said as he grasped her hand and gave it a shake.

"Please use my office," Dr. Metra said. "I have rounds to make." She rose from her desk and exited the office, closing the door behind her.

"Please have a seat," Marc indicated a seat at the conversation seating that was in the corner of the office. Dr. Sharmila sat down, and her daughters crawled onto the couch where the picture books were that Dr. Metra's assistant must have found for them. Marc took the seat opposite her. "Could you explain how you think we could help your daughter?"

"First, I would like to apologize for lying to your people," Dr. Sharmila said. "I told them that my daughters were here to visit their grandfather. I knew that you were treating Dr. Ahluwalia here, so since he's Indian, they assumed we were related."

"Nothing that I wouldn't do for my own daughter," Marc said, waving his hand to dismiss the issue.

"Thank you for your understanding."

"Again, how do you think we can help?"

"Your ex-wife and I are good friends," Dr. Sharmila said. "I was working at UCSD medical when she came to work there, and we've gotten close."

Marc nodded his head and rolled his hands to indicate she should continue.

"After she came back from here with her grandparents, we were having lunch one day. She was telling me how wonderful it was to have them back in her life. They were still staying with her at the time. Anyway, I broke down crying. It was difficult to hear such wonderful news right after Aalia started having to use crutches to walk. It broke my heart and her sister, Prisha's, heart as well."

"I can imagine," Marc said.

"After I explained it to Linda, she was very understanding. I told her I would do anything for such a cure for my little girl."

"Okay."

"Linda asked me if I really meant that. I said, of course I did. She pressed me further, asking if I would give up my career in San Diego, my life in the U.S.," Dr. Sharmila said. "I told her I would give up my life if my little girl could just be like her sister."

Marc nodded his head, guessing where this was going.

"Linda said that she thought there was something more to your cure for Alzheimer's than you were willing to say. She wouldn't explain further, but said if I was willing to come here and stay, that maybe you would have some way to help my girl."

"That's a lot to take on faith," Marc said.

"All I have left is faith," Dr. Sharmila said.

"What about your husband?"

"I kicked him out," Dr. Sharmila said. "He couldn't deal with Aalia's problem once it became worse. Somehow he thought it reflected on his manhood."

"I'm sorry to hear that."

"It was a reflection of his character," Dr. Sharmila said. "I don't want my girls exposed to such a poor example."

"Would there be any issues with the girls being here away from him?"

"He doesn't know where we are."

Marc sighed. "Dr. Metra is looking into whether there might be something we can do for Aalia, but we don't know yet. It could be a while."

"We have her entire life to wait."

Marc closed his eyes to think; after a moment, he nodded his head. "We could definitely use another doctor," he said. "What was your specialty?"

"Orthopedic surgery," Dr. Sharmila said.

Marc smiled, "Well, that is fortuitous. But Linda was right; this would be a one-way ticket. If we hire you and treat your daughter, you'll need to sign an NDA and commit for at least five years. You wouldn't even be able to tell Linda any specifics."

"I am happy with that."

"Okay, Dr. Metra says she's very hopeful. She has done some previous research on genetic diseases. I'll ask my lawyer to come see you. Where are you staying?"

"We are at the Wellesley Hotel."

"I'll have her contact you there. Her name is Samantha Newman," Marc said.

"I cannot thank you enough," Dr. Sharmila said. Tears were streaming down her face.

"Please call if you have any issues or need anything." Marc handed her his business card. "I only hope we can help."

"I have faith," Dr. Sharmila said.

Marc handed Dr. Sharmila and her two daughters off to Dr. Metra's assistant, who then showed them off the ship. A moment later, Dr. Metra came back into the office.

"Well, how did it go?" she asked.

"Tough," Marc said. "Do you think you'll be able to help?"

"I am confident. It really is only a matter of time."

"That's good to hear. She's an orthopedic surgeon."

"She told me. That will be very helpful when we start the surgeries," Dr. Metra said.

"I thought so. Keep me posted, please."

"As always, Captain."

Chapter 24 Soccer Friends

"Oh, quit whining," Liz said. "You'll have fun and get a chance to meet some new friends."

"I know, but I'm busy," Catie whined.

"Well, you're going to have to find a way to make a couple of hours of soccer fit into your daily schedule. Your father didn't seem negotiable on the subject."

"Yeah, yeah," Catie looked around the soccer field. There were three groups, the under ten group, her group ten to thirteen, and then the fourteen and older group. Each huddle was just forming as the players and their parents arrived. She felt a little conspicuous as the only white girl on the field. And having light brown hair made her stand out even more. The other girls weren't avoiding her, but they weren't coming over to say hello either.

"Hi."

Catie turned around and saw two girls. She was sure they were twins; they looked so much alike. One was slender and athletic looking, the other was using crutches to walk and seemed smaller, but Catie figured that was because of the crutches.

"Hi, I'm Catie."

"We know who you are," the one with crutches said.

"You do?"

"Sure, I think everybody knows you. Whenever you go by, somebody points and says there's Dr. McCormack's daughter," said the other twin.

"They're right, he's my father. Are you joining the team?" Catie asked, pointedly looking at the twin without the crutches.

"We both are."

"You are," Catie said. She was a bit surprised that the one with the crutches would be joining the team.

"Yes, Dr. Metra says I'll be able to play in a month."

"I'm glad to hear that. She's a great doctor."

"We think so. Our mother is a doctor and works with her now."

"Oh right, Dr. Sharmila," Catie said. "I remember my father mentioning her."

The twins giggled. "I bet he was mad."

"No, he wasn't mad," Catie said. "He was talking to Uncle Blake, and he said something like, Linda, that's my mom, sent me a doctor today. I'll have to return the favor."

"Mummy will be happy to know he wasn't mad," one twin said.

"Where are you living?" Catie asked.

"We live on Banyan Way."

"Hey, that's just down the street from us," Catie said.

"Cool, what position do you play?" the other twin asked. Catie had to look to see which one was talking. Their voices sounded identical, and they segued between who was speaking so smoothly that she didn't notice they had switched, without looking.

"I like to play second striker," Catie said. "And you?"

"We like to play winger," they both said together, or at least it looked that way to Catie.

"Here comes your coach," Liz said. "I'll be right over here, have fun." Liz looked across the field at the two members of their security team who were using cricket bats to pitch the ball between them. They were looking pretty inconspicuous, which was the plan.

After practice, Catie and the twin who was playing ran over to Liz and the other twin. "Well, that wasn't so bad," Liz said.

"I guess not," Catie said.

Catie turned to say goodbye to the twins, but they were engaged in an argument with an older Cook Islander. "Do we have to go shopping?"

"No shopping, no food tonight," the woman said.

"But we have homework."

"Plenty of time for homework after dinner."

"Aww."

"Ask your mother if you can come over to my house," Catie said. "You're close to us, and Liz is taking me home right now."

One twin had her cellphone out immediately and was texting her mother. "She says it's okay," she said, showing the older woman the message.

"Okay. But you behave yourself," the woman said.

"We will."

They all got into the car, and Liz drove them home. The twins pointed out the house they were living in when they drove by it. When they turned the corner into the compound, both twins gasped.

"You live in a mansion," they said.

"It's a big house, but there are seven of us," Catie said.

"Well, there are three of us," the twins said.

"But I'm the only kid. We have to have six bedrooms for us, and I bunk with Liz."

"Oh, that is a big family."

"We're not exactly a family, well three of us are. My Uncle Blake lives here, my dad, Liz, Samantha, Fred, and Kal. We all work for MacKenzie Discoveries."

"Even you?"

"Yes, I do."

"What do you do?"

"I work on some designs, picking out the interiors for our jet, things like that," Catie downplayed her work, not wanting to sound like she was bragging.

They established that the twins were going to St. Joseph School; they were ten years old; they were both in the fifth grade. They both wanted to be doctors like their mom, and they both hated math. It was 6:30 when Dr. Sharmila stopped by to pick them up. The twins were just finishing their homework and were asking Catie about what TV shows she liked to watch. They wouldn't believe her when she said she didn't watch TV, but the discussion was cut short when their mother showed up.

"They were nice," Liz said after the twins had left.

"Yeah, they're kind of cool, but weird. Sometimes it feels like there is only one of them, but in two bodies."

"I know what you mean. When I was listening to you guys, it really seemed like there was only one girl visiting, they sound so alike. They're in perfect sync when they're both talking, and they seem to finish each other's sentences."

"Yes, and did you notice they never seem to talk to each other. It's like they're telepathic."

Chapter 25 Board Meeting – Feb 4th

"I'd like to call this board meeting of MacKenzie Discoveries to order," Marc said.

"My, my, aren't we getting fancy," Blake laughed.

Marc gave Blake an indelicate finger salute, "I'm just trying to be in sync with our fancy new boardroom," Marc said. He swept his hand around the dining room in the mansion they were renting.

"It is nice," Samantha said. "And a little more convenient than the Mea Huli."

"Hey, I liked meeting on the Mea Huli," Catie said.

"Yes, it was nice," Samantha said, "but it added a couple of hours to the meeting since your father is so paranoid about being listened in on that we had to go out five miles before we could talk business."

"Hey, an ounce of prevention is worth a pound of cure," Marc quipped. "And we have had some eavesdroppers before."

"Are we going to use up the whole two hours we're saving, arguing?" Liz asked.

"I think not," Marc said. "Blake, you start."

"Our manufacturing building is up, and we've completed the characterization of the polysteel process. We start production on Monday."

"That was fast," Liz said.

"Yeah, the process dialed in right away. It just took the week, and I think half the time was spent running the test a second time just to verify results."

"Do we have enough workers lined up?" Marc asked.

"Yes, we're going to start with just one shift on one line until we iron out how to move the material around and resolve any other logistical issues," Blake said. "We'd like to avoid any industrial accidents."

"How are you going to handle the islanders' tendency to decide that today's a better day for fishing than for work?" Fred asked. "As I recall, that drove the businesses in Hawaii nuts."

Blake and Kal laughed. "Kal, why don't you explain."

"Sure, what we've done is hire two pools of workers, regular staff who are on the schedule and about half as many temporary staff. If a regular staff member decides they'd rather go fishing today, they call into the office, and we pull in a temporary staff person to substitute for them."

"What happens if the temporary staff guy also thinks it's a good day to fish?"

"We just call the next one; that's why the pool is fifty percent of the regular staff size. The temporary guys get a thirty percent bonus for days they work."

"Why wouldn't they all decide to be temporary?" Fred asked.

"Three twelve-hour shifts a week guaranteed, versus trying to hope you get two temp days a week isn't a good bet. People have to eat. The temp staff is mostly made up of the wives, brothers, or kids from the regular staff. Makes a good household income," Kal explained. "A lot of families are interested in doubling up, one takes the first three days and the other one the second three days. We're considering letting regular workers do one temp day a week, when they're off shift, to augment the temp pool."

"I like it," Marc said. "Sam, do you see any issues?"

"No, Kal worked with me to set it up," Samantha said. "The government really likes the idea."

"Moving on," Marc said. "What about battery production?"

"We're shifting them to the same schedule and rules that Kal came up with starting Monday," Blake said. "Workers are really excited about that. We have one hundred fifty thousand batteries ready to ship out."

"That's an impressive ramp up on the batteries," Marc said. "I hope you threw a small party for the team."

"Small party, I threw a big party," Blake said.

"My mistake, big party. Do you have anything, Kal?"

"Some of the workers are really pushing us to get the dorms added. They like the idea of coming on day one, spending two nights, and going home on day three. The forty-five-minute commute on the ferry is a bit much."

"That would make the 'I'm going fishing today' syndrome less of a problem," Fred added.

"Sounds good," Marc said. "Blake, can we expedite the construction?"

"Already on it. We've poured the concrete pad, so it will go up fast."

"Catie?" Marc said.

"We have a big battery order from Tesla, but we need to get another customer. The phones, pads, and notebooks look promising, but I think we have to do an in-person visit to close the deal. We're eventually going to need more customers than I can find via the internet; I'm not sure how to do that. We could take the batteries to a trade show, but who would we send?" Catie said. "Same thing about visiting the tech companies, who goes?"

Samantha and Fred were really impressed with all that Catie was handling, but the rest knew she was getting a lot of help from ADI. Of course, they also knew that ADI couldn't do it all, especially thinking of things like trade shows and tech reps.

"That's on my list," Marc said. "We need a salesperson to do the meet-and-greet part. Working through the internet works pretty well to start, but we really need someone who can walk in and close the deal. Trade shows are a great idea; otherwise, we might miss a big market we never realized existed."

"And why aren't we selling batteries to GM and Honda?" Liz asked. "They also have electric cars."

"Because I want to start an electric car company," Marc said.

Everyone was taken aback. "What, are you crazy?"

"No, just hear me out," Marc said. "I want to start a company; we'll be majority owners, but I want to get someone else to actually run it. I want to locate its manufacturing in second-world countries exclusively. Force the G7 to import from them since only Tesla will be competing with the same quality product. We can reign in Tesla by limiting their batteries, that will force them to stay in the high end."

"I like this," Samantha said. "Balance out the world's wealth a bit more equitably."

"What about third-world countries?" Catie asked.

"We have to walk before we can run," Marc said.

"You do know that first, second, and third world are outdated terms," Samantha said.

"They are?" Catie asked.

"Yes, it's better to think of them as high income, upper middle income, lower middle income, and low income," Samantha explained. "Those terms are less politically loaded and more accurately show where the wealth disparity is."

"So, we have two big things to deal with," Marc said. "First, find ourselves a sales and business rep, and two, we need an industrialist to start up a car manufacturing business."

"You're not asking much are you," Blake said.

"It's what we need. Sam, do you think you can come up with some people?"

"I can," Samantha said. "Are you expecting the industrialist to kick in capital?"

"I don't know. What do you think?"

"Since you're trying to spread the wealth, maybe what you need is someone to run the business. You can have the countries where you locate the plants kick in the capital in exchange for profit-sharing from the plants you locate there."

"Won't that encourage corruption?" Liz asked.

"Not if you structure it right," Samantha said. "If you're willing to pick up and move if they try to coerce you, and you make it a straight profit share to the treasury with public disclosure."

"Doesn't that set us up for looking corrupt?" Liz asked. "Remember, these countries have a long tradition of the big guys taking more than their fair share and lying to the rest about how much they're sacrificing."

"You're right," Samantha said. "Why not do it as public bonds, and base the bonds on the US dollar. The countries have to fund the plant, we pay off the bonds over ten years, and they get that revenue, plus all the taxes and jobs."

"I like that better," Marc said. "If we start small, we can adjust as we grow."

"So, we start with electric cars," Samantha said.

"What about electric scooters?" Catie said. "If we want to help the environment, getting all those scooters off the roads would be a great start."

"Do we have a design for an electric scooter?" Marc asked.

"We kinda do," Catie said. "It's not finalized, but I've been working on it."

"How big are they?" Liz asked.

"From the equivalent of one hundred ccs to two thousand ccs," Catie said. "But we should start out with the small ones."

"That would be a great way to start out the whole manufacturing partnership," Samantha said. "Get the scooter model up and working in a couple of countries in the next few months, and expand to cars later in the year."

"Okay, find us someone who wants to run a big business," Marc said. "Actually, I guess, find us a couple of people."

"Why don't you just buy a small international company and expand it?" Kal asked.

"We'd get all the baggage with it," Marc said.

"But you get lots of good infrastructure," Kal countered. "You could lop off the top few levels of management and rebuild a pretty decent company in a lot less time."

Marc looked at Samantha. "Sure, I can look at some potential companies to buy."

"Some that are already into small engines or scooters," Blake suggested.

"Moving on, how about our planes?" Marc asked, looking at Catie.

"Uncle Blake says he can start the shells next week. We're going to print one and take it all the way through the process and prove it out before we start a second."

"Why wait?" Marc asked.

"We don't want to waste a bunch of material if we have to change something," Catie replied.

"Can't we recycle the material?" Marc asked.

"ADI?" Catie asked.

Samantha looked up from her tablet, "Who is Adi?"

"Our tech consultant," Marc said. "She's usually available on the comm, and she usually listens in on the meetings."

"We should list her on the roll," Samantha said.

"I'd rather not," Marc said. "Is there a problem with that?"

"If she doesn't vote, then it's okay," Samantha said a little skeptically.

"ADI says we have to build a recycler," Catie said. "It looks easy to do."

"I'll put it on the list," Blake said. "We'll probably have other reasons to use it. I should have thought of it before."

"Thanks. How about power?" Marc asked.

"The arrays are up and running," Blake said. "I'll send you the specs." Blake's eyes darted up in his HUD, and he blinked. The power specs for the solar array showed up in Marc's HUD along with the specs for the small fusion reactor they had brought in from the Sakira. Blake had quietly installed it in a corner of the building. It was only a two-meter cube and was hidden behind the battery backup system and power panel for the building.

"I see we won't be running low," Marc said.

"I don't think so," Blake said. "We should be able to run a night shift."

"Good."

◆ ◆ ◆

"Admiral Michaels."

"Come in, Captain. An update from the Cook Islands?"

"This isn't actually from the Cook Islands," the captain said. "The FBI picked up some information that MacKenzie Discoveries is offering an Alzheimer's treatment."

"They are? Is it effective?"

"I had some checking done. McCormack's daughter's great grandparents on her mother's side were diagnosed with Alzheimer's four years ago. Apparently, they were quite advanced last year. The agent who visited them last week says they're sharp as a tack and look and move about like they're in their sixties instead of their eighties. There are two other cases that seem to have miraculously been cured after a trip to the Cook Islands; they're in the file. We have indicators of several others, but we can't get any confirmation due to the security around them."

"Security?"

"Yes, sir, it seems they are all very wealthy individuals."

"And how much does this service cost?" Admiral Michaels asked.

"Rumor is that it cost five hundred thousand dollars."

"Pricey."

"The FBI says they don't think they'll have trouble finding clients. The CIA is interested since it seems they're picking up a few clients from Europe, including Eastern Europe."

"Russia?"

"Can't tell."

"I assume you've alerted our man down there."

"Yes, I have, but I expect that the CIA will be sending someone. Do you want to keep our man in place?"

"Yes, but tell him to be extra discreet. I'd prefer the CIA didn't notice we have an asset in place."

"Yes, sir."

"Anything else?"

"Dr. McCormack has picked up several more scientists, all rumored to be suffering from Alzheimer's, and all were at the top of their field. We also picked up some rumors of a new jet certification being prepared for New Zealand."

"What's so special about it?"

"It's rumored to be a supersonic passenger jet."

"I wonder whose it is," Admiral Michaels said. "We know several companies are working toward that, but New Zealand would make one think of MacKenzie, wouldn't it?"

"It does, sir."

"Very well, carry on."

"Hello, Aalia," Dr. Metra said. "How are you feeling?"

"Okay," Aalia said.

"She's not okay," Prisha said. "She has to use crutches!"

"Now Prisha, it's not the doctor's fault," Dr. Sharmila scolded.

"Well, let's see what we can do about that," Dr. Metra said, giving Dr. Sharmila a nod. "I need to give you some shots, is that okay?"

Aalia nodded her head, and Prisha moved over next to her twin, grabbed her hand, and held it.

"Since we have to give you a bunch of shots, I'm going to put this in your leg, that way I only have to stick you once. Is that okay with you?"

Aalia nodded bravely as Dr. Metra showed her the peripheral venous catheter, a PVC, that she would insert into the vein.

"We're going to put it in a vein in your leg," Dr. Metra said. "That's the biggest vein, so we'll be able to put lots of medicine in. So, hop up here on the bed."

Aalia hopped onto the bed with help from Prisha, who refused to let go of Aalia's hand.

"Are you ready?" After Aalia nodded her head, Dr. Metra swabbed the area with an antiseptic and a numbing agent. Then she inserted the PVC into the vein. "Now that wasn't too bad, was it?"

"No," Aalia said. "Is that all?"

"Now we have to give you the injections," Dr. Metra said. "But they go into the valve we put in, so they won't hurt one bit."

"Okay."

"First, we're going to get rid of all those bad genes that gave you this disease," Dr. Metra said. She injected Aalia with a large syringe of genetically modified viruses. They would transport the replacement gene to the site of all the bad genes and replace them with the gene they had pulled from Prisha's DNA. "See, that didn't hurt at all, did it?"

"No, it just felt funny," Aalia said.

"It did, well I guess that's okay," Dr. Metra said. "Now since Prisha doesn't like you having to use crutches, we're going to give you a few shots to help you build your muscles back up. Do you like that idea?"

Aalia and Prisha nodded their heads vigorously.

"This first shot is going to go find those weak muscles and give them some extra protein." Dr. Metra gave Aalia a massive injection of nanites. These were carrying neutral muscle tissue that would be directed to her leg muscles. Dr. Metra used the scanner and the field generator that was built into the bed Aalia was lying on, to direct the nanites to the muscles she wanted to enhance. Once they were there, she dropped the suppression field, and they immediately deposited their load into the muscle tissue.

"Okay, and the last thing we need to do is let all this get inside you so it can help all your muscles start to get better fast," Dr. Metra said. Then she hung an IV bag next to the bed that was full of pluripotent stem cells made from Prisha's blood. They would start repairing all the damaged tissue in Aalia's body. "You have to lie there for one hour. Can you do that?"

Aalia and Prisha both nodded their heads solemnly.

"I'll leave you with them," Dr. Metra said as she removed her gloves.

"How long will it take?" Dr. Sharmila asked.

"She should start regaining strength right away. I would estimate a week before she's strong enough to go without the crutches."

"That soon?"

Dr. Metra nodded her head. "Yes, I'd think so. If you prefer, you can remove the PVC when the drip is done. Otherwise, I'll be back in an hour to check on you."

Dr. Sharmila hugged Dr. Metra. She was crying but didn't want her daughters to notice.

Chapter 26 Spies on the Beach

Blake and Kal were having drinks at the local bar, letting a little steam off after work. Blake was seeing if his luck with the local women would continue after he'd had his scars repaired. He'd been having a difficult time getting a date when he and Marc were in Hawaii. He had blamed it on the extensive scarring on the left side of his face and neck. When they had moved to the Cook Islands, Blake had discovered that the women here viewed the scars as a badge of honor. He'd been having a lot more success getting dates, but then Dr. Metra had fixed his scars.

"Are you worried you won't appeal to the locals anymore?" Kal teased.

"No, with my good looks, I'll be having to beat them off with a stick," Blake shot back. "How about you? You're not going to be able to use sympathy to pick anyone up."

"As if I ever had to go for the sympathy date," Kal shot back. "I've never had trouble finding a girl."

"Hey, I've always been able to find them," Blake said, "It's getting them to go out with you that's hard. I hear it's even harder for you to get a second date."

"You wait until we're doing some training with Liz. I'll show you some moves," Kal threatened.

"Well, those are probably the only moves you can use to get a second date."

"Put your money where your mouth is," Kal said. "You pick the girl. If I get two dates, you owe me five grand."

"You're on," Blake said. "You want to play it the other way too?"

"Sure, I'll pick one out for you. I can use an easy ten grand."

"We'll see who's laughing next week," Blake said. "And no throwing money around to act as honey."

"Agreed."

Both of the guys started looking around the bar. Both were trying to find the most attractive woman there, one who would be the least likely to go out with the other.

"I see just the woman for you," Blake said. "See that blond over there?" Blake nodded at a tall blond woman with a gorgeous figure. She was sitting at a table alone but working on her phone. He figured she was quite a bit taller than Kal.

"I see her," Kal said. "I'm still looking for your date; ah, I see her now." Kal discreetly indicated a Chinese woman who'd just entered the bar. She was slender, but with a shapely figure. She had a face that would stop traffic, definitely out of Blake's league.

"Okay, we have our targets," Blake said. "May the winner be me," he said.

"Good luck," Kal said. "You're going to need it just to get a first date."

Both men got up and moved toward their selected woman.

"Hi," Blake said. "You look like you're lost?"

"I'm looking for a nice restaurant to eat dinner," the Chinese woman said. "Someone recommended this place."

"This is a nice bar, but just an okay place to eat," Blake said. "I prefer Flambé myself."

"Is that French?"

"More international, but they have some nice French dishes," Blake said.

"Could you tell me how to get there?"

"I can walk you there if you like," Blake said. "I was just going over there to have dinner myself. My name is Blake, by the way."

"I'm Ying Yue."

"It's nice to meet you, Ying Yue," Blake said. "What brings you to Rarotonga?"

"I am writing an article for my magazine," Ying Yue said. "Rarotonga has become a vacation destination for people from China."

Blake held the door open for her as they left the bar. He took a quick glance over his shoulder to see how Kal was doing. He saw Kal just sitting down at the table with the blond.

"Hi, my name's Kal. You look like you might like some company."

"I might," the blond said in a deep sexy voice, her accent was obviously from Eastern Europe. "Why would you be someone I would want for company?"

"Well, I've been in Rarotonga for a little over four months, so I know the lay of the land, but with a newcomer's perspective. I can help point out where the interesting things are."

"And what do you think I might find interesting?"

"The nice places to eat, especially the places that cater to the locals," Kal said. "I know a bit about where to shop; where to fish, if you're into that; the best swimming beaches or where to go snorkeling."

"Snorkeling, I would like to do that," she said. "Do you know where I could find someone who could take me out to a good spot?"

"Well, I have access to a big yacht," Kal said. "It's my boss's, but he lets me use it."

"Then, sit down and tell me about this yacht and where we could go snorkeling."

It was the third week of soccer practice when Aalia came carrying her crutches.

"Hey, Aalia, no crutches today?" Catie called out as the twins made their way over to her. The twins were continuing to go home with Liz and Catie after soccer practice. There they would study and get some help from Catie once in a while. Catie had been watching Aalia getting stronger for the last week. Nobody said anything, but she assumed that Dr. Metra had started treating her.

"I hate these things," Aalia said.

"I hate them too," Prisha said. "We want to burn them."

"You can't burn metal," Liz said while stifling a laugh.

"Why not?" both twins said together. They were clearly upset at not being able to make the symbolic gesture of burning the accursed crutches.

"Well, we can ask Dr. Scheele if he can burn them for you," Catie said.

"Yes!"

While the girls were practicing, Liz checked with Dr. Sharmila to see if it was okay for the twins to go over to Dr. Scheele's lab and destroy the crutches. Dr. Sharmila only asked that Liz take a video of the momentous event.

After practice, Liz drove them to Dr. Scheele's lab.

"Dr. Scheele, this is Aalia and her sister Prisha," Liz said, introducing the two girls. "I think you already know Catie."

"I know of her, but we haven't met," Dr. Scheele said, giving Catie a nod. Catie was quietly pointing to the twins to let Dr. Scheele know that it was their show.

"Now, what can I do for you young ladies?" Dr. Scheele said as he sat on his heels so he would be the same height as the twins.

"We want to burn these crutches," Aalia said.

"She doesn't need them anymore, and we hate them," Prisha added.

Dr. Scheele looked at Liz. She nodded to let him know it was okay to destroy the crutches.

"Let me see one," Dr. Scheele said. Aalia handed him one of the crutches. "Hmm, aluminum. Well, we certainly can burn them," he said.

"Oh, boy!"

"You'll need to wear some glasses," Dr. Scheele said. He looked around his lab until he found two pairs of welding goggles that would protect the twins' eyes from the bright light of burning aluminum. He gave them to Liz while he took the pair of crutches and placed them in a metal box on the workbench.

Liz helped the twins put on their goggles. She and Catie adjusted their specs to provide the necessary protection, and they all lined up in front of the workbench.

"Now, I'm going to start up the plasma torch," Dr. Scheele said. "Then you can take this handle here and steer the beam until it burns up those nasty crutches."

The twins gasped as they realized they would get to do the deed. After Dr. Scheele started the torch up, they both took hold of the control handle. They guided the torch over the crutches, moving it slowly as they giggled. The aluminum would burst into flames and disappear. They kept moving it to the right as they gradually vaporized both crutches completely. The plastic and rubber parts of the crutches continued to burn for a while, but the aluminum was utterly vaporized.

"That was so cool," they said together.

"I'm glad you liked it," Dr. Scheele said. "Is there anything else I can do for you?"

The twins shook their heads.

"Thank you, Dr. Scheele," Catie said. "It is a big event for them."

"I could tell. Someday you can explain it to me better, but now you should go and celebrate."

"Celebrate!" the twins squealed.

"How about ice cream," Liz suggested.

"Yeah!"

Both Blake and Kal had managed four dates that week, neither of them cared that they'd each lost the bet. They were just having a great time. On Saturday, Blake was heading out for another date when Marc snagged him before he could leave the house.

"Blake, ADI tells me you have a new girlfriend."

"Oh yeah, and man is she hot," Blake said.

"She also told me she tried to access your comm last night."

"Yeah, she tried, she didn't get anywhere."

"Why do you think she tried to get into your comm?"

"I suspect it's because she's a Chinese spy."

"If you think she's a spy, why are you going out with her?"

"What part of HOT did you not understand?" Blake asked. "Besides, what was she going to find out? You can't hack our comms."

"Well, she could find that out!"

"What's going on?" Kal asked as he came down the stairs.

"We're talking about how Blake has been letting a Chinese spy lead him around by the nose," Marc snorted.

"Oh, yours is a spy too!" Kal laughed.

"What do you mean by 'yours is a spy too'?" Marc asked.

"Well, I'm pretty sure the blond Blake thought wouldn't go out with me is a Russian spy," Kal said. "Who outed you?" he asked Blake.

"ADI had to tell the Captain that Ying Yue tried to open my comm," Blake said. "If the Russian's a spy too, why haven't you been outed yet?"

"Oh, I'm playing hard to get," Kal said. "She hasn't had a chance to get to my comm yet."

"Is she as hot as she looked in the bar?"

"Smoking."

"Wait! Are you two nuts?" Marc shouted.

"What's your problem?" Kal asked. "You had to know that spies would start nosing around. The best way to put them off the scent is to play dumb."

"What are you guys yelling about?" Liz asked as she walked into the dining room where Marc had been working.

"Yeah," Catie echoed.

"Spies," Blake said.

"Oh, I'm hoping for a French one," Liz said. "Or at least a British one."

"So far, we have a Chinese and a Russian," Blake said. "Both are women."

"Hot?"

"Smoking!"

"I'm still hoping," Liz said. "Maybe they'll send two, assault from both directions."

Blake gaped at Liz, "What?"

Liz blushed, "I meant a male and female," she stammered. "Try to ply the women in the crew as well as you men."

Catie was giggling uncontrollably.

"They have to know we just keep you two around for your muscles," Liz said. "They're going to have to send someone to get to the brains here."

"Catie's too young," Blake said. "Besides, she's always got a bodyguard with her."

Liz threw a cushion at Blake, "That was mean."

Catie was rolling on the floor by now. "Poor Daddy, he's always got a bodyguard too, that or Samantha."

"Alright," Marc laughed. "I can't believe this. ADI, as captain, am I allowed to order summary executions?"

"Only in extreme situations," ADI replied.

"ADI has a sense of humor," Catie squealed.

Marc put his head in his hands and groaned. "What did I do to deserve this," he said as he tried to stifle his laugh.

"I don't know, but you must have been a pretty bad boy," Liz said. "When did the spies show up?"

"Last week," Kal replied; he was struggling to control his laughter. "Blake and I made a bet about who could get a second date with a woman picked by the other. We both selected a spy. Can you believe that?"

"Then, the French and British can't be far behind."

"Enough! Enough!" Marc barked. "As funny as this is, it is serious. Can I at least get you three overgrown teenagers to give reports on any spy activity? That way, we can have ADI track them, and we can correlate notes among everyone."

"I've had ADI tracking my girl," Kal said.

"ADI?" Marc asked.

"Captain, I detected the unusual interest in MacKenzie business by the Russian woman when Cer Kal started dating her. I notified him of it and have been tracking her since. The same is true for the Chinese woman."

"Has there been any unusual activity?" Marc asked.

"Besides their interest in Cer Blake and Cer Kal, none," ADI said.

Liz and Catie started laughing uncontrollably again.

"ADI, you wound me," Blake said.

"I could not have," ADI said. "I didn't use any weapons."

Catie squealed. "ADI has wit even."

"Dry wit," ADI replied.

"There must be an American spy here," Marc said.

"Oh yes, he's been here quite a long time," ADI said.

"Who is it?" Marc asked.

"He is the man who is usually sitting in the Surf's Up bar," ADI said.

"You mean that scrudsy looking white man in the Hawaiian shirt?" Liz asked.

"If you mean by scrudsy, that he needs to shave and take a bath," ADI said, "then that is him."

"He's never tried to talk to me," Liz said.

"He has confined himself to taking photos and talking to the locals and any of the construction crew or the people working for MacKenzie Discoveries," ADI said. "He seems to prefer to sit there and drink beer all day."

"Oh, this is too much," Marc said. "ADI, please track and advise me whenever you detect any suspicious persons who are likely to be a spy."

"Yes, Captain," ADI said. "Captain and Cer Liz, I must advise you that a British man landed on Rarotonga this afternoon. He has been behaving suspiciously, asking the locals questions about production on Manuae."

"Yes," Liz pumped her fist.

Chapter 27 Board Meeting – Feb 18th

"I call this meeting to order," Marc said. "How is everybody doing?"

"Not as well as Uncle Blake and Kal," Catie giggled.

Marc gave Catie a harsh look, while Kal, Blake, and Liz laughed. "What am I missing?" Samantha asked.

"Just some beach action," Blake said.

"Catie, are you spying on your uncle?" Samantha admonished.

"Not me," Catie giggled, looking all innocent.

"Enough," Marc said. "Let's get on with business. You five can go to the bar afterward to carry on your salacious giggling and gossiping. Blake, how are the construction crews coming along?"

"I've got them coming in as fast as I can put them to work," Blake said.

"That does bring up an issue," Sam said. "The government on Arutanga is not happy with their new guests. It seems they're a bit overly boisterous for the small island. Is there any way we can put them on Rarotonga?"

"That's a long commute," Blake said. "But I can sympathize with the locals for not wanting them around."

"Can we put them up here on Manuae in the dorms?"

"We can, and I have a few staying there, but you get the same problem."

"Why don't you put them on a ship?" Catie said. "Some old cruise ship, where they can have their own bars with entertainment and a cafeteria to eat at. Then they can go to Rarotonga on their days off."

"I like that idea," Samantha said. "I'm sure we can find one of the smaller cruise ships for sale. If we set it up right, we can make half their wages back by providing restaurants, bars, and entertainment."

"I don't care about the wages. Find someone on Rarotonga to run it; giving them a piece of the action will keep them happy. But I agree, let's buy a ship. Next: Where are we with our discreet inquiries?"

"It is amazing how many wealthy people are hiding the fact that someone in their family has Alzheimer's," Samantha said. "Plus, the number of corporations where their CEO is coming down with symptoms. I hate to say it, but we should raise the price."

"Sure, why not, more money is a good thing," Marc said.

"We have fifteen patients coming in this month, and as many as we have open slots for next month," Samantha said.

"What do you think we should raise the price to?"

"One million," Samantha said. "We'll see if that throttles the demand."

"Okay, go forward with that."

"Don't forget, I'm holding you to fifty percent charity cases."

"I won't forget, do we have any?"

"Can I start looking now?" Samantha asked. "I thought we had to wait until we moved to the new clinic."

"Hey, we're not hurting for money that much. We can take whoever you find."

"Is it okay if it's friends or friends of friends?" Samantha asked.

"Of course," Marc said. "That goes for everybody. If any of you have a relative or family friend who needs help, we'll take care of them."

"Now I remember why I like you so much," Samantha said.

"Me too," Catie giggled.

"Blake, how are we doing with production?"

"Isn't this Fred's problem?" Blake asked, hoping to avoid the grilling that he knew was coming.

"Hey, I manage the orders," Fred shot back, "but it's your job to figure out how to deliver them. Besides, this is just internal demand."

Blake ran his hand over his face as he sighed. "I know you'd like better results. We have production of the polysteel up. As I estimated before, we're over three months away from being able to start construction on Delphi City."

"What's the bottleneck?" Marc asked.

"Those damn beams and columns," Blake said. "They take up a lot of space to manufacture, we need lots of them, and the process is kind of slow since we can only deposit a few millimeters of polysteel at a time."

Catie sat forward in her seat with a jerk. "Why is that a problem?"

"We have to run the plasma head the entire two hundred meters of the beam," Blake said. "Then we have to stop and add the foam to form the 'I' part of the beam, adding a layer of it every twenty passes."

Catie shook her head, "I don't understand. Why are you adding foam?"

"Because it's an I-beam," Blake said. "Once we finish the base, we have to mask off everything except the 'I' part until we get to the top plate. Why are you confused, would you do it a different way?"

"I assumed you would extrude it," Catie said.

Blake tilted his head up and looked at the ceiling. He shook his head and leaned forward, extending his hands, forming a chokehold. "I'm going to throttle you!"

"No reason to be so extreme," Marc said. "If she misunderstands the constraints, just explain it to her."

"It's not that," Blake rasped, "she has just tripled, no probably quadrupled our capacity. What do you know about extrusions, anyway?"

"ADI explained it to me when I asked her how fiber-optic cables were made. I even wrote a paper on it for one of my classes."

"I got stuck," Blake explained. "I started with the plating and the pontoons. I was spraying them on a form, so I just extended that process to the beams and columns. It never occurred to me to wipe the slate clean and look at other processes. By extruding the beams and columns, we won't have to worry about floor space since we can stack them. Plus, we're not constrained by the two-millimeter limit; we can continuously deposit the polysteel while we pull the beam away from the die."

"Yadda, yadda, yadda," Samantha said. "What does it mean to the schedule?"

"I think it means we can start building the city in four or five weeks instead of two or three months," Blake said.

"Now that is cause for celebration," Marc said as he got up and opened the cabinet and brought out the Glenlivet.

"Wow, you must be happy if you're pouring the scotch," Blake said.

"Hey, you guys are usually giving me headaches, which, although that calls for scotch, it doesn't call for a toast," Marc said. He poured each of them a finger of scotch, he gave Catie just a splash. "To Delphi City!"

"To Delphi City!"

"Sam, how is your search going for a company to buy?" Marc asked after everyone had a chance to finish their scotch.

"I think I found just the company," Samantha said. "They're German. They make specialty scooters, which works well with Catie's idea to start with scooters. They have a manufacturing facility in Malaysia, and they're struggling with all the new competition from China."

"What about the owner?"

"His name is Peter Johansson. He's fifty; took over the company from his father; he's been very employee conscious, even in Malaysia. He looks like a really smart guy. He's struggling with how to compete against cheap Chinese labor and government subsidies that are designed to force him out of business."

"Have you contacted him yet?"

"I've sent out a feeler. I'll know more next week."

"Okay. Catie, how is your scooter design going?"

"I've finished the first two models, the Vespa-type scooter and then the motorbike," Catie said. "I think those will be the most popular. They've both got significantly more power than the competing models, and of course, they're all-electric."

"Wow, you are a wonder," Samantha said.

Catie blushed, "As soon as we have the fuel cells ready, we'll be able to add them to the bike. There's lots of room where the engine was. I've left the fuel tank alone; it's cosmetic on the all-electric model."

"That's great," Samantha said. "We'll see if Herr Johansson is interested. I suspect he'll be excited to be able to stick it to the Chinese. I also found us a sales rep."

"You have been busy," Marc said.

"I have too much free time," Samantha said. "Anyway, she's an old roommate from college. She was a dynamo in sales before she got married and had kids. She's looking to get back into it; but she needs something where she's not on the road all the time. A private jet flying her around would really make things work for her. She could take the kids and the nanny with her when they don't have school, and when they have school, she can leave them with the nanny or teach those lessons herself. She was in technical sales, so she knows most of the players we're interested in now. She used to set up tradeshow booths for a while after she had the first kid."

"She sounds perfect. What do you need to close the deal?"

"The private jet."

"Can we just have her charter one when she needs it?"

"That would work," Samantha said.

"Then do it. Closing another deal on the batteries will make that cost look like small change."

"Done," Samantha said. She'd obviously had an email ready to send and just pressed send on her specs with her eyes.

The next day Kal took Marc and Catie on a tour of the dorms on Manuae; he wanted to see what the locals were complaining about. Liz came along to provide security for Catie.

"I can see why the locals aren't happy with these guys," Marc said. Looking around, he could see that the construction workers were dominating all the community space. The TV room was full of them, and they were watching some raucous game show. The café had several tables of construction workers sitting around drinking coffee, some of them telling stories. Their voices were loud, and the laughing even louder.

"Are the others the same?"

"Pretty much," Kal said. "We try to separate them, but they make friends with some of the locals, and eventually, they're occupying all the space again."

"I see," Marc said as they walked into the cafeteria.

"Hey, one of you want to play some poker, we need a fifth." A group of four workers was sitting at one of the tables in the cafeteria playing cards.

"What happened to your fifth? You didn't just show up hoping to find another player," Kal asked.

"He opted for some overtime," one of the men said. "He probably needs it to cover his losses."

"Well, we're on a tight schedule here," Kal said. "Maybe some other time."

"Bawk, Bawk," the guy clucked. "Afraid of the competition?"

Marc, Liz, and Kal both rolled their eyes at the juvenile antics. "I'll play," Catie said.

"We play for money," the guy said.

"So, do I," Catie said.

"I don't think it'd be legal for some kid to play."

"I'm the mayor here," Marc said. "I can assure you there's no problem with her age."

"Umm . . ."

"What's the matter, you guys afraid of a little girl?" Kal asked.

"Of course not!"

"What's the buy-in?" Catie asked.

"One thousand," the guy said. He got some startled looks from his friends, but they didn't say anything.

"Can I borrow some?" Catie asked her father. "I'll have Betsy send some over, but that will take twenty or thirty minutes."

"Sure," Marc said. "Hundreds, okay?"

Catie looked at the guy, "I'll have change in thirty minutes."

"We're happy to take your money in any denomination."

"Kiwis or US?" Catie asked.

"US," the guy said.

Catie sent a quick text to Betsy, their local administrator, asking her to send five hundred dollars in ones, fives, and twenties. Marc quickly counted out ten $100 bills and gave them to Catie.

"We'll be leaving in a couple of hours," he said. "Do you think you'll be ready by then, or will I have to send the plane back?"

"I think I'll be ready," Catie said as she sat down. Liz took a seat at a table in the corner and started working in her HUD.

"Yeah, I don't think it will take us that long to take her money," one guy joked.

"See you later," Marc said. "Have fun."

Catie sat down and handed her money to the first guy, he started counting out chips. "Whites are one dollar, the blues are five, the greens are ten, and blacks are one hundred. By the way, my name's Bill."

"I'm Catie. What are you playing?"

"I'm Gary," the guy next to Bill said. "We're playing Texas Hold 'em. Pot limit. And you need to take those fancy glasses off."

"No problem," Catie said as she took her glasses off and hung them around her neck with the lenses pointing backward.

"I'm Jalin, and that's Howie. Do you know how to play?"

"Sure," Catie said. "I play with my uncle all the time."

"Good," Gary said as he shuffled the cards, "Ante's ten bucks, minimum raise is five."

Catie nodded her head as she watched him deal the cards.

When Marc and Kal stopped by two hours later, Catie was sitting there with most of the chips. Only Gary still had any, and he looked like he was down to about fifty dollars.

"It looks like you're about ready to go," Marc said as Gary finished dealing the cards.

"Yep," Catie said. "I think just this hand."

Gary just shook his head as he picked up his cards to look at them. He smiled at Catie and said, "I might be ready for a comeback."

"I don't think so," Catie said. "I'll bet twenty."

"Call," Gary said as he matched Catie's bet. He flipped over the flop, an ace of hearts, a two of diamonds and a five of clubs. He smiled. "Would you mind if I bought some more chips now?"

"That or use cash," Catie said. "I don't mind."

"Alright, your bet."

Catie pushed a small stack of chips into the pot, "Sixty."

Gary pushed his pile in and pulled some money from his wallet. "I'll see your sixty and raise you a hundred."

"I'll see your raise and raise you another hundred," Catie said.

"Call."

Gary showed the turn, a five of diamonds. He really smiled at Catie now. "Still your bet."

"I'll bet five hundred," Catie said as she gave Gary a steely look. "You can declare all-in if you want."

"I'm good," Gary said. "I'll call." He peeled five $100 bills off of his roll and tossed them in the pot.

"Now for the river card," he said as he turned over the last card, the four of diamonds.

"I bet five hundred," Catie said.

"I see your five and raise you one thousand," Gary said as he peeled off a wad of hundreds.

"Call," Catie said. "I don't want to take all your money." She pushed a stack of black chips into the pot.

"I don't think that flush of yours is going to be good enough," Gary said. "Full house, aces over fives." He flipped his two cards over with a flourish and leaned back with a big smile. "Told you I was ready for a comeback."

"I'm confused," Catie said.

"We'll let me explain it to you," Gary said. "Hands go, one pair, two pair, three of a kind, straight, flush and **then** a full house. A full house beats your flush."

"But where I've played, a straight flush always beats a full house," Catie said. "And I knew you didn't have four aces since I have the ace of diamonds and the three of diamonds." Catie flipped over her two cards.

Gary's face fell. "You had to wait for the river to fill that hand. What . . . why did you bet so much?"

"I felt lucky," Catie said. "Now I need to cash my chips so I can catch my ride home."

Gary popped all the money out of the card box and threw it into the pot. "There you go."

"You're mean," Marc whispered to Catie as they made their way out of the cafeteria.

"He was kind of an ass," Catie said. "The other two were at least polite."

"Well, he's a much poorer ass right now," Marc said. He gave Catie a hug as he laughed. "Our very own Ms. Manners."

Chapter 28 Jungle Paintball

"Kal, how are your new legs?" Catie asked, "I mean besides letting you chase Russian spies."

"They're good," Kal said. "I've been training, and I think I'm back up to the same performance I had before I lost them." He looked around to see if Fred or Samantha were close by since they weren't supposed to know about his new legs yet.

"They just left for Sydney," Catie said. "Some contract thing Sam's taking care of there."

"Oh," Kal relaxed. "They left early."

"Shopping."

Kal laughed, "Should have guessed. Where's Liz?"

"Right behind you," Liz said as she smacked Kal in the back of the head. "What's up with your situational awareness?"

"There is nothing wrong with my situational awareness," Kal said. "I could sneak up on you and put a cap in your ass before you knew what was going on."

"You wanna bet?" Liz demanded.

"Oh, any day, girl, and twice on Saturday," Kal shot back.

"You want in on this Catie?" Liz asked.

"I just want him to teach me how," Catie said. "But I'll take your bet."

"You mean you're betting on Kal?" Liz asked with surprise.

"I'm pretty sure he's going to win," Catie said.

"Ooh, I'm wounded. When, cowboy?" Liz asked.

"Pick a day," Kal said. "If we take Catie with us, then we can have the rest of the team guard Marc and the compound."

"You're on, how about Thursday? Catie has a soccer game on Saturday. Where do you want to play?" Liz asked.

"Manuae," Kal said. "You get a thirty-minute head start from the dock."

"Wait, wait," Catie said. "I want Kal to teach me how to do it."

"Not a problem," Kal said. "After I take care of Liz, I'll show you both how to track and hide."

"Paintball pistol, no fair using a sniper rifle," Liz set the rules.

"You're on, night or daytime?" Kal asked.

"Daytime if you're so hot," Liz snapped.

"See you at 0600," Kal said. "We'll take the Mea Huli there."

"We should go the night before," Catie said, "We can sleep on the Mea Huli. It takes almost four hours to get there."

"Okay, check with your father," Liz said.

"I already have," Catie said.

"We'll head out at 22:00," Kal said. "I'll get one of my guys to drive the boat, so we can all sleep. We might as well time it, so we hit Manuae at 06:00 since we're not in a hurry."

Liz and Catie had elected to wear their shipsuits under their cammo. With the hood, it would provide an extra layer of protection from insects as well as avoid some problems that might arise from too much coffee. Liz literally did not want to be caught with her pants down.

"Okay hotshot," Liz said as she prepared to leave the Mea Huli in her quest to evade Kal. "How long do you want?"

"Make it two hours; no using alerts on your HUD; no using the surveillance drone; physical tag or pistol paintball ends the game; you get a thirty-minute head start."

"Surveillance drone?" Liz looked puzzled.

"I'm putting it up so I can watch," Catie said.

"And no communication either," Kal added.

"As if," Liz said. "What's the bet?"

"One thousand!"

"You're on. See ya in two hours," Liz headed out toward the trees.

Catie went up to the sun deck so she could watch while Kal sat down and waited.

Catie watched as Liz started out with an easy run into the trees, she obviously wanted to create as much buffer between her and Kal as possible. She made her way along a dry streambed that she came across. After ten minutes, she paused and cut off a branch from a bush; she started sweeping her footprints as she walked along the streambed, while she tried to stay on the larger rocks that presented themselves.

After another five minutes, she passed some larger rocks that came out of the ground to the left of the streambed. She continued on for a few minutes then doubled back, carefully trying to avoid any sign that she was retracing her steps. When she got to the big rocks, she hopped onto the closest one. After inspecting the streambed for any signs of her leap, she moved on, hopping from rock to rock until she reached the end of them. She then worked her way between the trees until she found a small clump of bushes that had a space between them where she could lie in wait. There she settled down to wait.

After the thirty minutes, Kal headed out. He jogged along the same streambed as Liz had, stopping every minute or so. He was a few hundred yards from the rocks Liz had used to leave the streambed when he stopped for a long time. Catie watched as he just sat there. Then Kal gathered some twigs and branches from the nearby bush and stuck them in his hat and out of his cammo in various places. Then to Catie's surprise, he started off very quietly to the left of the streambed. It was hard to follow him as he moved along; eventually, Catie lost sight of him. She couldn't bring the drone in closer since it might tip off his position to Liz. She decided just to watch the area around Liz and also put up a few windows showing the output of Liz's and Kal's spec cameras.

Kal's camera just showed the bushes and indicated when he paused for long periods as he made his way along. Liz's camera just showed her looking around the area where she was hidden.

Twenty minutes after Kal left, Catie noticed a small motion on Liz's rear spec camera. It was barely perceptible, and she didn't think Liz had seen it since she would have to have been looking at that part of the display to notice it. Then she saw Kal's hand reach from behind a tree and tap Liz on the shoulder. Liz jumped about two feet in the air.

"Shit! How did you do that?"

"Skill, girl, pure skill."

Catie talked into the comm. "That was so cool! I want to try."

"Which one?" Kal asked.

"I bet you can't sneak up on me before I catch you," Catie said.

"You sure you want to make that bet?" Liz said.

"Sure, you don't learn without putting something on the line. Same rules, Kal?"

"Same rules; same bet?"

"Sure," Catie said. "Liz, you want to get in on this?"

"How about it, Kal, you wanna bet you can tag Catie?"

"You're taking her side of the bet?" Kal asked incredulously.

"We girls have to stick together, and besides, I make it a policy to never bet against her."

"Okay, it's your money."

"Time starts now," Catie said. "I've got plenty of head start on you."

"One point, you can't go in the water," Kal said.

"No problem, I plan to stay dry," Catie said. "See you in a few."

Catie turned off all the displays on her HUD, closed her comm, and hopped off of the Mea Huli. She headed to the left and jogged into the woods. She only went about ten minutes before she found the spot she was looking for. It was a small clearing in the trees, with a few big chunks of lava rocks in the middle. Obviously, what little soil had once covered this area had been eroded away, leaving the clearing and the rocks. She settled down against one of the rocks and waited. She figured Kal should be there in about fifteen minutes. She turned on the infrared channel on her spec cameras and raised her head up. She'd pulled her hood down and covered it with some grass to disguise herself. She started turning her head slowly from side to side, so her cameras covered the entire area.

Right on time, she saw a heat signature approaching her from the east. She dropped down and arranged herself so she could track the signature. It approached very slowly and circled to the north. She had selected this spot because Kal would have to try and take a shot at her from the bushes. There wasn't enough cover for him to get close enough to tag her without her seeing him. Her plan was simple, she would know where he was, but he wouldn't know she knew. So, when he was preparing to take a shot, she would roll to the ground and start blasting at his location. She figured she could get off at least four shots before he had cleared his weapon.

Kal surprised her again. Instead of preparing to take a shot from the edge of the clearing, he was slowly moving the edge of the clearing toward Catie. He'd constructed a blind out of the branches from local bushes and was moving it into the clearing an inch at a time. Even a foot would dramatically improve his shot angle. But to Catie's advantage, the tedious work tied up his hands. She waited until he was moving the blind again, then she rolled out of her sitting position, her gun was already in her hand against her chest. She extended her arm as she rolled and fired off shots continuously.

"Okay, you witch, I'm hit," Kal yelled.

"Sore loser," Catie shot back.

"How did you cheat?" Kal asked indignantly. Both of them could hear Liz laughing into their comms.

"I didn't cheat," Catie shot back. "I followed the rules."

"Let me rephrase, what did you see that Liz and I missed?"

"You concede?"

"Yes, I concede," Kal said. "So, what did we miss?"

"Infrared."

Kal rolled his eyes and sighed, "Don't tell me the cameras on our specs have an infrared channel?"

"Okay, I won't, but they're super sensitive."

Liz laughed, "I thought you wanted to learn from Kal."

"I do, but I thought I should give you a chance to get your money back."

"What about my money?" Kal asked, trying to look all hurt.

"I'll buy us all dinner," Catie said. "Now show us how you can be so sneaky. How did you know where Liz was? You went to the right way before she did."

"I listened," Kal said.

"I wasn't making any noise," Liz said.

"Not much, I suspect," Kal said. "I listened to the sounds of the forest. Birds, even insects, make different sounds after they have been disturbed. You just have to listen to find where the sound is different."

"Really, show us."

Kal spent the rest of the day and into the night showing Catie and Liz how to make stealthy approaches. He showed them how to detect slight variations in sounds; to spot telltale signs that showed what someone was doing and how they were walking. Catie immediately found ways to use their specs to supplement their natural senses. They allowed them to do an even better job of detecting where someone was. Of course, the infrared was one of the best things once you were relatively close.

Chapter 29 Emergency Aid

Liz was watching Catie and the twins playing soccer on Rarotonga. The twins had taken to playing soccer with gusto. Aalia had regained all her muscle mass, and it was impossible to tell the twins apart anymore. Catie had just scored a goal, and the twins were giving her a high five when there was a loud pop from the adjacent field where the under-ten kids were playing.

Liz rushed over to see what had happened. She ran toward the small crowd that was gathered in the middle of the field. They were surrounding a young girl lying on the ground writhing in pain. Another girl was kneeling down next to her, crying, "I'm sorry, I was tackling the ball," she whined as tears ran down her cheeks.

Liz could tell immediately that the girl had a compound fracture of her tibia. "Let's take her to the Virginia Henderson. Dr. Sharmila will be able to fix her right up," she said once the stretcher arrived.

"Are you crazy, she's got a broken leg," the ambulance attendant said.

"I'm sure it's just sprained," Liz said. "But Dr. Sharmila is an orthopedic surgeon, so either way, she'll be able to take care of her."

The ambulance attendant just shook his head as they loaded the girl onto the stretcher and into the ambulance.

"Where are her parents?" Liz asked the second girl.

"She's with me," a woman said. "I just called her mother and told her to meet us at the ship. Are you sure Dr. Sharmila will be able to take care of her?"

"Of course, she will," Liz said. Catie was standing next to Liz by this time with the twins right behind her. She nodded her head to confirm what Liz had said. Everyone knew Catie, and with her confirmation, the woman gave a sigh of relief.

"What is her name?"

"She's Sefina Marsters."

"Thank you. I'll see you at the ship."

Liz signaled for their car, and she, Catie, and the twins climbed in. Liz instructed the driver to get to the Virginia Henderson before the ambulance, then called Dr. Sharmila on her HUD.

"Dr. Sharmila, we have an ambulance heading your way, a little girl was injured at the soccer field. Leg's broken, but I want everyone to think it's just a serious sprain. That way, you can fix her up. Her name is Sefina Marsters, if that's any help."

"I understand," Dr. Sharmila said. "Quick thinking. I'll go down to meet the ambulance and see if I can avoid any misconceptions. I'll just use her fingerprint to pull up her records. Half the people on the islands are named Marsters."

She was waiting outside when the ambulance arrived. As they brought the stretcher out, she used a portable scanner to grab the girl's thumbprint then she examined the girl's leg. "Oh my, that is serious," she said.

"It's broken," the ambulance attendant said.

"No, I don't think so. All the swelling would make you think so, but I'm sure it's just a bad sprain; maybe some muscle tearing," Dr. Sharmila said. "Let's get her onto the ship, and I'll be able to tell better after an x-ray." She signaled for two of the staff to take over the stretcher and thanked the ambulance attendant for being so fast to get the girl to the ship. Liz and company arrived about this time, and the twins piled out of the car and ran over to their mother.

"Are you going to be able to fix her?" they asked.

"Of course I am. Why don't you run up to my office while I take care of her. Then you can come down and visit her. Are you her mother?" she asked the woman who'd accompanied the girl in the ambulance.

"No, just the neighbor. Her mother is on her way. She should be here in a few minutes."

"Why don't you wait here with Catie and Liz," Dr. Sharmila said. "They can show you up to the treatment room when her mother arrives. I'll just go and see what I can do right now."

Dr. Sharmila left everyone on the pier while she climbed the gangplank back onto the Virginia Henderson. Once she was out of sight, she ran to catch up to the stretcher that was carrying the little girl. She signaled the two men pushing the stretcher to pause for a moment. Once they were stopped, she injected a painkiller into the little girl's leg. The girl immediately stopped crying and moaning, settling down into a light sleep.

"Treatment room four," she instructed.

Once in the treatment room, she had them transfer the girl to the bed and asked them to leave. She strapped the girl to the bed, checked her vitals, and reviewed her records before proceeding. She took a quick blood sample and put it into the analyzer that was mounted to the wall of the treatment room. Then she brought an arm with a scanner on it down from overhead, like what is used in a dentist's office. She strapped a clamp to the girl's leg above the knee, and one to the leg at the ankle. Then she flicked her eyes up and engaged the imager. She could see the break clearly on her HUD. "Nasty," she thought. She had the clamps pull the two ends apart until she was able to bring the broken bones into alignment. She carefully twisted them until they lined up perfectly. She injected nanites along the broken edge of the bones and let the clamps ease the two ends back together. Then she used another syringe to inject nanites around the pieces of bone that were buried in the leg's tissue.

Dr. Sharmila relaxed while she waited for the nanites to do their job. The first set would deposit neutral bone material along the fracture before deactivating themselves so they could be flushed out. The second set would dissolve the bone fragments and let the body expel them. The first injection she'd given the girl had blocked the pain receptors in the area of the break and also had released a mild sedative. After five minutes, she prepared for the last part of the procedure.

Dr. Sharmila could hear a woman she assumed was the mother talking to the nurse outside the treatment room. She injected the last set of nanites into the girl's leg. These would deposit neutral muscle and ligament tissue in the various tears around the break. She needed another three minutes before she could complete the treatment. She wanted to do that before the girl's mother entered the room, but she could hear the voices being raised. Just as she was ready to give up and let the mother in, she listened to her daughters talking to the mother.

Smiling at how well they distracted the mother with their chatter, each one saying half the words while the other filled in the blanks. Listening to them through the wall, it was almost impossible to tell that more than one person was talking.

Checking her watch, she prepared the last injection. It was a large syringe of stem cells that had just been manufactured from the blood sample she had taken at the beginning. The stem cells would find the neutral biomaterial and lay the girl's own DNA into them to restore the injury.

After giving the injection, she opened the door to the treatment room. The girl's mother and the woman who'd accompanied the girl to the ship were anxiously waiting while the twins were chattering away.

"Hello, I'm Dr. Sharmila."

"I'm Jenny Marsters," the mother said. "How is she?"

"She'll be fine. She's going to need to use crutches to get around for a couple of days, but after that, she can work her way back to playing soccer."

"They said it was broken."

"Oh no, just a bad sprain and some tearing," Dr. Sharmila said. "I gave her a sedative for the pain, but she should be waking up about now. Why don't you come in and see her?"

The mother gasped with relief. "Oh, I was so worried." She rushed into the room, grasped her daughter's hand and stroked her hair.

Her touch woke her daughter up, "Mommy, my leg."

"The doctor says it's going to be just fine. Does it hurt?"

"Not anymore; you mean, it's not broken?"

"That's right, the doctor says just a couple of days on crutches."

"Oh, good. We're in the playoffs next week. I'll be able to play, won't I?"

"We'll see. Right now, you need to rest. I'll go see about taking you home."

"Okay," Sefina said. She was very drowsy and fell back to sleep once her mother left.

◆ ◆ ◆

Catie was sweating and swearing. Liz had just thrown her for the third time, and she hadn't even seen it coming, and worse than that, they had an audience.

"Don't give her any momentum to work with," Kal hollered. He was openly laughing at her.

"Maybe you should show me how instead of just laughing at me," Catie snapped.

Kal looked at Liz, questioning what she thought about it.

"Come on mister big mouth," Liz said. She was bouncing on her toes to keep loose.

"Okay sister, let's see what you've got," Kal said.

Liz just grinned, *"this is going to be fun,"* she thought. Kal was always making some smart remark about her training and Krav Maga in general. It was like he believed that his Marine hand-to-hand combat was so much better. Well, plenty of times, she had wiped the floor with Marines who had thought that.

"Okay," Kal said. "You want me to stand here?" He took the spot on the mat where Catie had been.

Liz nodded her head and smiled again as Kal held his hand up in front of himself like a boxer, but with his hands open.

"So, what do I do? Try to hit you or just stare you to death?" he asked.

"It looks like you're trying to talk me to death," Liz shot back.

Kal laughed, "I was always taught that taking out the opponent without making contact is always the best way."

"Come on, smart ass. Just try to hit me," Liz said.

Kal walked closer to Liz; when he was within reach, he snapped out a left jab. Liz started to block it and stepped in close to Kal, preparing to throw him, but he wasn't there. Then her legs shot out from under her, and she landed on her butt. "Oomph."

She looked up for Kal, but he was already back where he'd started from.

"Sorry, I missed," he said.

Liz got to her feet with as much dignity as she could manage. "Okay, let's try that again."

Kal moved in and threw a left jab again. Just as Liz blocked it, he hit her with a right cross to the ribs, she deflected it with her elbow, but it still made contact. Kal had already retreated to his starting spot. Catie was just standing there with her mouth open.

"Again," Liz shouted.

Kal moved in once more. He threw a quick left-right combo that Liz easily blocked. He started to rush her, leading with his left. She set up to take the charge when Kal disappeared. Again, she felt her feet fly out from under her. This time she landed on top of Kal, who had her in a sleeper hold around her neck with his legs wrapped around hers pinning them down. Liz slapped the mat with her hand, tapping out.

Kal helped her to her feet. "Did I do that right?"

"You bastard, they didn't teach you that in the Marines."

"No, I'm Hawaiian," Kal said. "Aikido, eighth Don."

Liz was rubbing her butt, although the second time she'd actually landed on top of Kal, he had managed to take her weight on the point of his hip.

Catie was applauding, "Finally, Liz is the one rubbing her butt! I'm going to take lessons from Kal too. Maybe between the two of you, I'll learn something."

"You've been training," Liz said.

"Sure, there's an Aikido Master on the island. I go there twice a week," Kal said. "It took a while to shake the rust off, but it came back quickly."

"Well, I'm properly humbled," Liz said.

Kal laughed, "You'll be ready next time. You've slowed down a little, not enough competition."

"Well, you should join us in the mornings," Liz said.

"I'd be happy to."

"Oh boy, I'm going to love not being the only one to be hitting the mat," Catie said with a giggle.

"Just remember, you're the one who's definitely going to hit the mat," Liz threatened her.

Chapter 30 Pilot Training

Blake, Catie, and Liz were putting on their wetsuits so they could go to the Sakira. "This would be a lot easier if we could just land the Lynx at the airport," Liz complained.

Blake laughed, "Marc would have a heart attack."

"The Lynxes almost float," Catie said.

"Close but not close enough," Blake said. "What's her min surface speed?"

"Twenty knots," Catie answered.

"We could almost jump from the Mea Huli," Liz said. "Problem would be if we missed."

"Why don't we use the tender from the Mea Huli?" Catie asked.

"I know your dad pulled that stunt with the wave rider, but he'd have a fit if anyone else tried it."

"Not fair."

"Fair has nothing to do with reality," Blake said. "Haven't you learned that yet?"

"Yeah, but . . ."

"Dive," Blake said.

It only took them a minute to swim over and climb into the cargo hold of the Lynx. It took another three minutes before everyone had cycled through the lock into the main cabin.

"Now we can relax," Blake said. "Catie, are you going to drive it?"

"No. Just tell ADI to take us down."

"Okay."

"Hey, I have an idea," Catie said.

"Oh no," Blake said with mock fear.

Liz slugged Blake, "Give her a chance. She usually has good ones."

"I know, but they typically mean more work for me," Blake complained.

"Uncle Blake!" Catie groaned. "This one's easy."

"What do you have?"

"We could have the Mea Huli pull a dock," Catie said.

Blake crinkled his forehead. "A dock?"

"Yeah, some kind of inflatable thing that the Lynx could drive on top of that would give it enough buoyancy to float. Then we could just walk from the Mea Huli into the airlock."

Blake's eyes floated to the top of his head as he thought about that. "That probably would work. I'll work with ADI on a design."

"Cool."

The next week when they were going to the Sakira, they wore their regular clothes. Blake had ADI hold the Mea Huli at twenty-two knots as he kicked the dock off of the rear platform. He opened the valve on the air compressor so the dock would fill with air, and five minutes, later it was floating and staying steady behind the Mea Huli.

"How's that work?" Liz asked.

"It has a sea anchor to keep it stable. When the Lynx pops her nose up on it, we'll close the sea anchor to maximize buoyancy, then we'll pull it in close."

"How does the Lynx get off the dock?"

"When we're aboard the Lynx, Kyle will drop the sea anchor and speed up the Mea Huli. That'll pull the dock down a bit, and the Lynx will slide right off."

"This is so cool," Catie said as she watched the Lynx surface and track behind the Mea Huli. It popped up on the dock, and Blake had the winch pull the dock forward until it was pressed against the Mea Huli. The Lynx just followed behind. Then ADI let the Mea Huli's speed bleed off until she and the Lynx were coasting along at a sedate five knots.

"After you," Blake motioned to Catie to go first.

Catie scrambled onto the dock and made her way to the forward hatch of the Lynx. It was open since ADI had opened it once the Lynx and Mea Huli were stabilized. She crawled in and waved at Liz and Blake.

"This is so much more dignified," Liz said as she followed Catie.

After the Lynx docked in Flight Bay Two of the Sakira, they had to wait for the thirty minutes it took to drain all the water out. Then they made their way through the lock and up to Flight Bay One. They had to wait until ADI got clearance from Marc for them to enter the flight bay.

After they made their way into Flight Bay One, Liz said, "If we could dock the Lynx in here, we wouldn't have to wait for all the water to get pumped out. Just enough so we could wade to our planes."

"That's clever," Blake said. "ADI, can we dock the Lynx in here?"

"No, Cer Blake," ADI said. "Flight Bay Two is the only one that is allowed to be opened remotely unless we're under operational status."

"Why?"

"It's protocol," ADI said.

"Figures," Liz said.

"ADI," Catie interrupted. "Can we move the Foxes to Flight Bay Two?"

"If the captain gives permission, I can move them," ADI said. "How many do you want to move?"

"Three?" Blake suggested.

"Why not all four?" Catie asked.

"We shouldn't put all our eggs in one basket," Blake said. "Besides, we only need three; if we get a fourth pilot, we can use the Lynx."

"Would we be able to do our training simulations without having to get the captain's permission?" Catie asked.

"Yes, only operations in Flight Bay One require the captain to sign off each time," ADI said.

"If we bring a dinghy," Catie said, "we can save a bunch of time by only pumping the bay down halfway."

"I like the way this girl thinks," Blake said. "ADI open a comm to Marc."

"What's up?" Marc said. "You guys can't be through yet."

"We've come up with a big time-saver," Blake said. "If you have ADI move three of the Foxes to Bay Two, we can do our simulations without having to ping you. We'll cut an hour off of the transit time because we won't have to pump the bay dry."

"Who came up with that idea? Catie?" Marc asked.

"No, Liz thought about docking where the Foxes were; Catie figured out how to work around the constraints."

"Okay, ADI, please move the Foxes to Flight Bay Two," Marc ordered.

"Only three of them," Catie interrupted, "and after we're through for the day."

"ADI, when they are through with their training, move three of the Foxes to Flight Bay Two."

"Yes, Captain," ADI replied.

"When will the new Lynx be ready?" Blake asked.

"Two weeks," Catie said. "The shell is done, we're mounting engines tomorrow, then we'll build out the cockpit and main cabin. The flight simulator for the Lynx is ready, but it's nothing like what these babies provide."

"Great, what's the run for today?" Liz asked.

"Two on one," Blake said. "We'll each get to go against the other two. The side with two will be restricted to F35 specs, lone wolf gets the Fox."

"Worst time to down both enemy planes, buys dinner."

"You're on."

"Hey, Liz, you have a hot date?" Catie asked. She'd walked into their room as Liz was putting on a little black dress.

"A certain British gentleman has invited me to dinner at Tamarind House," Liz said.

"Oh, fancy place. He must really like you," Catie said, giggling.

"We both know what he likes," Liz said, giggling along with Catie.

"Well, since you can't give him that, you'll have to come up with something else to interest him."

Liz picked a throw pillow off the bed and threw it at Catie. Then she picked up her high-heels and walked to the stairs. Catie ran after her and dashed down the stairs. "Guess who is taking Liz to Tamarind House?"

"Who?" Blake asked.

"You mean she's finally got a date!" Kal added.

"Yes! Some British guy has found her irresistible," Catie giggled.

"Just remember we have a training session tomorrow morning," Liz reminded Catie.

"Don't worry, Catie, I'll protect you," Kal said.

"Any helpful hints about dating a spy?" Liz asked.

"Well, mine asked to borrow my phone. When I lent it to her, she dropped it on the pavement," Blake said.

"Did it hurt the pavement?" Kal asked.

"Not much," Blake laughed. "Ying Yue was amazed and disappointed that the phone survived."

"Sasha got our phones mixed up once," Kal said. "ADI called me, and Sasha's like, 'oh shit, what do I do now?' as my ring tone is coming from her purse."

"What did she do?"

"She's pretty good with her hands," Kal said.

"I bet she is," Blake said with a big grin.

"Yes, she is. She made it look like her bag was sitting on top of my phone. She just handed me my phone like nothing was happening," Kal said.

"Liz, you can't go out like that," Catie said.

"Why not?"

"You need to have some jewelry," Catie said. "Wait, I'll get my pearls."

"No, they're your special . . ."

Catie ignored her and ran upstairs to grab the pearls from her jewelry box. "Here put them on," she said. "They're going to look great with that black dress."

"But . . ."

"They're made to be worn," Catie said. "Wait, put this flower in your hair. It's a camera; that way, ADI can keep an eye on things for you. You won't be able to wear your specs dressed up like that."

"Where did you get this?"

"ADI made it for me," Catie said. "I mentioned that I felt exposed when I couldn't wear my specs. She said she could put a camera in anything, so we came up with this."

"Is he picking you up?" Kal asked.

"No, we're meeting at the restaurant," Liz said. "I thought it would be easier that way."

"You mean easier to get out of here and back without getting noticed," Blake said.

"I was hoping for a little less attention," Liz said.

"Don't worry, I've got a date tonight," Blake said. "I don't expect to be back until morning."

"I'm stuck guarding Catie," Kal said. "You're welcome for the night off."

"Why thank you," Liz said. "Now, I have to get going."

"Don't hurry home on my account," Kal said as he gave Liz a wave.

◆ ◆ ◆

"Hello, Liz, you're looking lovely," the British spy said.

"Hello, Logan, you're looking lovely too," Liz said. Logan was dressed in a black tuxedo, very James Bondish.

"Well a man has to compete," Logan said. "Shall we?" he offered his arm to Liz. She took it and let him escort her into the restaurant. "Reservations for Logan Marlowe."

"Right this way," the maître d' said. He led them to a lovely table in the corner of the restaurant, overlooking the beach. The moon was just above the water.

"How was your day?" Logan asked.

"Oh, nothing special," Liz said. "Just managing orders and production schedules." Liz listed off work that ADI took care of, avoiding the work she actually did, like babysitting a couple of nuclear physicists.

"Sounds dreadful."

"It's hard to have a dreadful day down here," Liz said. "What did you do today?"

"Looked around at real estate," Logan said. "The boys in Auckland think we should open a local stock brokerage here, make it more convenient for the locals to invest."

"I thought you were from Britain."

"That's home, but I've been working out of Auckland for a few years now. We're an international concern. One has to do a foreign tour to make the big boys happy."

"Well, you have to keep the big boys happy, don't you?"

"Needs must," Logan said. "Say, you guys sure have a lot of activity going over there for just producing batteries."

"Oh, I think Marc plans on doing more than batteries," Liz said. "He's putting lots of infrastructure in ahead of some other plans."

"Anything interesting, these other plans?"

"I wouldn't know," Liz said. "Right now, my life is just batteries. He plays his cards pretty close to the vest. Wouldn't want to pre-announce anything now, would he?"

"Oh, I'm sure he wouldn't," Logan said. "You really need to be quick to get a jump on the big corporations. He really has them scrambling with those batteries."

"Did you find anything?"

"Find what?"

"Real estate?"

"Oh, a couple of offices we could lease. I'd like to get something close to the beach in case I get tasked with starting it up."

"I hope you do," Liz said, "get tasked with starting it up. Then I would get a chance to see more of you."

◆ ◆ ◆

"You're home early," Catie said as Liz was carefully trying to get into bed without waking her.

"Were you waiting up for me?"

"Moi?"

"It's one o'clock," Liz said. "Were you going to stay up all night?"

"No, I told ADI to wake me when you got in. So how was he, and why are you home so early?"

"This is not early," Liz said. "And he was very nice and inquisitive."

"Curious about what?" Catie asked with a snicker.

"Just go to sleep, I'm not talking about my date with a thirteen-year-old."

"How am I going to learn?" Catie giggled.

"When you're older," Liz said. "Goodnight!"

Chapter 31 Board Meeting – March 4th

"Come on, settle down," Marc shouted. "Let's get going. First order of business, how is progress going with Herr Johansson?"

"We've reached a preliminary agreement," Samantha said. "He's interested in the partnership, but he'd like to see a bit more of what we're bringing to the game. Catie and I are going to meet him in Auckland this week. They'll do a design review of her scooters, and if that goes well, we will sign a contract."

"Catie, are you going to be ready?" Marc asked.

"No pressure," Catie laughed. "I'm ready. ADI and I are just doing some revisions to take advantage of the tooling he already has. It will make it faster to get the scooters into production. We'll be finished before we leave for Auckland."

"Good, are you flying?"

"Of course," Catie said. "That is, if Fred lets me."

"I'll even let you land there," Fred said.

"Wait a minute, I'm on that flight," Samantha teased.

"Don't worry, you know I won't crash," Catie said. "At least not before the design review."

"I'll check with Sam about how it went before I let you fly home," Fred said, continuing with the joke.

"Okay," Marc said. "How's the search for a cruise ship going?"

"I bought one," Samantha said.

"Already?" Marc squeaked.

"Blake is in a hurry," Samantha explained. "It's the Sky Princess. It can handle five hundred passengers, and it is in transit right now. I've arranged for them to do as many of the repairs and refit as they can during the trip here. Once it's here, Blake will have to figure out how to finish them. But the ship should be able to handle his construction crew right away."

"How about managing it?" Marc asked.

"One of the hotels on Rarotonga wants that contract. They seem pretty excited about it. They've even mentioned that they might like to buy it when we're finished with it. They think that with the money flowing into Rarotonga and the eventual population increases around the islands, there might be a niche market for short cruises."

"How is your old roommate doing?" Marc asked.

"Marcie has locked Apple into a short-term exclusive on batteries for laptops and phones. Another exclusive with Milwaukee Tools for their batteries. That charter company is loving her."

"That's excellent," Marc said. "She has really been doing a bang-up job. We need to come up with more things for her to sell."

"I'll pass that along to her," Samantha said.

"Kal, security?" Marc prompted.

"We're up to ten on active status," Kal said. "We have six more who are going through medical. Some of them need a little time to clean up, but Dr. Metra says she feels good about them all."

"Labor situation okay?"

"We're doing great," Kal said. "We'll need to start talking about importing labor soon, but we need to see how many Cook Islanders decide to come back from New Zealand before we go there."

"Okay. Liz, how are our scientists doing?"

"Those physicists are finally talking to Dr. Scheele about making a plasma field generator. They're also talking to Dr. Zelbar about making a containment vessel. I'm arranging for extra lab space for them," Liz said. "I assume you want their labs to be on Manuae."

"Definitely," Marc said. "Are they going to be okay living there?"

"I'm not sure they know where they're living now. So, a different island won't be too serious a change. As long as somebody feeds them."

"Okay," Marc said. "Dr. Metra has some surgeries scheduled, so she bowed out of today's meeting. She's happy with the progress, would love more nurses."

"We have some coming next month," Samantha said. "You do realize that they have to move."

"I'm just the messenger," Marc said.

"You know these meetings are getting boring," Catie said.

"I agree," Blake seconded.

"You guys remember what happened the last time you were complaining about meetings being boring?" Marc said. "I'm happy with boring. Hopefully, we continue to keep a relatively low profile."

"Yes, you should remember the old Chinese curse, 'May you live in interesting times'," Liz said.

"Oh, now you've jinxed us," Samantha scolded.

"Sorry kids, practice is canceled," the coach said. "The field is too soft after the rain last night. I'll see you back here tomorrow."

"Oh pooh," the twins said.

"Hey, do you want to play paintball?" Catie asked. The twins had been asking about it since they'd seen Catie's gear a few weeks ago.

"Yes!"

"Shouldn't you have asked their mother first?" Liz said.

"I did," Catie laughed. "A couple of weeks ago. I've just been waiting for the opportunity."

"Okay, do you want to go get our gear, or should we just rent some like the twins?"

"Let's just rent stuff."

After getting everybody geared up and showing the twins how to use the paintball rifles, they paired off. Catie and Aalia against Liz and Prisha.

"Let's just use the obstacle course," Liz suggested.

"You're on," Catie agreed. "Two minutes to go over strategy and get in place. We'll take the north side." Catie grabbed Aalia's hand and led her around the outside of the obstacle course.

"Are you ready?" Catie asked.

Aalia nodded her head.

"Now they're going to try and sneak up on us, so we have to do a better job of sneaking up on them," Catie explained. She paused and looked around the course. The walls were only six feet tall, "Hmm, what do you think about riding on my shoulders so you can see above the wall?"

"I like that," Aalia said.

"Okay, but you need to duck down below the top of the wall until I tell you to peek, okay. Then you look up and tell me if you see them. But be really quiet."

Aalia nodded her head.

Catie bent down and let Aalia sit on her shoulders. "Okay, I'm going to stand up, but you need to bend down so they can't see you. Tap my head once for yes and twice for no."

Aalia tapped Catie's head. Catie worked her way around the first two walls until she was by the left side of the room. "Okay, peek for just a second . . . Did you see anyone?"

Aalia tapped Catie's head twice.

"Okay, now we'll try to sneak around this wall." Catie dodged around the wall and stopped against the next wall. "Okay, peak again."

Aalia tapped Catie's head once.

"You saw them."

One tap.

"Do you think you can shoot one of them?"

One tap.

"Okay, get them."

"Out," Liz called out.

"I said, I'm out!" Liz yelled as she came around the corner with Prisha on her shoulders. Prisha immediately shot Catie.

"Hey, why didn't you shoot her?" Catie complained to Aalia, right as Prisha shot her again.

"Out! What's up with this?" Catie complained. "You guys are supposed to shoot each other, too." Catie knelt down to allow Aalia off of her shoulders. Aalia immediately went after Liz again. Liz had dropped Prisha, who was now taking aim at Catie.

"Oh, that's how it is, is it!" Catie squawked as she started unloading on Aalia.

Liz immediately started shooting Prisha, "You traitor!"

After thirty seconds of continuous fire, they were all out of ammo. They collapsed on the floor, giggling.

"You should have known better than to pair them off against each other," Liz said. "You'll never get one to go against the other."

"You're right, I should have known better," Catie said. "Wow, we didn't do anything except get paint all over each other."

"It's hard to train when you have a couple of traitors in your midst."

"We're not traitors, we're twins," the twins echoed together.

"Yeah, we finally get that," Catie said.

Chapter 32 Parts for All

Miki Sunamoto knocked on the doorjamb of Takurō's hospital room, "You awake?"

"Miki!" Takurō cried out. "Why didn't you tell me you were coming?"

"I wanted to surprise you. Kal said you'd be able to receive visitors today."

"Well, you're my first since they lifted the isolation. Come in."

Miki walked in and sat next to Takurō's bed, grasping his right hand and holding it to her cheek. "You look good."

"When have I not looked good?"

"I mean, you're alert. Every time we talked on video, you looked pale and spaced out like you were on dope or something."

"I was on something. Good stuff, too," Takurō said.

"Knock! Knock!" Dr. Sharmila said as she entered the room. "How is my patient doing?"

"Great!"

"How's the hand?"

Miki looked shocked, "What happened to your hand?" she said as she looked at the hand that she was clasping.

"She meant this hand," Takurō said as he lifted his left hand out from under the covers.

"Oh my god!" Miki cried. "It looks real." She reached across and gently clasped the other hand. "It feels so real too . . . But this is your hand!"

"Of course, it's mine. No repos, right, Doc?"

"No, even if you don't pay, we'll let you keep it. May I?" Dr. Sharmila asked as she held her hand out, asking Miki to relinquish Takurō's left hand.

"Any feeling? Could you feel your sister's hand?"

"I kind of think so, but it might be wishful thinking."

Dr. Sharmila surreptitiously poked his finger with a pushpin.

"Ouch!"

"Not wishful thinking," Dr. Sharmila said.

"Explain this!" Miki demanded.

"Kal told you it was a new experimental process," Takurō said.

"But that is your real hand. Not some replacement. I'd recognize it anywhere."

"I know, cool, isn't it?"

"But how?"

"They printed it on a three-D printer then attached it," Takurō said. "Then they pumped me full of stem cells, and those little buggers replaced everything with new cells, just like they're supposed to do."

Tears started streaming down Miki's cheeks. "They regrew your hand! What about your leg?"

"It's coming along just fine," Dr. Sharmila said as she lifted the sheet off of Takurō's legs. "How's this knee feeling?" she asked as she probed his right knee.

"That's his good knee!" Miki said.

"Well that's debatable," Dr. Sharmila said. "We had to do extensive repair on it after all the wear and tear from compensating for the prosthetic."

"It feels good, Doc," Takurō said. "I've been doing the exercise whenever I've been awake."

"Okay, I'll have them do a full panel on you tonight. If it comes back all clear, we'll unhook you from everything, and you can use a wheelchair to get around and visit your friends."

"When can he come home?"

"Next week, if things go well. We need to keep him here, so we're able to pump him full of stem cells while the regeneration finishes up. After that, he just has to come in every day for another week to do PT."

"Then, you'll be able to walk and everything?" Miki asked.

"Unfortunately, not everything," Takurō said with a frown.

"What won't you be able to do?" Miki gasped.

"Won't be able to dance for shit."

"We can't fix two left feet," Dr. Sharmila said.

"Oh, you nut!" Miki said as she slugged her brother on the shoulder. "You never could dance."

Miki walked behind Takurō's wheelchair as they made their way to the recreation room in the hospital. As she entered the room for the first time, she noticed just how many amputees were milling about. She knew Kal was collecting as many veterans as he could convince to join up with Delphi City Security, but seeing so many in one room, still hampered by the injuries, tore at her heart.

"Come on Sis," Takurō said. "There's cake over on the left. Let's get some, and I'll introduce you to some of the guys."

Takurō placed a drink in the cup-holder on his wheelchair then grabbed a big piece of chocolate cake. "Miki, grab one and follow me."

"Takurō! You old dog, where did you find that fine lady?"

Miki spun around and saw a large black man in a wheelchair pulling up to her brother. He was a double amputee. The mine he'd hit had torn up the muscles in his hip so he couldn't manage a prosthetic leg; he'd been stuck in a wheelchair ever since.

"Barry, this fine lady is my sister, Miki. Miki, this is Barry, we served together."

"Barry, nice to meet you." Miki shook hands with him.

"Nice to meet you too, Miki. Tell me how an ugly mutt like your brother could have such a fine-looking sister?"

"Well, he used to be good looking, but then he started drinking and hanging out with guys like you," Miki retorted.

"Good one! Well Takurō, that leg looks mighty good. When will you be walking on it?"

"I've got PT every day. I just took my first steps today. Feels weird since I don't have complete feeling in my foot yet, but the doc says not to worry."

"That's good to hear. They just started making my legs today. In two weeks, I go in to get them attached."

"You sure they can make 'em that black?" Takurō asked.

"Bro, they can make them pink, as long as they work."

"I hear you," Takurō said as he gave Barry a fist bump.

"Like the new hand," Barry said. "How's it working?"

"Hand is just fine. Seems like I never lost it now."

"That is good to hear. Miki, Takurō is proving out the process for the rest of us. I had to wait extra-long because it took them more time to tune the process so that it could reproduce the fine musculature of a black man."

"You are so full of it, Barry," Takurō laughed. "Anyone here for you?"

"No man, once I get patched up here, I have to do some calls and see if I can patch things up with the wife and kids," Barry said with a deep sadness in his voice.

"You'll do fine. Just keep up the good attitude," Takurō said.

"I will do that. It's much finer than that bad attitude I was carrying around," Barry said as he turned his wheelchair around and headed off. "See you around. Especially you, Miki."

"Bye."

"What was that about?" Miki asked.

"PTSD, he was homeless for a couple of years. His wife kicked him out when he wouldn't get help for it."

Chapter 33 Design Review

"Herr Johansson, this is our scooter designer, Catie McCormack, and our associate Liz Farmer," Samantha introduced everyone as Peter Johansson joined them. They were meeting in a conference room at the SKYCITY Grand Hotel in Auckland.

"But she's so young," Herr Johansson said. "How can she do such a wonderful design?"

"Be careful, Peter, she might take offense and ask you to play gin," Samantha said.

"Oh, I love gin," Herr Johansson said.

"Don't say I didn't warn you. I've reserved the room for two days in case you need more time. I'm off to do some shopping, so have fun," Samantha waved as she exited the room.

"I meant no offense," Herr Johansson said.

"It's okay," Catie said. "I get that a lot. Was there any place you'd like to start?"

"The brakes," Herr Johansson said. "They are the most important part of any vehicle, and these are very unusual."

"The front brakes are just induction brakes; that way they can return the braking energy back to the batteries," Catie said. "And they need almost no maintenance, and they don't wear out."

"That is especially important for our market."

"I thought so too. Now the rear brakes are just the induction motor running in reverse, just like you see on all electric cars. We're connecting the rear wheel via a shaft and screw, so we have lots of torque and again very little maintenance, unlike a chain."

"Yes, I like that," Herr Johansson said. "But let's look at the induction brake design, please."

◆ ◆ ◆

Four hours later, Catie and Herr Johansson were still at it.

"I changed the design of the front cowling so that it matches the tooling you already have," Catie said as she flipped the page to bring up yet another of the spec details to answer Herr Johansson's questions. She was starting to think that the design review would never end.

"Ah, I see that, very clever," Herr Johansson said.

"Eventually, I would like to switch over to polysteel, but we have limited capacity right now."

"Polysteel, I have never heard of it," Herr Johansson said.

"It's a new material invented by MacKenzie Discoveries," Catie said. "It is much stronger than steel and way lighter. It's also corrosion-resistant, kind of like titanium. When we have the capacity, we can form the main body as a monolithic shell. That will reduce the weight and increase safety.

"The electric motor delivers twenty-five horsepower, the batteries charge in ten minutes and will last for two hundred miles," Catie continued.

"I see you've designed it so that one only has to purchase the correct charging cord, and it will accept any voltage level," Herr Johansson said.

"Yes, of course it charges slower at a lower voltage, but hopefully gas stations will start adding charging pumps. Since they charge so fast, it should be economical for them to do that. We're worried that some people won't have the ability to charge their scooters at home."

"That is also my concern, which is why I am so happy to see such fast charging times. And one would assume that time would be much faster if the batteries are not completed discharged."

"Oh yes, some people would only need to charge theirs for two or three minutes if they charge before the battery is at fifty percent."

"Knock, Knock," Samantha came in. "You guys have been at it all day. How's it going?"

"Excellent," Herr Johansson said. "I am most pleased with what I have seen."

"Will you need the room tomorrow?"

"Oh yes, we still need to review the design of the motorbike."

"Okay, more shopping time for me," Samantha said. "But now, why don't we break and have dinner."

Chapter 34 They're awake

It was 03:00 when ADI pinged Marc's comm. It took him a moment to figure out what was going on. He rolled over and looked at his clock. "What's up, ADI?"

"Captain, we have an emergency. Commander Centag has been brought out of stasis."

"How is that possible?"

"I don't know. He has just brought three other officers out of stasis. I am analyzing the code to see how it has happened."

"What are they doing?"

"I do not know," ADI said. "I am trying to lock down the medical bay, but there is some override in the system that I cannot shut down."

"Wake Dr. Metra!"

"I'm on the comm," Dr. Metra said.

"How did they get out of stasis?" Marc asked.

"I don't know. Commander Centag must have programmed a backdoor and put it on a timer," Dr. Metra said.

"ADI, can you lock the bridge down?"

"I have," ADI said. "They have just exited the medical bay and are heading toward the officer quarters."

"Can you stop them?" Marc asked.

"I have that area of the ship locked down," ADI said. "I'm using the doctor's quarantine orders to isolate them from the crew areas."

"Is it working?" Dr. Metra asked.

"Yes, they tried to get into the bridge, but my lockout held. Now they're heading down toward the flight bays," ADI reported.

"How are they able to operate the elevator?" Marc asked.

"I don't know," ADI said. "They have somehow overridden my lockouts. I'm trying to analyze the code now."

"Do you have the flight bays locked?" Marc asked.

"I do, but I still don't understand how they overrode my lockout on the elevator," ADI said.

"Captain, they have overridden my lockout on Flight Bay One," ADI said. "I was unable to depressurize the bay fast enough."

"What would that have done?"

"The lock will not work with a pressure differential," ADI said. "All four are now through the lock. I am continuing to depressurize the bay."

"Can you prevent them from launching the Fox?"

"I should have been able to prevent them from exiting the medical bay," ADI said. "Since they were able to override my program, I cannot say. I am continuing to analyze the code to search for their overrides."

"Can you disable the Fox?"

"I am trying to," ADI said. "They have destroyed the communication pod on the Fox and are now boarding."

"All four?"

"No, Captain, just Commander Centag and Lieutenant Magals," ADI said. "The other two are trying to get back out of the flight bay."

"Trying?"

"I have depressurized the bay sufficiently that the lock will not cycle."

"Good. What is Commander Centag doing now?"

"He has just triggered an emergency launch sequence. I cannot override it. The bay doors are opening now."

"What about the other two crewmen?"

"They are drowning," ADI said. "Commander Centag has launched the Fox."

"Can you track it?"

"Without the communication pod, I will not be able to track the Fox."

"Launch the Lynx and try to follow him," Marc said.

"Captain, if he surfaces with the Fox he is in, he will be able to shoot the LX9 down," ADI said.

“Use it to track him underwater,” Marc said. “Bring the other three Foxes up to rendezvous with the Mea Huli. Alert the team that we need them on the Mea Huli now.”

“Yes, Captain. Launching the Lynx now. I should have him on sonar once it is out of the Sakira.”

“What’s up?” Blake said into the comm loudly.

“We’ve got an emergency,” Marc said. “We need our pilots to get to the Mea Huli and be ready to fly the Foxes. I’ll brief you when you’re aboard.”

Everyone scrambled out of their beds and raced downstairs. They grabbed a couple of jeeps and were tearing down the street toward the Mea Huli. It only took three minutes before they were climbing the ramp onto the Mea Huli.

“What the hell happened?” Blake asked as he and Marc ran to the bridge.

“One of the Foxes has been stolen!”

“How?”

“Commander Centag had some kind of sleeper code running. It woke him and his friends up and then let them into Flight Bay One.”

"I bet they were surprised to only find one Fox, good thing we moved the others to Flight Bay One," Blake said as he fired up the engines on the Mea Huli. "We're going to piss the port authorities off," he said as he pushed the throttle forward and freed them from the dock. Once free, he pushed the throttle all the way forward. The Mea Huli was quickly exceeding the five-knot speed limit.

“Yeah, especially, the two crew who couldn’t get into the Fox,” Marc said.

“What happened to them, stuck on the Sakira?”

“Drowned,” Marc said. “The commander did an emergency launch and flooded the bay. They were trapped there by ADI.”

Blake cocked his jaw, “Well, at least we only have one Fox and two hostiles to worry about.”

"ADI has the Lynx following them," Marc said. "The three Foxes are headed our way."

"You know the Lynx isn't a match for the Fox," Blake said.

"Its weapons don't work underwater," Marc said. "If they surface, we'll have one of the Foxes peel off and track them."

"Captain," ADI interrupted. "I've lost Commander Centag and the Fox."

"Why?"

"They've gone silent," ADI said. "Without an engine signature, the Lynx's sonar cannot see them."

"Did they stop and go to the bottom?"

"Possibly," ADI said. "It is a greater probability that they're coasting along on their last vector."

"Add two of the Foxes into the search pattern, bring the other one close to the Mea Huli, so if we locate our quarry, we can put a pilot on it quickly."

"So, what now?" Blake asked.

"You're the combat pilot, you tell me."

"We need to set up a rotation. We need to have a fresh pilot available when we locate it," Blake said. "Liz, Catie, and I can go on eight-hour shifts, so one of us is always well-rested."

"I'm not happy about putting Catie into a combat situation."

"Why? I'm our best pilot!"

Marc looked at Blake. Blake shrugged his shoulders; "She keeps kicking our asses in the simulations. She was working on the simulator before I realized there was one available on our comms."

"Well, what are the odds of one of you winning a dogfight with the commander?" Marc asked Blake.

"With Liz, ADI would actually do a better job; either way, the chances are fifty-fifty you lose a Fox and the pilot."

"With you?"

"ADI says, eighty-twenty, I outfly the commander."

"And Catie?"

"Ninety-ten."

"But a ten percent chance of losing my daughter," Marc groaned.

"What if ADI flies it?"

"Like I said, fifty-fifty," Blake said. "Seventy-thirty if she has two Foxes to engage with."

"Anything we can do to improve the odds?"

"ADI has the commander's flight records; we'll start reviewing them to see if we can learn his patterns."

"How much will that help?"

"I'll probably get up over ninety percent," Blake said. "Catie will probably top ninety-five. She reads the other pilot's tendencies like a seer."

"See, I told you!" Catie jumped in. "You can't ground me."

"Okay, we'll see what happens," Marc said. "First, we have to find them."

After a week, Marc called off the search. He knew the Fox and Commander Centag would eventually surface. He only hoped that his team would find them before they surfaced in the wrong place. He had ADI maximize surveillance in the southwest Pacific by moving one of their stealth satellites into the area over Australia to increase the resolution of coverage. He also had her sifting through all the communication they could intercept, looking for any indication of the Fox or Commander Centag.

"ADI, can you explain why Commander Centag was trying to reach the officer quarters first?" Marc asked. He was doing an after-action review with his core team.

"Yes, why head for his quarters before trying to take the bridge?" Kal asked.

"Something in his quarters that he needed," Blake suggested.

"There must be," Marc said. "We need to search his quarters. Do we know how he got out of stasis?"

"I am still analyzing the code," ADI said. "I need to coordinate with MADI, so it is taking longer. We do know that the stasis chambers were actually turned off and then opened, which was very dangerous."

"We need to search his quarters," Blake said.

"Take Kal with you," Marc said.

"Well, what did you find?" Marc asked.

"We found a relay unit," Blake said. He and Kal were standing in Commander Centag's quarters aboard the Sakira.

"Where was it?" Marc asked.

"It was under a hidden panel in the floor," Blake explained.

"How did you find the panel?"

"We didn't. ADI sent one of those little bots in, and it scanned everything. It found the little hollow space in the floor, so we pulled the panel up. The only thing in it was the communication relay."

"Can you be more specific?" Marc asked.

"Captain, it is half of a quantum pair. It is not one of the ones registered to the Sakira, and the other half is likely on Paraxea, or in Commander Centag's possession," ADI said. "It has a battery, so it is self-contained."

"Is it active?" Marc asked.

"No, Captain, it is not communicating," ADI said.

"I do not recommend trying to use it," Dr. Metra cut in. "We should just have ADI monitor it, but don't plug it into her communication board. It might have some vicious code in it."

"I agree," Kal said. "But how can ADI monitor it if we don't plug it in?"

"Cer Kal. It has an LED that lights up when it is active. I can monitor that if you'll place it on the bridge at one of the comm stations. That will put it on one of my normal sensor checks."

"Okay, we'll do that," Kal said. "I think we just wait and see whether anything comes across."

Chapter 35 Board Meeting – March 18th

"Let's start with updates, Samantha?" Marc opened the board meeting. They were holding this one on Manuae, so everyone could get a look at the new facilities.

"The prime minister approved the construction of the local apartment block on Arutanga," Samantha said. "You can start construction in two weeks. I've also completed the purchase of the Sky Princess. She should be here in two weeks."

"That is great news," Marc said. "Blake, are you ready to put some construction workers on her?"

"I wish she could get here sooner," Blake said. "But we'll make do with the space we have available in our dorms here."

"I didn't realize you needed space that soon."

"We've been stocking polysteel for months. I'm ready to start using it to build something."

Marc raised his eyebrows in surprise, "You are, huh?"

"Look out the window over there," Blake said.

Everybody got up and ran to the window. Outside, they could see a barge being loaded with polysteel beams. It already had four five-meter-diameter polysteel tubes on it, and four huge polysteel pontoons lashed down beside them.

"You've been holding out on me," Marc said.

"Just building up to a surprise," Blake said.

"ADI, why haven't you corrected Blake's status reports?"

"Captain, you never asked me to certify their veracity," ADI said. "Cer Blake assured me that you would be delighted at the surprise."

"How did you pull this off?" Marc asked.

"The third shift started last month," Blake said. "You've been a bit distracted, so you didn't notice, and I thought I'd let it slide."

"When are they placing the pontoons?"

"They're heading out in one hour," Blake said. "We should have the first quadrant ready for plating in one week."

"You're going to attach the pontoons on the barge?" Marc asked.

"Yeah, they'd be a bit unwieldy otherwise," Blake said. "We attach the foot, pump a few thousand gallons of water into it then kick it over the side. We can get all four done today."

"Then we're going to go watch," Marc said as he headed toward the stairs. "Do we have plenty of Champagne on the Mea Huli?"

"We're always fully stocked," Fred said. "We also happen to have one of the finest chefs in the Cook Islands engaged for the next three days."

Marc ran like a little kid, beating everyone onto the pier and out to the Mea Huli. As he got close, he realized that the boat was covered in streamers and balloons. He just laughed as he climbed aboard and made his way up to the bridge.

"I have never seen your father this animated," Samantha said to Catie. "We need to have more surprises."

"Good idea."

"You've really done some planning," Marc said as he came up to the bridge a few minutes later.

"The party was Catie's idea. She got Sam to help."

"You like it, Daddy?" Catie asked as she and Samantha reached the bridge.

"I love it!"

"You looked like you could use a party," Samantha said. "I thought Catie had the perfect idea."

Fred went to the pilothouse and started the Mea Huli's engines. After they'd warmed up a bit and everyone had a glass of Champagne, he had the crewman cast off, and the Mea Huli headed out after the tug and barge.

Catie took a few pictures of the tug and barge as they got underway, then she joined the festivities with a glass of apple cider. "To Delphi City," she toasted.

Everyone raised their glass. "To Delphi City!"

They spent the afternoon watching the beginning of their new city. The massive crane on the one-hundred-fifty-meter barge lifted the first of the pontoons. It held it sideways just off the end of the barge. The construction workers pushed one of the five-meter-diameter pipes, so it hung over the edge of the barge and butted up against the ellipsoid pontoon. After they attached the temporary clamps, they started welding the pieces together using the special plasma torches. The torches joined the polysteel as though it had been formed as a single piece. It took an hour for the two welders to weld the pieces together. They pumped two thousand gallons of water into the pontoon, and the crane slowly let the pontoon sink into the water. Once it stabilized and was vertical, the polysteel tube was sticking up out of the sea twenty meters.

"How long was that thing?" Samantha asked.

"The tubes are eighty meters long," Blake said. "Once it's done, we'll float the deck at ten meters above the water. That way, it doesn't interfere with the natural wave action against the Manuae reefs."

"Dr. McGenty strikes again," Samantha laughed.

"Yes, he's really serious about the environment."

"How are you going to keep it from floating away?" Samantha asked. "Don't tell me Dr. McGenty is going to let you anchor it to the ocean floor."

"No, each quad is designed to have four small waterjet engines attached to its four outside pontoons, they will hold it in place," Blake explained. "This is just a quarter quad, so we'll use a tug to keep it in place until we get the other three pieces ready."

"They're getting ready to lift the second pontoon," Catie shouted excitedly.

Everyone turned and watched as the second pontoon was lowered into the water. "Are they going to attach them together?" Catie asked.

"After they get all four of them up," Blake said. "They'll just cable them together for now."

Over the next three days, they watched as the workers assembled the first quarter section of the city. The two-hundred-meter spans of polysteel were braced against the columns in four directions. Two sides of the quarter section had fifty-meter overhangs, while the other two sides terminated at the column waiting for the two hundred-meter span of polysteel to connect it to the next part of the quad. The last piece of decking was being lowered into place, as everyone stood with glasses ready to toast. Soon they were looking at a two-hundred-fifty-meter by two-hundred-fifty-meter platform that would support the start of their new city.

"To Delphi City," Marc toasted as he raised his glass.

Everyone raised their glass in reply, "To Delphi City!"

"Why are there so many holes in this deck?" Samantha asked as she walked around.

"This is the underdeck," Blake said. "We'll be adding a ten-meter-tall wall around the perimeter, with support beams. Then we'll put the main deck down. All the utilities and equipment will be down here."

"Oh, so why the holes?"

"Less weight, better airflow. We can seal any areas we want, but most of this is just going to be pipes and conduits."

"Then why have the decking? You could just hang that below the main decking and build rooms where you need them."

"Unfortunately, sometimes waves come along that are bigger than ten meters," Blake said. "We wouldn't want all our plumbing and such to get torn up by one of them."

"Ah, I didn't realize that."

"Neither did I until Dr. McGenty pointed it out during the first pass design review."

"Hey, he's earning his money then."

"He's still a pain in the ass."

"Here's to pains in the ass, may their visitations be brief," Samantha toasted.

"Hear, hear!"

"You can see why we need the Sky Princess," Blake said. "We need room for all the workers who will put the infrastructure in place. We want to do that before we put the main decking down."

"It looks like you'll have the first section completed by the time it gets here," Marc said.

"Yes, the cargo ship with all the fixtures should be here next week," Blake said. "We can at least get them unloaded. We're going to store all the equipment up here."

"Aren't we a little close to Manuae?" Liz asked. "I thought we were going to put the city out about a mile."

"We are," Blake said. "Once we have the first quad done, we'll put a polysteel production facility on it, and then we'll use those waterjet engines to push it out farther. Right now, we want to minimize transit time. That barge is really slow."

"What are you going to put in the first quad?" Samantha asked.

"Catie, this is your question," Blake said.

"Oh, sure. Uncle Blake already told you we're putting in a fabrication facility for the polysteel. We're also going to move all the other fab from Manuae to the first quad. We'll keep the polysteel going in both places until the first section is finished. Then we'll start restoring Manuae. The first quad will be six hundred forty thousand square meters. That's about sixty-four city blocks or one hundred sixty acres," Catie said. "It's mostly the wharf area and manufacturing, but we're going to put some greenhouses and farming areas on it so we can grow our own food. We want it to be self-sufficient as soon as possible."

"You're going to grow food on it?" Samantha asked incredulously.

"We're even going to plant trees. This quad's only going to get about ten trees since it's going to be mostly industrial," Catie added. "But I've got some really cool trees planned."

"What are you going to do for water? Is it going to rain enough?"

"We're putting in a desalination plant," Catie said, "but we'll recycle the water and capture rainwater whenever we get rain."

"Recycled water, for the greenhouses, right?"

"No, for everything," Catie said. "It gets filtered so well that it's foolish to separate it. It's going to be like a spaceship, everything will get recycled, and there will be almost no waste."

"Okay . . . ," Samantha said, still not convinced.

"Then, of course, we'll have a couple of office buildings and dorms for the workers to use while we build the other quads," Catie said. "Nothing will be over ten stories. The next quad will have apartments and condos, then it will start to look like a real city. And of course, we'll be adding more manufacturing."

"I know I'm supposed to know this, but how many people do you think will be living there?"

"When it's finished, it's going to be one square mile of city. It will be able to house twenty to thirty thousand people, depending on how tall we make the condos," Catie answered.

"That's more people than live in all of the Cook Islands."

"That's because everyone goes to New Zealand for jobs. Maybe some of them will come back. And of course, we'll have lots of immigration from other parts of the world," Catie said. "Once we build the floating airport, we'll be able to add three more sections, then we'll be up to around sixty thousand."

"My, I forgot how ambitious we were," Samantha chuckled. "I have a meeting to go to. Fred, can you fly me to Wellington?"

"Sure," Fred said. "We'll see you guys tomorrow."

"Bye," Marc said as he gave Samantha a quick kiss.

"Bye-bye," Samantha said.

"Maybe we should go back to the Mea Huli and have lunch, then we can finish that board meeting we were having," Marc said. As they made their way back, Marc got Catie alone, "Thanks for the party, it almost makes me forget about the disaster we're having."

"Oh, Daddy, we'll find them."

Once they were back on the Mea Huli, Marc restarted the updates. "Back to work. Where are we with Herr Johansson?"

"He loved my design, and Samantha's going to close the deal right now," Catie said. "She says she'll bring the contract back for you to sign. I think he's hoping to have new scooters coming off the line in a month."

"While it's just the five of us, how about an update on our spy situation?" Marc asked.

"Logan is a pretty good dancer," Liz said, making Catie giggle.

"I was thinking more in the line of what they have learned and what kinds of questions they're asking," Marc said.

"Well, Sasha has become quite enamored with Manuae," Kal said. "She's always looking for an excuse to come here."

"Why is that?" Marc asked.

"You don't think she wants to admire our architecture?" Blake quipped.

Marc gave Blake a steely look, then he turned to Kal and rolled his hands, signaling him to continue.

"She's bringing this small computer with her," Kal said. "She keeps trying to hack into our comm network."

"You didn't think I should be apprised of that?" Marc scolded.

"You have enough going on," Kal said. "Besides, ADI has it handled. She's created a fake network for Sasha to try and hack into. She's tracing all her work back to the source."

"ADI?" Marc called out.

"Yes Captain," ADI said. "I'm building a map of all the Russian hacking sources as well as a library of their various hacks."

"What about the Chinese?" Marc asked.

"Ying Yue has just started to bring a computer along on her dates with Cer Blake," ADI said.

"Apparently I managed to keep her entertained longer than Kal did Sasha," Blake said.

"Oh, get real!" Kal said.

"Do you anticipate any problems?" Marc asked.

"I've got her covered," Blake said.

"I was asking ADI."

"No Captain. The Chinese code doesn't appear to be as sophisticated as the Russian code. But I'll continue to map out the sources of all their computers," ADI said. "We can use that later if you decide you would like to send a virus attack their way."

"What about the British?"

"No activity there, outside of Cer Logan's dates with Cer Liz," ADI said.

"Any unusual questions?" Marc asked the group.

"I don't think so," Liz said. "Logan is interested in our production capacity and what we might have coming next."

"Pretty much the same here," Kal said. "Other than trying to hack the network, just the standard what do you do questions."

"What about our American spy?" Marc said.

"Oh, he's been here, but he's not done much," Kal said.

Chapter 36 Take Down

Day 1 14:10 CKT

ADI pinged Marc's comm.

"Yes ADI?"

"Captain, I detected a reference to an advanced fighter jet in a communication with the Chinese Consulate in Perth, Australia. It is a vague reference about the opportunity to purchase an advanced fighter."

"Put two surveillance drones in that area," Marc instructed.

"It would be more efficient if I transported them in the LX9," ADI said. "They could be in place within two hours."

"Do it."

"Which pilot should I use?"

"Who's on-call?" Marc asked. Even though he'd given up the search, he'd kept his three pilots on a rotation so that a well-rested one would be available should the need arise.

"Commander Blake," ADI responded.

"Send him."

ADI pinged Blake's comm and gave him the instructions.

"Hey, Bro. Good news?" Blake asked.

"Maybe. ADI picked up a communication about an advanced fighter for sale. Sounds like Centag is trying to sell the Fox to the Chinese," Marc said.

"I bet an invitation to bid is going out to the Russians as well," Blake said.

"ADI?"

"I have instituted additional communication surveillance on all the embassies and consulates in Australia," ADI replied.

"Any idea where the communication originated from?" Marc asked.

"It appears to have originated within Perth via cellphone," ADI replied.

"Where's the cellphone?"

"It is currently turned off."

"Who is it registered to?"

"It was purchased yesterday in Perth; you would call it a burner phone. I am accessing the surveillance cameras in that area to try and determine who purchased it," ADI explained.

"Blake?"

"I'm already halfway to the Mea Huli," Blake said. "Should be airborne in thirty. Kal's with me to drive the boat."

"Thanks," Marc said. He gave a big sigh and rested his head in his hands, "Finally."

Day 1 14:40 CKT

"Okay guys, we have a lead," Marc said to open the meeting. "Blake and ADI have two surveillance drones hovering over Perth. Now that we have a general location, we need a plan."

"My guess is that they landed next to one of those big farms or sheep stations back there. Then they took the farmer's family hostage and are using their home as a base," Kal said.

"How could they get away with that?" Catie asked. "Wouldn't the neighbors notice?"

"Neighbors are miles apart out there. They probably don't go into town that often," Kal said. "You could land the Fox on one of the roads and drive it into a barn or shed."

"ADI, check to see if there's any chatter about a family that's dropped out of sight in the last three weeks. Or changed their town visiting habits during the same time period," Marc instructed.

"Yes, Captain."

"What do we do if we find them?" Blake asked.

"Yes, and do we know how they overrode all the command codes and bypassed ADI?" Liz asked.

"Yes," Marc said. "ADI explain for everyone."

"Yes, Captain. I discovered the virus that Commander Centag placed in the systems. It was a very sophisticated piece of code. It contained the previous captain's credentials and exploited a defect that allowed them to still be active. Commander Centag placed the code into the systems sometime before Dr. Metra ordered the quarantine. It bypassed the controls on the stasis chamber and deactivated the four of them. It was a very dangerous move since there is a high probability that the subject in stasis will die when the chamber is simply turned off and opened."

"Can you fix it?" Catie asked.

"I have removed the code," ADI said. "If we can establish a comm link to the FX4, I can reestablish control over it."

"How do we do that?" Kal asked.

"We need to get a comm within four meters of the spacecraft."

"That's close," Kal said.

"What if it's underwater?" Catie asked.

"There would have to be contact between the FX4 and one of the other spacecraft or a drone," ADI replied. "Then I would have a direct link to the system's communication."

"Nothing like making it easy," Blake said.

"Could we put an arm or something on the Fox so that it could extend a comm out?" Catie asked.

"The FX4 and the LX9 both have remote arms beneath the cockpit," ADI said.

"How long does the contact have to be?" Catie asked.

"Five seconds."

Catie sat back and smiled at everyone. "We just have to herd Centag's Fox. Once we find it, with the Lynx and three Foxes, we should be able to get one close enough to make contact."

"That sounds dangerous," Marc said. "He's desperate and might do something that would destroy his Fox and whichever one is close to him."

"Then we wait him out, stay on his tail until he runs out of food, water, patience," Kal said. "With three Foxes and ADI driving the Lynx, we should be able to hound him into the ground."

"Okay, so how do we find them?" Marc asked.

"We watch, we listen, and we wait," Kal said. "We should put some assets on the ground around Perth. We might be able to pick up some clues about where they're hiding."

"Who?"

"I'll take a team of three," Kal said. "It's not the same as Afghanistan but the same principle, and they speak English."

"Are you sure about that," Liz said. "Have you tried talking to an Aussie?"

"Oh, they kind of speak English," Kal laughed. "I'll see if any of our guys speak Aussie. ADI, can you link in my team?"

"Ready," ADI said.

"Guys, we have some work to do down by Perth. Anyone familiar with the area, especially if you can speak the local patois, send me a message. Thanks, ADI."

"Of course, Cer Kal."

"Okay, assets on the ground, sniffing around. We have ADI monitoring the communications, and the probes giving us up-close surveillance," Marc said. "Anything else?"

"Time," Kal said. "Oh, I just heard back. We have a woman on the security team who used to date a guy from Perth. She's been there a few times and says she's comfortable with the accent. I'll add her to my team."

"Good," Marc said. "Have Fred give you a ride over."

Day 3 04:32 CKT -- 22:32 AWST

A comm alert came up on Marc's HUD. "Yes, ADI."

"An ATM machine was just robbed in northeast Perth."

"Our guys?"

"Based on surveillance video, they used a plasma torch to open it," ADI said.

"A Paraxean device?"

"Yes, Captain."

"How much did they get?" Marc asked.

"The machine was just filled; they got seventy-two thousand Australian dollars."

"Whoever they're camping out with must have run out of cash."

"A high probability," ADI said.

"Inform Kal and the rest of the command team."

"I have, Captain."

"Thanks, ADI."

Day 4 21:32 CKT -- 15:32 AWST

Marc's HUD pinged him with an alert from Kal. "Hello, Kal, good news, I hope."

"We think we know where they're hiding out," Kal said.

"How?"

"Jen's been chatting with the women at the local market here in Tigwell. They've told her that this guy Boswell hasn't been to town as much as usual in the last few weeks. Apparently, he usually brings one of his kids with him, and the last two times he's been in, no kids and some big guy hanging around."

"You think the guy is our missing commander?" Marc asked.

"I'm pretty sure. He always wears one of the Aussie sun hats that cover the neck and ears," Kal said.

"Makes sense," Marc said. "What about the nose?"

"Jen says one of the women said he must have whacked himself on the nose because he was wearing a Band-Aid on it."

"Okay, so where's his place?"

"Forty klicks east of town," Kal said. "We're sending a drone over that way."

"Okay, I'll get our pilots ready."

Day 4 22:32 CKT --16:32 AWST

"Kal is confident that they know where our missing Fox is," Marc said as he met with his three pilots.

"Good," Blake said. "We're ready. We'll go ahead, get underway, and get our planes over in that area. When we know for sure he's there, we'll wait until dark and come in fast from three different directions."

"Everyone, be careful. It's 17:00 in Perth right now, dark at 19:00," Blake said. "Let's go get our babies in the air."

Marc looked at Catie in her flight suit. It was hard to imagine that the woman there was his thirteen-year-old daughter. "You be careful," he said to her.

"Don't worry, Daddy," Catie said as she gave her father a quick hug and ran out after Blake.

Day 4 11:32 CKT -- 17:32 AWST

"We're outside the ranch," Kal said. "Everything's quiet right now. Sun's just setting."

"Good," Blake said. "We're cruising off the coast, skimming the deck to avoid detection."

"We think the Fox is in the barn. There are a few wide tracks going into it that fit with the Fox's landing gear."

"We'll pop up in thirty," Blake said. "We'll come in high at Mach five; circle once to bleed off our speed; then we'll tighten the noose."

"Copy."

Day 4 00:40 CKT -- 18:40 AWST

"On our way," Blake announced as the three Foxes tilted up and tore into the sky, accelerating to Mach five.

"Captain, I have a text to the Chinese Consulate from the Boswell ranch," ADI announced over the comm.

"What did it say?"

"It said 'now,' and gave a set of coordinates in the Philippine Sea."

"Did everybody copy?" Marc asked.

"Copied," Blake said.

"Copied," Kal said. "We have movement! They're making a break for the barn!"

CRACK! CRACK!

"One Down!" Kal barked. "The other is hit, but he made it into the barn!"

"The Fox is coming out! She's airborne!"

Day 4 00:52 CKT -- 18:52 AWST

"It just flew under me!" Catie yelled, "I'm circling to follow!"

"Right behind you, girl!" Liz responded.

"What's the situation on the ground?" Marc asked.

"We've got one down; we'll police the body and get out of here. The rancher's family is safe, and he just wants us gone."

"Any worries about police?"

"Don't think so," Kal said. "He's pretty adamant that he just wants to wash his hands of this mess. And I think he's hoping to keep the sixty to seventy thousand sitting in a bag in his pantry."

"Okay, clear out; I'll send Fred to pick you up," Marc said.

"It will take us a few hours to get back to Perth. We'll meet him at the airport," Kal said.

Day 4 01:00 CKT -- 19:00 AWST

"I'm on his tail, I can't get into weapons range," Catie said. "We need someone to go up high to make up the distance."

"On my way up," Blake said. "Liz, go up high too."

"Copy," Liz replied.

Day 4 01:20 CKT -- 19:20 AWST

"We're ahead of him," Blake announced. "Liz, come down on his tail, I'll circle and come at him head-on. Weapons free."

"Copy."

"He's dropping to the deck!" Catie barked. "I think he's going to go submarine."

"Stay on him," Blake commanded. "We don't want to lose him again."

"Copy, he's not getting away from me."

Catie followed the other Fox down to the ocean surface; they were both skimming the surface at Mach five. "He's going to turn and dump speed so they can submerge!"

"Do you know which way?"

"Not yet!"

Catie studied her quarry as they both raced across the surface of the ocean. "Which way are you going to go?" she whispered. She continued to watch him as she watched Liz's and Blake's Foxes approaching. "Liz, cut west and drop to the deck!" Catie ordered.

Catie watched as Liz's Fox dropped to the surface and cut to the west blocking their quarry's path. Just as Liz was drawing into weapons range, their opponent popped off of the deck, banked hard, and turned north. "Gotcha," Catie said as she was already banking her Fox to the north. Using the turn to bleed off speed as fast as possible, in seconds, Catie was going slow enough to skim the water. She had closed the distance with their opponent but still was outside of weapons range. "He's going to go under any second!"

The other Fox dropped down and submerged. "First time, huh," Catie whispered as she submerged. She was able to accomplish it without having to drop off nearly as much speed as the other Fox. Her Fox was only fifty meters behind his once they leveled off at eighty meters. "I'm on him!" Catie announced. "He's got nowhere to go!"

"That's great, but you're not going to be able to catch him," Marc said.

"Not yet," Catie said. "We can try to have one of the others get in his way, slow him down."

"I want that Fox back," Blake said. "I say we wait him out!"

"Wait him out?"

"Like Kal said, he's got no food, or at least not much. How long do you think he can last?"

"How long can we last?" Marc asked.

"We can rotate," Blake said. "Catie takes four hours, then I'll ride his tail. Between the three of us, we can stay rested, fed, and just wear him out."

"Captain," ADI broke in.

"Yes, ADI."

"The Chinese aircraft carrier Liaoning has left its homeport of Qingdao and is steaming toward the Philippine Sea."

"How long until they can meet up?"

"Eighty-six hours," ADI said.

"About three-and-a-half days," Marc did the math for everyone. "Can he last that long?"

"He gave them the coordinates," Blake said. "He must think he can hold out that long."

"If he's got water, it would only take a few granola bars and some chocolate, and he'd be okay for food," Kal said.

"Okay. Blake set up your rotations; we have three days to figure out what to do about the Chinese Navy."

Day 5 20:00 CKT -- 14:00 ACST

"I've got overwatch," Catie announced as she flew up on Liz.

"Copy," Liz acknowledged. "Blake, I'm on my way."

"About time," Blake replied. "I really need some sleep. I wonder how our disreputable commander is making out."

"I'm sure he has it on autopilot," Catie said. "We keep making up a little distance on him each shift, so he's not paying too close of attention."

"Well I wish we could get close enough to tag him out," Blake said. "This is getting old."

"What's your distance?" Liz asked.

"I'm at twenty meters," Blake replied.

"We won't make it before he reaches the Chinese carrier," Catie said.

"If he tries to surface, we'll be close enough to take out his engines," Blake said.

"I think he knows that," Catie said. "What do you think he's hoping for?"

"Maybe he doesn't think we know how to fly," Liz said.

"Probably, he's making it up as he goes," Blake said. "He wasn't expecting us."

"Then why did he pick a rendezvous out in the middle of the Philippine Sea?" Catie asked.

"He knew ADI was trying to catch him from when he launched from the Sakira," Blake said. "So he needed to stay under until he was close enough for a handoff and could get the Fox out of sight. The carrier must have been his worst-case backup plan. Three Foxes coming in on him had to spook him."

"You think he was that well prepared?"

"He was planning this, or something like it for a long time," Blake said.

"I'm with Uncle Blake on this one," Catie said.

"I'm here," Liz announced, "You're relieved, Commander Blake, go get some sleep."

"You don't have to ask me twice."

Day 7 10:00 CKT -- 04:00 ACST

"I've got two bogies approaching at Mach one point two!" Catie yelled. Catie was in her third hour of overwatch for Liz. "ADI alert the staff. Liz, are you okay down there?"

"I'm good," Liz replied. "Does this mean I'm going to get paid overtime?"

"I would count on it," Catie said. "We'll handle things up here, you stay on Centag down there."

"I'm on my way," Blake announced. "I'll be there in thirty."

The Mea Huli had been working its way from Rarotonga for the last three days. It was now just off Papua New Guinea, so Blake was just a few minutes' flight away.

"Copy."

Day 7 10:21 CKT -- 04:21 ACST

"I've got missile launches!" Catie barked. She put her Fox into a corkscrew to the right and punched the throttle. "ADI, take out the missiles!"

"Yes, Cer Catie." As Catie corkscrewed around the two missiles, ADI fired the forward lasers taking out the first one, then the second.

"Missiles destroyed," Catie announced. "I'm going to come around on him and nail his engines with the plasma cannon."

"Watch out for his wingman," Blake yelled.

"I see him, I'm up to Mach three; he's too far for even a missile launch." Catie continued her corkscrew until she was under the incoming Chinese fighter. She pulsed the plasma cannon for half a second and punched the throttle to max. As she screamed by the fighter, she could see two chutes.

"One down, crew has ejected!" Catie announced. "I'm rounding on the second one, I'll be there in two."

"The carrier has launched another fighter," ADI announced. "And a second is preparing to launch."

"I'm on them," Blake announced. "I'm going to go wide and come across their tails. If I'm good, I'll get both their engines before they realize I'm coming."

"You've never been good," Liz laughed.

"I'm so bad, I'm good," Blake countered.

"I'll give you that," Liz laughed. "Now be careful."

"Always."

Day 7 10:24 CKT -- 04:24 ACST

"I'm crossing him now," Catie announced. "He's launched two missiles. I'll take him out first then deal with them."

Catie pushed her throttle up until she was doing Mach 5. She corkscrewed up to the left. When her Fox reached the top, she broke off of the spin for one second and then corkscrewed down in the opposite direction. "Ha, knew you would fall for that," she laughed as she saw the missiles lose target lock.

Catie was just coming into range when the fighter launched another two missiles and dove hard for the deck. "No way, buster!" Catie banked hard and got her nose turned around as she fired her plasma cannons. "Gotcha!" she said with relish as the rear of the Chinese jet's engine exploded. She watched with concern to see if the crew would be able to eject. Finally, she saw two chutes. The four missiles that had been launched were searching for a contact after losing the target lock provided by the fighter. It only took Catie two minutes to knock them down.

Day 7 10:27 CKT -- 04:27 ACST

"Uncle Blake! How are you doing?"

"Coming up on our two new friends now," Blake replied. "Catie, I want you to drop to the deck; come in on the carrier at Mach three. When you get into cannon range, pop up; blast their launch deck; then get the hell out of there, go straight up."

"Copy!" Catie confirmed.

"Liz, how are things down there?" Blake asked.

"I'm just sitting on his tail. No activity down here," Liz said.

"He's blind while he's underwater," Catie said.

"Copy that," Liz said.

◆ ◆ ◆

"I'm on the deck now," Catie announced.

"Good, I'm getting ready to cross the tails of our two new fighters in ten, . . . five . . . one . . . I scorched their tails; both have lost their engines. I see chutes."

"I'm coming up on the carrier," Catie announced. "Ten . . . five . . . one. Plasma locked on; firing; going vertical." Catie's Fox shot into the air corkscrewing as the carrier launched their air defense missiles. Within five seconds, she was doing Mach 5.2 and leaving the antiaircraft missiles behind.

"The Chinese carrier is turning around," ADI announced.

"Good," Marc said. "What about the pilots?"

"They've sent out a search and rescue helicopter to pick them up."

"Catie, head back; I'll relieve you," Blake commanded.

"I'm supposed to relieve Liz," Catie said.

"Trust me, you need to take a break," Blake said. "I'll switch places with Liz."

"You just got yanked out of bed," Catie said.

"I'll let ADI fly and take a nap until you can rotate back in. We'll get back on cycle after that."

Day 8 02:10 CKT -- 08:10 EST

"Admiral, there was an incident in the Philippine Sea yesterday. Four Chinese Shenyang J-15 jets appear to have been shot down," a commander said as he knocked on Admiral Michaels' door.

"When did this happen?" the admiral asked.

"Approximately four hours ago."

"How did we find out?" Admiral Michaels asked.

"We picked up comm traffic between the aircraft and the carrier Liaoning. The pilots reported an aircraft approaching, they said they gave the signal as instructed and did not get a response, so it appears that they assumed it was hostile."

"So, they were expecting a friend?" the admiral asked.

"It seems so. The Liaoning left port in a hurry and steamed at full speed to the Philippine Sea."

"So how did this result in them losing four planes?"

"The first two pilots reported that they launched two missiles once they didn't get the proper response."

"No provocation?"

"Correct sir."

"They must have wanted a private party with their friend," Admiral Michaels said. "And then?"

"The approaching fighter instituted evasive maneuvers, shot down the two missiles, and then took out the first plane's engines."

"What was the second plane doing?"

"It was trying to circle around to pin the other fighter in. The pilot reported that the enemy fighter accelerated away at Mach five. He says it outran his missiles."

Admiral Michaels sat up straighter and leaned forward. "That's not believable."

"He also claimed that he could barely get a target lock on it, that it had almost no radar signature."

"How did he get shot down?"

"That enemy plane circled around and dropped out of sight. When he saw it again, he launched two missiles, the plane evaded them, so he launched two more. He says the plane was doing Mach five when it banked behind him and destroyed his plane."

"Where do the other two come in?"

"They were launched as soon as their first plane declared hostilities, sir."

"How were they taken out?"

"The pilot reported a second plane came up off the deck and destroyed their engines with cannon fire. They said they couldn't respond in time because it was also doing Mach five."

"So, are these pilots telling stories to save face after being shot down?"

"I don't know, sir, but satellite imagery shows the Liaoning returning to port. She's missing the end of her jump ramp."

"So, the planes launched a missile at the carrier?"

"Pretty surgical strike to just take out the end of the ramp, sir."

"And where are our friends?"

"The Mea Huli is off of Papua New Guinea."

"A bit far from their new home."

"Yes, sir. They turned around and headed back toward Rarotonga right after the incident with the carrier was reported."

"Now that is interesting," Admiral Michaels said.

"That's what I thought. I assumed you would like to know. I don't see how the incidents are related, but it is a strange coincidence, sir."

"Yes, it is. Thank you," Admiral Michaels said.

Day 9 01:10 CKT -- 19:10 ACST

"Uncle Blake, are you ready?" Catie asked as she flew, prepared to replace Liz in overwatch so that Liz could replace Blake in dogging their wayward Fox.

"Definitely, I'm bored to tears."

"Any change in course?"

"No, he's on the exact same course as he was yesterday."

"No pop-ups or jogs?"

"No. Liz, have you noticed anything up there?"

"No."

"Catie, what are you thinking?" Blake asked.

"I'm thinking it's time to try and bump him," Catie said.

"Okay, you and Liz both come down and line up in front of him. Let's see if he tries to dodge," Blake commanded.

"On our way."

Catie and Liz dropped onto the water and let their Foxes slow until they could dive. Then they dove down in front of Blake and their quarry, proceeding on the course at their top underwater speed. Once they were synced up on course, Catie was positioned ten meters to the right, and Liz was ten meters to the left.

"We're synced up," Catie said. "Slowing now."

"He's not moving," Blake said. "Maybe he fell asleep."

"It's been over three days," Catie said. "He's been sleeping before. What's changed?"

"ADI?"

"I can detect no changes," ADI said. "He last came up to recalibrate his course fourteen hours ago."

"That's a big gap," Blake said.

"Yeah, he's been popping up every eight to nine hours," Catie said.

"Let's see if we can bump him," Blake said.

"I'm sliding over," Catie said. She continued to let her Fox slow down as she eased it over next to their target. "Extending the arm . . . contact."

"I have control," ADI said. "I detect no life signs on the Fox."

"Where's Commander Centag?"

"He appears to be in the pilot seat," ADI said. "It seems he is dead."

"Get the Foxes back to the Sakira," Marc broke in. "We'll figure out what's going on there. Dr. Metra and I will meet you there with the Lynx."

Day 9 14:10 CKT

As soon as the Lynx and the Fox were in the flight bay and the water level was below the port, Marc and Dr. Metra were in the dinghy rowing over to the Fox.

"Hey, you closed the door on us," Catie snapped.

"Use Flight Bay One," Marc retorted. "We're busy here."

"Yes, sir," Catie muttered in a surly tone.

"I heard that!"

"Sorry."

"ADI, raise the canopy on the Fox," Marc commanded. "Any signs of life?"

"Canopy rising, Captain. And I still do not detect any life signs."

"Can he mask his life signs?"

"It is unlikely," ADI replied.

As the dinghy bumped up against the Fox, Dr. Metra stood up, grasped the edge of the cockpit, and looked inside. "He's not masking them," she said.

"Dead?"

"Very."

"How?"

"His oxygen mask is off," Dr. Metra said.

"That would explain it," ADI said. "I detected no cabin oxygen when I established contact. He had cut off the cabin air when he submerged the plane. I assume it was to prevent me from doing the same or introducing a sleeping gas into it."

"You could do that?" Marc asked.

"Yes, Captain," ADI replied. "There is a failsafe sleeping gas canister to deal with potential problems."

"Couldn't you have injected it into his air supply as well?"

"Normally, I could, Captain, but he seems to have modified the system."

"Okay, so why shut off his own mask?"

"I have no data; however, he did so twelve hours ago."

"That explains the lack of maneuvering, and his not popping up to recalibrate," Catie said over the comm.

"ADI, continue to evacuate the water," Marc said. "We'll deal with him here, then decide what to do."

"Yes, Captain."

Day 9 15:10 CKT

"Dr. Metra, what do you make of the situation?" Marc asked. The team was meeting in the conference room in the captain's cabin aboard the Sakira.

"I don't know. The commander and the three he released with himself were the main trouble makers on the Sakira," Dr. Metra explained. "I would assume if he had other allies, he would have brought them along. With the four FX4s he expected to find inside Flight Bay One, he could have taken seven others."

"That makes sense," Marc said. "What did you find on his body?"

"I did not find the other half of the communication relay," Dr. Metra said.

"So, it's probably on Paraxea with his allies," Marc suggested.

"I would assume," Dr. Metra said. "There must have been more to his plan than just killing the captain."

"Do you think that the rest of the crew are safe?" Marc asked.

"Do you mean their health, or if can you trust them?" Dr. Metra asked.

"Whether we can trust them," Marc answered.

"I'm not sure. We are far outside of standard protocol. Although with you as captain, I'm not sure what they can do. Maybe we should ask ADI."

"ADI, given our current situation, are there any circumstances where a member of the crew could violate my orders and try to communicate with Paraxea?"

"No, Captain. They would need your permission to access the external communications."

"Are there any circumstances where they could trigger a protocol so that you would communicate with Paraxea?" Marc asked.

"I am sending the standard updates to Paraxea now, Captain. The crew would not be able to change how I do that," ADI said.

"Are there any circumstances where you would communicate more to Paraxea than you have currently been instructed to by Dr. Metra or me?" Marc asked.

"That would only occur if all members of the command crew were dead as well as the doctor," ADI said. "There are five of you now."

"Is there a way to prevent that?"

"Only by ensuring that there is always a living person to assume command," ADI said.

"I'm good with staying alive," Blake said.

"Huh," Marc said, "I am too. Okay, so back to the crew. What would the advantage be of bringing them out of stasis?"

"There are one hundred forty-five remaining crewmembers," Dr. Metra said. "ADI, please list the officers and their qualifications."

"Yes, Doctor. There are eighteen officers left in stasis: four intelligence, officers who are essentially analysts; the chief engineer; two pilots; the propulsion engineer; the communications engineer; the robotics engineer; the weapons engineer; the reactor engineer; two hydroponics engineers; the science officer; the navigator; the electronics engineer; the environmental engineer; and the chief steward."

"That is a nice collection of knowledge," Marc said. "But explain the chief steward."

"The chief steward is responsible for life inside the Sakira. All the cleaning, the cooking, food supplies, the hydroponics and environmental systems, and all non-ship-critical maintenance."

"I see. That makes sense. That is a lot of talent."

"Yes, it takes a lot of specialized knowledge to run a starship. We also have a contingent of civilian scientists."

"ADI, please list the scientists," Marc asked.

"There is an architect, a chemist, an energy scientist, an environmental scientist, an anthropologist, an astrophysicist, and a physicist," ADI iterated.

"And the crew?" Marc asked.

"ADI, please list the crew for ship operations first," Dr. Metra instructed.

"There are six ship pilots, eight weapons specialists, eight propulsion specialists, ten electronics technicians, four reactor specialists, four maintenance chiefs, four communication specialists, and forty crewmen," ADI listed. "Under the chief steward, there are four environmental specialists, four nurses, two cooks, a supply chief, and twenty maintenance stewards.

"Nice skill sets there," Marc said. "Are you familiar with any of them?"

"I am friends with the chief steward, the anthropologist, and the astrophysicist. I've worked with the environmental scientist on a previous mission," Dr. Metra said. "I don't like the chemist, but the energy scientist seems like a nice person. The other crew members I'm familiar with only as regards their medical conditions."

"Okay, that's good for now," Marc said. "I think we'll postpone the decision about waking the crew for now."

"What do we do with Commander Centag?" Marc asked.

"I'll take care of the body," Dr. Metra said.

"What else?" Marc asked.

"Well, the Chinese certainly know something is up," Blake said. "They're pretty good at containing secrets, so it might not go any further. They don't have a reason to connect it with us, but as soon as you unveil the new Lynx, they're going to assume this was us."

"But what can they do?" Liz asked.

"Nothing specific, I don't think," Marc said. "But they're obviously interested in the technology, so they might come looking for it."

"We've been preparing for that eventuality for six months," Kal said. "I think this just steps up the timeline."

"Could they get more aggressive?" Blake asked. "Come in with commandos instead of spies?"

"That is something we need to be prepared for," Marc said. "Kal, I want a plan in two weeks."

"You'll have it."

Chapter 37 Board Meeting – April 1st

Samantha gave Marc a quick kiss as she entered the meeting room. "You look better."

"What do you mean by that?" Marc asked.

"Every time I've seen you in the last three weeks, you've looked exhausted. You've been terrible company whenever we went out, but now you look like you just got back from vacation. You didn't go somewhere without me, did you?"

"I've been here the whole time," Marc said. "Must have been working too hard."

"Yeah, I'm sure that's it," Samantha said, not believing one word of it.

"Hello, Catie," Samantha said. "Where did you guys go in the Mea Huli?"

"We sailed over by Australia," Catie said. "Liz and I wanted to work on our tans. I think Uncle Blake was hoping to find a sheila," she laughed.

"No doubt," Samantha laughed with her. "Hey, Kal, when did you get back?"

"Yesterday," Kal said. "We had a good training exercise down in Perth."

"Drink much beer?"

"Our fair share," Kal said.

"Let's bring this meeting to order," Marc said as Blake finally arrived.

"Hey, don't look at me," Blake said. "I'm five minutes early."

"Remember, Dad always said you were late unless you were fifteen minutes early," Marc said.

"And I followed that advice dutifully while I was at home and during my career in the Navy. But now I'm trying to enjoy this island paradise and not let work ruin it for me."

"The meeting," Marc said. "Where are we on construction?"

"We have the Sky Princess here, so we're moving the construction guys onto her. We've started with the ones on Arutanga first; hopefully, that will relieve some of the pressure that the locals are putting on Sam."

"It's already helping," Samantha said. "They can at least see the light at the end of the tunnel."

"Quad one is complete. We're putting the buildings up as fast as we can. They're all mostly prefab, so it's going fast. We can come back later and replace those we want, but this gets us off the ground the fastest."

"That's great," Marc said.

"Our first Lynx came off the line yesterday," Blake continued.

"Hey, that was my announcement," Catie hollered.

"Payback is hell," Blake said.

Catie stuck her tongue out at Blake, "Just remember that," she muttered.

"Oops! I forgot that flows both ways," he laughed. "Anyway, back to construction. Our polysteel production is really accelerating. Once we open the facilities on Delphi City, it will really start picking up. We're going to need to double that workforce," Blake said, giving Kal a look.

"Sam?" Marc said, trying to move the updates along.

"For those of you who have been out of touch for a while," Samantha said, "we have closed the deal with Herr Johansson. He's ecstatic about the scooters, and we'll have the first prototype here on Rarotonga in two days."

"I'll bet you can't wait until we've moved to the city," Blake said.

"Yeah, then at least I'll get a little more leash to move about," Catie gave Liz a mean look, thinking about the last week of virtual imprisonment.

"How are we doing on patients?"

"We are keeping the facilities full," Samantha said. "Price increase didn't do anything to the demand."

"Liz?"

"Just keeping my head above water," Liz said.

"Catie?"

"Well, as you heard from Uncle Rat Fink, the first Lynx is off the production line. It's passed the first round of ground tests with flying colors. It will be ready for test flights next week," Catie said. "I'll be the test pilot."

Marc rolled his eyes. "I was kind of assuming that you would be. Sam, will there be any problems with the government on that?"

"She'll need to have an adult copilot," Samantha said. "But since she's taking off and landing on Manuae, I don't see any issues."

"Sounds like you're good, Sweetie," Marc said.

"Dad!" Catie groaned.

"I mean Cer Catie," Marc corrected himself. "And?"

"We've submitted the design info to New Zealand to begin the certification of the airplane. Once we have verified its flight worthiness ourselves, we'll begin that process."

"That sounds good, anything else?"

"Not much, just helping out the car design team; ADI's doing most of the work."

"Fred?"

"Just tracking our orders. Johansson just put in a pretty big one for batteries," Fred said. "He's asking about the fuel cells, but we still don't have a design ready there."

"It's coming," Liz said. "Dr. Nikola is very confident she'll have something within the month."

"Okay, with that, I'm going to close the meeting," Marc said.

"Here we are," Blake said as he gave a flourish and pointed to the Sky Princess. Marc had asked for a tour, and Catie had decided to tag along. Of course, that meant Liz had to come as well.

"Our very own cruise liner," Catie said. "Is it really seaworthy?" The ship did look a bit worse for wear.

"It made it here, didn't it?" Blake said, "and you can see that it's still floating."

Marc laughed at Catie. "Are the modifications done?"

"Yes," Blake said. "It was mostly repairs; we didn't need to modify much. Putting that new septic system on her was the biggest effort. Now even Dr. McGenty wouldn't complain."

"Good thing," Marc said. "That man can really try one's patience."

"Yes, but he was a good sport and tried out the toilet prototype for Tomi," Catie said.

"You couldn't manage to flush him down it, could you?" Blake asked.

"No, but Tomi did suggest we see how the treatment plant would process his body," Catie replied.

"Yep, that's our Dr. McGenty; he can make enemies faster than a speeding bullet," Blake said.

Marc laughed. "Enough already, let's check our ship out."

Blake led them up the gangway onto the ship. "There's a pool on the upper deck, the guys like that. The women even come over once in a while to use it."

"What's the matter with the beach?" Catie asked.

"I don't know, I think it has to do with the bar and the lack of sand," Blake said. "It's a saltwater pool, so no chlorine sting and also no children or surfers."

"I guess that would be attractive," Liz said. "I might have to try it out."

"I'll go with you," Catie said.

"Ahh, I'm not sure I like that idea," Marc said.

"We'll come when they're all at work," Catie said.

"Don't worry, I'll keep her safe," Liz whispered to Marc.

Marc shook his head and sighed. The problems of being a father with a teenage daughter. "Let's see what the accommodations look like."

Blake led them down the passageway. "Here is the basic room," he said. "We converted them all to singles and put new beds in them. We converted the suites into small public spaces so the guys can watch TV in small groups or play cards."

"Cards?" Catie asked.

"You don't think you've burned your bridge there yet?" Marc said.

"You never know," Catie said. "They might not have wanted to admit they lost to a girl."

"Maybe, but for now, why don't we stay focused on the tour," Marc suggested.

"This is the main dining room," Blake said. "It's set up like a cafeteria; basically, there's food here all the time. Since the guys work a rotating shift, five days on, two off, we've got crews at work seven days a week. There's always someone here on their day off."

"Okay, you have to feed them," Marc said. "How about if they want something different?"

"We have two restaurants on the ship that they can go to and spend their own money," Blake said. "So far, they've been pretty full every night. There are also two bars and two nightclubs."

"Two nightclubs?"

"Yeah, one of them features some kind of music each night. Amazingly these construction workers keep it full. The other does comedy. Half the time, it's a professional, the other half, it's open mic. Some of these guys are pretty funny."

"Everyone has their hidden talent," Marc said. "Have there been any complaints?"

"The only one I've heard is that the booze isn't free."

"Well, that would be plain stupid," Liz said.

"I agree," Marc said. "Free booze, we'd be up to our necks in industrial accidents."

Blake laughed. "Do you want to go up and see the pool?"

"I'll see it some other time," Catie said as she motioned to Liz.

"Are you serious?" Marc asked.

"Come on, Daddy. I never can get anyone to play."

"And why do you think that is?"

Catie made a 'who me' face.

"Go ahead. Did you bring money?"

Catie nodded her head, then led Liz toward the elevator. They went up to deck six and started checking out the small public rooms. There had to be a card game somewhere.

Chapter 38 Lynx Test Flights

Catie was nervous as she taxied the Lynx onto Manuae's runway. Blake was sitting next to her in the copilot's seat, but he was keeping quiet. Slowly she ran through the various items on her checklist. Verifying that each system was working as expected. She finally got to the engines; she held the brakes as she pushed the throttle forward. The engines roared as the jet fuel flowed through the superheating coils and into the combustion chamber.

"Seems like she has plenty of power," Blake said, finally breaking the tension in the cockpit.

"She'd better," Catie said. "Are you ready for this?"

"As ready as I can be," Blake laughed. "Do you want to call the tower?"

"Lynx Two to Manuae Control, requesting permission for takeoff."

"Manuae Control, Lynx Two, skies are clear, you are cleared for takeoff."

Catie released the brakes and pushed the throttle forward. The Lynx raced down the runway. After sixteen hundred meters, Catie adjusted the flaps and pulled the nose up gently, and the Lynx smoothly rose into the sky.

"Manuae Control, nice takeoff, have a good flight."

"Thanks, Daddy," Catie said.

Catie climbed to five thousand meters, then leveled off and started testing the Lynx's turning. She did sweeping-turns in each direction, tightening the radius each time. "She turns nice."

"That's a good thing," Blake said. "How does the yoke feel?"

"Steady as a rock," Catie said. "I'm going to take her up to twenty thousand meters and Mach 0.9, then we'll head back."

"Cautious," Blake said.

"Of course. The ground crew will inspect everything tonight to make sure there are no stress cracks or loose components. Then tomorrow, if all checks out, we'll do a supersonic run."

"Hey, how did you do the other day on the Sky Princess? Did you find a poker game?"

"Yeah, we found two," Catie said.

"Two!"

"Well, they don't last that long," Catie said. "So, after the first game ran out of money, we found a second one."

"How much did you take them for?"

"Six hundred at the first game. They were nice guys."

"And the second game?"

"Well, they started making comments and trying to push me out by betting big. They were kind of jerks."

"So, how much?"

"Three thousand."

"You are evil."

"Not evil," Catie said. "Just a little vindictive."

"Okay, let's go home, I've got a bottle of Champagne waiting for us."

The whole board was inside the hangar waiting on them to taxi in and deplane. As soon as Catie stepped off the ramp, her father handed her half a glass of Champagne. "Here's to a new era in aviation and the woman who launched it!"

"Cheers!"

Marc had a photographer taking pictures the whole time. Catie was surprised at how exhausted she felt. The excitement and tension of taking the new aircraft up for the first time was way more taxing than she had expected. And maybe she drank too much Champagne. *"Half a glass, what a wimp,"* she thought. But after an hour of chatting about the flight, all she wanted to do was go to bed.

The ground crew had given the Lynx a glowing review. No problems were found, and now they were watching as Catie and Blake taxied to take her back up. This time they would go supersonic.

"Let's get this show on the road," Blake said after Catie had finished her preflight checks.

"Lynx Two to Manuae Control, requesting permission for takeoff."

"Manuae Control, Lynx Two, skies are clear, you are cleared for takeoff."

"And away we go!" Blake said as Catie pushed the throttle forward.

The Lynx rose into the air quickly. This time Catie only used fourteen hundred meters of runway.

"Showoff," Blake said.

"We are supposed to be testing its capabilities," Catie shot back. She took the Lynx up to twenty thousand meters and leveled off. While both Catie and Blake carefully monitored the engine temperature and power ratings, Catie pushed the throttle forward.

"Approaching Mach one . . . Mach 1.2 . . . Mach 1.4 . . . Mach 1.6."

Catie held the throttle there and initiated some sweeping-turns. She adjusted the throttle to maintain their speed through the turns. After a few more turns, she straightened the Lynx out and started pushing the throttle forward more.

"Mach 1.8 . . . Mach 2.1 . . . Mach 2.3," Blake read off.

At Mach 2.8, Catie ran the Lynx through another set of turns before straightening out and taking her up to Mach four. There she did another set of turns, then turned the Lynx back toward Manuae.

"What, we're going to stop here?"

"We're recording all this to submit to the Kiwis," Catie said. "We'll do a flight tomorrow that's off the record." Catie was referring to the fact that the Lynx was actually designed to go Mach five, but they had a governor on the engines that would restrict the speed to Mach four. Mach four could only be exceeded if the pilot knew about it and could enter the code to disable the governor. Her father had decided that they would like to hold back some of the capabilities for the first year or so to give them an edge should something happen that threatened Delphi City. They had even hidden the fact that the Foxes could do Mach 6.2 when they had encountered the Chinese, not wanting to go above Mach five unless they had to.

After this landing, there was a lot less fanfare. Her father met her in the hangar and gave her a big hug, but then they all went back to work. Just a typical day at MacKenzie Discoveries.

Chapter 39 Board Meeting – April 15th

"I call this meeting to order," Marc said as everyone settled around the table.

"Kal, what do you have?"

"We had a great training exercise last week," Kal said. "We're making good use of that paintball arena Blake put in. I've got another team just waiting to take on the A-team."

"Bring it on," Liz said. "We've been getting stale without a real challenge."

"I'll set it up for next week. Be careful, these are all ex-military."

"I'm not scared," Catie said.

"I didn't think so," Kal said. "I've got another four that will be ready next week."

"Okay," Marc said. "Liz, you've taken over the offshore manufacturing and sales; how's it going?"

"Catie's scooter design is up. Johansson built a couple of prototypes last month and has them certified in India, Mexico, Indonesia, and the Philippines. China is still a problem. The first production run has just started; they're popping off the line as we speak," Liz reported.

"Cool," Catie said. "When can we have a few around here?"

"Fred is going to bring some on his next trip," Liz said, giving Fred a nod.

"That is if I'm properly compensated," Fred said.

"What do you want?" Catie scoffed.

"I just want you to buy drinks for once," Fred said.

"Done!"

"Back to Johansson. He has the car design done, so he's hoping to get a prototype ready for road qualifications in the US and EU starting next month. He's really burning through money -- good thing we're selling batteries as fast as we can make them."

"Catie, how was the test flight?"

"Things went perfect; we did three flights to get through all the tests. They're part of the package we're submitting to the Kiwis. Flybys by Fred verified we didn't have a shockwave; that was a relief. She passed them all. We did an off-the-books one yesterday that took her up to Mach five. The second unit is about ready, and we'll send this one to the Kiwis when they're ready to do certification testing."

"Anything else?"

"Yes, education. Sam hired four teachers to be coaches for anyone homeschooling their children. There are me, the twins, and six other students inaugurating the process."

"Okay," Marc said. "Blake, care to add some more to your previous update?"

"Sure thing. We should have the first city section completed in two months," Blake said. "It will take another two months to have the full four sections in place minus some of the infrastructure. We'll add that as we need to."

"What about our airport?" Marc asked

"Geez, aren't you ever satisfied?"

"Not when I know I can have more!" Marc said.

"I've hired the guy who worked on Japan's megafloat project. He wants to actually build one instead of just putting designs and prototypes together."

"Why do we need another airport?" Samantha asked. "Most of our stuff comes in on cargo ships, there's a perfectly good airport on Rarotonga, and you've got the small strips here and on Manuae that handle the G650."

"She makes some good points there," Blake said. "This airport is a huge investment. We'll need to pull in another billion to get it done. The Lynxes could use our strip here, just need to upgrade it a little. Or if you really want a floating one, you could do a much smaller airport than this monstrosity you're asking for."

Marc just sat there, smiling. He laughed a bit then, folded his hands together, and leaned on the table with his forearms. "I've been working on a little design project of my own. After our bit of excitement last month, I think we need to accelerate some of our plans. We need the extra runway length and support systems for this." He flicked up an image on the big screen using his HUD. Everyone turned and looked at it.

"What, you want to start using C17s to ship stuff?" Blake asked.

"That's not a C17," Liz said. "Look at the engines."

"What the hell . . ."

"This is our new Oryx," Marc said.

"Do we really need a supersonic transport?" Blake asked.

"It has to be supersonic," Marc said. "How else is it going to make orbit?"

"Finally!" Catie shouted as she pumped her fist.

"Orbit?!" Samantha squeaked.

"There's no way that thing can make orbit," Fred said. "Even if you strapped spare tanks to it, it'd never carry enough fuel."

"Ah, you make a fine point," Marc said. "But since these will never land anywhere but our airport, they don't need to be certified, so we can take some liberties with technology."

"What technology?" Fred and Samantha asked at the same time.

Marc looked Samantha in the eyes and clasped her hands, "Dear Samantha, I've been holding out on you," he chuckled.

Samantha tried to pull her hand free so she could slug Marc. "Spill, you bastard."

"As you know, we have a couple of renowned nuclear physicists working for us. They've been working on a fusion reactor. What you don't know is that we actually have a fusion reactor already; they're just trying to reinvent it."

"What, are you crazy!" Samantha was completely nonplussed.

"I don't think so," Marc said. "Blake and I found a spaceship last year; we've been working to introduce that technology to Earth. We're hoping to catch up and maybe get ahead before the owners come looking for it."

"You are crazy!"

"We'll take you on a tour of it later," Marc said. "But for now, just trust me. We, in fact, have several fusion reactors. One is small enough to fit in this plane and drive its engines. In fact, that's what drives the Lynx, at least the original. The ones Catie is working on are going to have to use standard engines."

Fred looked around the table; Catie, Blake, Liz, and Kal were just sitting there smiling. They acted no different than if Marc were telling them all that he'd just bought a new yacht.

"Marc, what's wrong with you?" Samantha said. She had an almost terrified look on her face.

"Sam," Fred said. "Sam, look at them." He pointed to their friends.

Samantha looked around the table. "He's not nuts?" she asked as she realized she was the only one showing any concern.

"Nope," Liz said. "He let Kal and me see it right before Christmas. It is amazing."

"And you're going to tell me that ADI is some kind of alien," Samantha said.

"No, Cer Sam, I'm an Autonomous Digital Intelligence," ADI said. "Dr. Metra is the alien, as you say."

"Ohhhh, I need a drink," Samantha said.

"Coming right up," Blake jumped up, grabbed a bottle of scotch and poured Samantha a healthy dose.

"What about me," Fred yelped. "I'm in shock too."

Blake laughed and poured another glass for Fred.

"We're going to have trouble finishing this meeting if you keep pouring scotch," Marc said.

"There's always tomorrow," Blake laughed as he poured a more moderate dose for the others at the table. Catie gave him a sour look. After getting a nod from Marc, Blake poured her a tiny dose.

"To the Oryx," Blake toasted.

"To the Oryx!"

"And I haven't even gotten to the very best part," Marc said.

"What, there's more?" Samantha groaned. She held her glass out to Blake for a refill.

"Why do you think we need a ship to fly into orbit?" Marc asked.

"To undercut SpaceX and Boeing?" Samantha said, hopefully.

Marc snorted. "No, to build Station Delphi."

"Station Delphi?"

Marc used his HUD to flick the screen to the next image. Everyone gasped as they looked at the image of a space station as it rotated on the display. It was a tall cylindrical can surrounded by three rings.

"How big is that thing?" Fred asked. Samantha just groaned again.

"The hub has a diameter of two hundred meters and is one hundred meters tall. It's for micro-G industry," Marc continued. "The outer ring has a diameter of one thousand meters. The ring itself is an ellipsoid, it is fifty meters by thirty meters with the long axis parallel to the hub. The station rotates at 1.35 revolutions per minute. That gives the outer ring a gravity of one G; the middle ring gets three-quarter-G; the inner ring only half-G, and the hub will see one-fifth-G."

"If it rotates, how do you have a zero-G industry?" Blake asked.

"The hub has an inner shell that isolates the zero-G area. It doesn't rotate, it's coupled to the outer shell via magnetic bearings along the axis. The spokes you see are elevators, so you have access between the three rings and the hub."

"That's huge!" Liz said.

"Yes it is," Marc said. "It's designed so we can stack four of them, one section on top of another to make it a bigger station if we need to."

"How many people do you think will want to live in space?" Liz asked.

"It will depend on how much manufacturing we need to do up there," Marc said. "Ten to eleven thousand people can live in the outer ring; depending on how many couples and children there are, three quarters that many in the middle," Marc continued. "Maybe a few thousand in the inner ring. We'll have to see how people feel about living in a half-G environment."

"And how much public space we allocate," Catie added.

"Correct," Marc said. "We will probably see between twenty to thirty thousand per section. We'll just have light-industry and some population in the half-G ring. So, the full station should house eighty to one hundred thousand people comfortably when it's fully built out."

"How are you going to lift that much material?" Blake asked.

Catie was squirming in her seat, beside herself with excitement.

"Do you have something to say?" Marc asked. He could tell she was bursting at the seams.

"Yes," Catie said. "Dibs! Double Dibs!"

Afterword

Thanks for reading **Delphi City**!

I hope you've enjoyed the second book in the *Delphi in Space* series. As a self-published author, the one thing you can do that will help the most is to leave a review on Goodreads and Amazon.

The next book in our series is **Delphi Station**.

Now the McCormacks are finally going to get into space. At least if the big governments on Earth don't stop them. They've managed to accumulate enough money to build a city, and now they're going to build a space station. That will create a safe place to manufacture their new technology, and a way to demonstrate to the world that humans have a future in space.

But as they demonstrate more advanced technology, they attract more interest from the world's governments. The people in power aren't too happy about sharing it with some small company in the South Pacific. What will it take to keep their dream alive?

Acknowledgments

It is impossible to say how much I am indebted to my beta readers and copy editors. Without them, you would not be able to read my books due to all the grammar and spelling errors. I have always subscribed to Andrew Jackson's opinion that "It is a damn poor mind that can think of only one way to spell a word."

So special thanks to:

My copy editor, Ann Clark, who also happens to be my wife.

My beta reader and editor, Theresa Holmes.

My beta reader and cheerleader, Roger Blanton, who happens to be my brother.

Also important to a book author is the cover art for their book. I'm especially thankful to Momir Borocki for the exceptional covers he has produced for my books. It is amazing what he can do with the strange PowerPoint drawings I give him; and how he makes sense of my suggestions, I'll never know.

If you need a cover, he can be reached at momir.borocki@gmail.com.

Also by Bob Blanton

Delphi in Space
Sakira
Delphi City
Delphi Station
Delphi Nation
Delphi Alliance
Delphi Federation – Fall 2020

Stone Series
Matthew and the Stone
Stone Ranger
Stone Undercover

Made in the USA
Monee, IL
05 February 2021